THE TUBMAN TRAIN

BOOK 3 IN THE UNDERGROUND RAILROAD SERIES

DOUG PETERSON

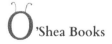

'Shea Books

For Jackson

Published by O'Shea Books

Champaign, IL 61821

www.bydougpeterson.com

ISBN: 978-1-7358151-0-7

DOUG PETERSON'S
UNDERGROUND RAILROAD SERIES

Book 1: The Vanishing Woman

Ellen and William Craft escaped when Ellen posed as a white man, while her husband pretended to be her slave. A true story.

Book 2: The Disappearing Man

Henry "Box" Brown mailed himself to freedom. He shipped himself in a box from Richmond to Philadelphia. A true story.

OTHER NOVELS BY DOUG PETERSON

The Puzzle People

A suspense novel that spans the rise and fall of the Berlin Wall. Inspired by real events.

The Lincoln League

The story of John Scobell, the first African American spy, operating deep within Confederate lines during the Civil War. Inspired by real events.

THE TUBMAN TRAIN

"God's time is always near. He gave me my strength, and He set the North Star in the heavens; He meant I should be free."

— HARRIET TUBMAN

BEFORE SHE WAS KNOWN AS HARRIET TUBMAN...

Before she was known as the She-Moses...
Before she was known as the General...
She was called...

MINTY

"I used to sleep on the floor in front of the fireplace and there I'd lie and cry and cry. I used to think all the time, 'If I could only get home and get in my mother's bed!' And the funny part of that was, she never had a bed in her life. Nothing but a board box nailed up against the wall and straw laid on it."

— HARRIET TUBMAN

1

Dorchester County, Maryland

Minty was freezing in her new dress. Her mistress had made the dress, but it wasn't much good for keeping her warm on a nippy night like this. She rode behind Mister Cook on the back of his big horse, moving through the darkness, into the swampy heart of the land.

Minty was six years old, and for the first time in her life, she was being separated from her Mama. She was torn up about it, but she told herself that at least she'd be away from her master, Edward Brodess, who wasn't fit to own a dog. Brodess had a devilish wife named Eliza Ann, whose main job was spending what little money they had on useless knickknacks to scatter around their house.

Minty was the daughter of Ben and Rit Ross; her given name was Araminta. But people called her Minty. The name conjured up pictures of a fine-smelling plant, but she didn't think of herself as a pretty thing. She felt more like a neglected weed.

She lived with her Mama and her brothers and sisters behind the Brodess house near Bucktown, but she hardly ever got to see her Papa. He was a valued timber inspector for her master's stepfather,

Mister Anthony Thompson. So Papa lived at the Thompson place, a good ten miles away, west of Church Creek.

Minty had already seen the second oldest of her sisters, Mariah Ritty, sold away—although she had been too young at the time to remember her. Still, Mama always told her how Mariah would play peekaboo with her. Her big sister would hold her hands over her eyes and say, "Where's Mariah? Where's Mariah, Minty?" And then Mariah would pull away her hands and squeal, "Here I am!"

Where's Mariah? It's like one day her big sister just opened her hands, and she was no longer there; she had completely vanished—whisked away. *Where's Mariah, Minty?*

She wished she knew.

Now, on this chilly autumn evening, Minty had also been whisked away, although she hadn't been sold. Mister Brodess had hired her out to the Cook family so she could learn to weave and bring in some extra money for Miss Eliza to spend. Minty had a big empty ache in her stomach the entire three-mile ride to the Cook house, and she kept feeling tears trying to burst out. She pushed them back until her eyes ached as well.

"Wait there, Minty," said Mister Cook when they finally reached his cabin. It was an isolated outpost in the Blackwater Swamp near Bucktown.

Minty stood there, just outside the cabin. She shivered in the dark and stared at the flickering light coming from inside while Mister Cook stabled the horse. She hugged herself for warmth, but she couldn't stop her teeth from rattling.

"C'mon. Inside."

Mister Cook, a large man, brushed by her in the dark, like the shadow of a ghost, and then he opened the door. She could see him outlined in black by the light inside.

"C'mon!"

Minty followed, wondering what kind of world lay inside. She stepped into the cabin, where Missus Cook and two boys sat at the table, having their dinner by candlelight. A fire crackled in the corner, giving out a sweet smell like roasting apples. Missus Cook gave her a hard stare, up and down. Minty was small for her age; everyone always told her that. She wondered if Missus Cook was thinking she was too tiny to possibly be any good around the house.

Minty stared at the food on the table. The Cooks weren't rich, that was clear, but they had bread and stew and, most enticing, cups of milk. She caught herself licking her lips.

"You want yourself a glass of milk?" Missus Cook said.

Minty was shocked. Was this some kind of trick? She had never eaten with white folks before, and she didn't trust them. Was Missus Cook going to offer her a glass of milk and then snatch it away the moment she reached for it? Something stubborn and flinty rose up inside her, and she found herself saying, "No, ma'am. I never liked sweet milk no how."

Missus Cook seemed just as surprised as Minty by what she had just said. The woman glanced over at her husband, who gave a slight shrug. The two boys, both of them older than Minty, stared at her in silence before looking down at their tin bowls and shoveling in another spoonful of stew. The victuals smelled tasty.

"You sure you don't want no milk?" Missus Cook asked.

"I don't take to the taste of milk. But thank you, ma'am."

As soon as Minty said the words, her mind squawked and demanded to know what she was doing. She was as fond of milk as any young shoat. So smooth and sweet.

"You don't like milk? Why I never heard such a thing!"

"You sure you don't want something to drink?" said Mister Cook, like she was a stray cat that needed a little bit of nourishment.

"I'm sure, sir. Thank you, sir."

"You're a strange little creature," Missus Cook said, shaking her head and turning back to her food.

"Strange" was the right word. This whole experience was strange, strange, strange. Minty wasn't exactly sure what drove her to say no to the milk, but she kind of felt like she had just won a battle. Missus Cook wanted to give her a glass of milk, and Minty had said no. Minty knew good and well she couldn't say no when it came to chores or much else. But this was one situation where she could win. She could say no to *good things* like milk.

Saying no made her feel strong. She knew it was strange to give up something she wanted, but that's how she felt.

Minty took a seat on a stool in a corner, near the fire, and she watched the Cooks finish off their dinner. Tomorrow she would be ordered to work, and that was a battle she knew she couldn't win.

2

Minty slogged through the cold, murky water, which came up to her waist and rattled her bones. Missus Cook had no patience for her clumsy attempts at weaving, so the Cooks finally gave up on her and sent her out to the marshes to gather muskrats from the traps instead. Minty liked being outdoors, and it certainly beat trying to weave. But it was late autumn and certainly not the day to be up to your waist in freezing water.

She had never felt so miserable in her life. Her body was a raging battleground of conflicting temperatures. She felt as hot as a stove, but her legs were ice cold. Her cough shook her aching body like a bear shaking a tree, and she spit up all manner of ugly stuff. She was sick as a dog.

Large trees, most of them stripped of leaves, rose out of the water all around her, an entire army of them stretching as far as she could see. Sloshing through the blackish water, she pushed through a clump of dark-green grass—the muskrat's choice for building lodges. Minty knew the marsh, every twist and turn. She also knew where to place her feet, but today she was feeling so sick that she had a hard time paying attention. She got careless, stepped wrong, and in seconds she found herself up to her waist in mud.

It was irksome, but she did not panic. This wasn't quicksand, but she had to grab onto a nearby branch and pull herself, inch by inch, out of the slurping mud. As she pulled herself free, it felt like it was trying to suck her back down. By the time she was free, she was exhausted to the point of fainting. She splashed cold water on her face to keep alert. If she fainted in this marsh, she just might drown.

Moving forward, more carefully now, she spotted a dabbling duck, dipping its head beneath the water to eat the plants below. She wondered if the duck felt as cold as she did. She had wrapped her feet in rags before coming out, but the rags had long ago soaked through and she could barely feel her feet. Today could be the day she loses some toes to frostbite.

Minty tried to be as quiet as possible while she checked the various float traps that Mister Cook had scattered up and down this stream. The only good thing about the cold was that at least she wouldn't encounter any snakes or snapping turtles this time of year. Tom Carroway, a nasty boy who lived with his Pa in the woods, loved telling her about the slave girl who got bit by a snapping turtle the size of a dog while wading in these waters. He claimed the turtle bit her entire leg off. Minty hated to admit it, but his stories scared her to the core.

Today, however, it was this sickness that scared her the most. She didn't want to die just yet.

Then Minty spotted it. A muskrat skimmed along the top of the water. Its wet fur streaked backward in the water as its nose and black-dot eyes peeped just above the waterline. The muskrat swam straight for one of the traps—a floating hunk of wood with a nail sticking up from it. The day before, she had jammed a corncob onto the nail to lure the animal, and it was working.

The muskrat came right up to the trap, which was partly submerged below the water. Then it hauled its wet, slippery body up and onto the wood to get at the corn cob. Clearly, it was not aware of the steel trap also sitting on the floating platform.

SNAP!

The jaws of the trap clamped down on the muskrat's leg, and the animal let out a ratty shriek before tumbling into the water. The weight of the trap and chain would keep the muskrat underwater so Minty lurked near the bank, watching and waiting for the animal to drown. She could see the chain, connected to the float, move around and scrape the wood. She could imagine the muskrat, head downward in the water, its bloody leg still jammed in the trap, trying to paddle back to the surface for air. Muskrats were fighters, just like her. But she knew the animal was in a losing battle. Soon enough, the chain stopped moving and clanking.

Minty started to shiver and shake until she thought all of her teeth were going to rattle right out of her head. Then she coughed so loudly that she probably scared away every other muskrat within a mile.

She looked as sorrowful as the drowned muskrat when she finally dragged her drenched body out of the marsh. She was covered in mud from the waist down. Numb and delirious, she trudged back to the Cooks' house, her feet and fingers aching like they had been hit by hammers. She carried three dead muskrats in her two sacks. The big, wet animals were as heavy as lead, so Minty had to drag them along the dirt. By now, her body was one big ache. Her head throbbed, and she felt herself burning up from the inside; her Mama could probably cook supper on her forehead. She could barely lift her legs to step forward and for the first time since coming to the Cooks' house, she got lost hiking back from the stream. Her mind wasn't working, and all she could think about was lying down and sleeping.

She was starting to think that maybe it would've been smarter to learn how to weave after all. She spun around in circles, trying to look for familiar landmarks. Where was the tree with the big broken limb sticking out from its side like a man's missing arm? Or the evergreen with one side all brown and dead? Nothing looked right.

As she whirled around, studying her surroundings, she made herself good and dizzy, and she nearly tumbled sideways onto the cold, muddy ground. She knew the Cooks' house was off to the south, and she knew her directions by looking at the sky. She did her best to sort herself out and started to trudge on again, hoping familiar sights would start popping up all around. To make things worse, it began to mist—a shivering spray.

It wasn't long before her body just gave up. Her legs throbbed with a deep soreness, and fever engulfed her. She took two steps and stumbled. Three more steps, another stumble. Then, just when she thought she saw a familiar tree up ahead, her head went spinning like a top, and she felt herself falling.

Minty didn't even remember hitting the ground.

...

As it turned out, the Cook family said she had measles. So the Cooks shipped Minty back home where she got to be with her Mama and brothers and sisters. A rash spread across her neck, arms, legs, and feet, and fever gripped her for several days. Master Brodess wanted to put her back to work, but Mama wasn't having it. She was tough that way, and she knew how to work the master. During that week and a half, Minty got in more sleeping than she could ever remember. Fever or no fever, she felt like she was basking in heaven being able to rest and be with family. Her homesickness at the Cooks had been worse than her measles, and she began to dread the day she got completely well. When the fever began to slip away, she started to panic. She told Mama she was still burning up, but she couldn't fool her. It was clear she was on the mend, although Mama did stretch out her illness as long as believable for Master Brodess. Minty prayed she would get another blast of the illness, but she just kept getting better. It was terrible.

When Brodess finally shipped her back to the Cooks, Missus Cook continued to get mad at her for not knowing how to weave. Her heart grew weary, and her whole world seemed to be sinking deeper into the mud.

Minty hoped if she did her chores poorly, they might finally realize she was a terrible worker and send her back home for good. Whenever Missus Cook told her to make up the beds, she would go into the room and start beating on the feather bed, making all kinds of racket and pretending to work hard. And then she'd hurl herself onto the soft bed like she was diving into a river. She got caught only once doing this.

Minty was determined to fail at her chores, and eventually all of her stubborn uselessness paid off. After much trying, she was ordered to return home. But it wasn't long before she was hired out again—hired out to a woman that made her wish she were back at the Cooks' cabin.

3

Minty was hired out next to be a nursemaid and house servant to a certain Miss Susan.

Miss Susan was as nasty a young lady as there ever was.

She kept a bullwhip up by the mantle for Minty to see, and she even slept with the whip beneath her pillow. So Minty decided she would try to do her chores properly this time. But there was no doing right in the eyes of Miss Susan.

Whenever Minty put the parlor in order, she would keep her eyes fixed on that bullwhip on the mantle, as if she were afraid it would leap down and start whipping her on its own power. Minty would shove the table and chairs to the middle of the room and then sweep with all of her strength, raising up a tremendous amount of dust. The moment she finished sweeping, she would snatch up the rag and start dusting until she could see her face in the polished shine of the wood. But when Miss Susan came in, that evil woman would run her finger along the table and piano, turning to stick her dusty finger in Minty's face.

"You call this clean?"

Then down would come the big whip, and the strokes would fall on Minty's head and face and neck. But she never hollered. Never once. Sometimes, Minty wore several layers of thick clothing, and Miss Susan wouldn't even notice that she had extra cushioning to protect her from the whip. But if the whip caught her on bare skin, especially on the face and neck, it burned like fire. Still, she didn't make a sound. She would *never* give Miss Susan that pleasure. *Make me strong and able to fight*, she prayed to God every single night. *Make me strong.*

If it weren't for Miss Susan's younger sister, Miss Emily, Minty would've gone on being whipped half to death. Miss Emily, a widow, lived under the same roof. At first, she said and did nothing about her older sister's ways. She probably thought it wasn't her place, with her being dependent on their hospitality. Miss Emily would be in the back room, sewing, always sewing, and surely she could hear the whip snapping. Even though she never heard Minty holler, just the sound of the whip must have rattled her nerves.

"If you do not stop whipping that child, I will leave your home and never come back!" Miss Emily shouted one afternoon, just when Miss Susan was fixing to give Minty her fifth whipping of the day.

"Then good riddance!" Miss Susan blasted back. "That child slighted her work on purpose!"

"Leave her to me," said Miss Emily, and her sister answered by storming out of the room, kicking up curses every step of the way.

Miss Emily watched carefully as Minty went through the steps of her chores once again. She stopped Minty after the sweeping, explaining that she needed to wait a spell for the dust to drift back down on the furniture. If Minty dusted before all of the dust had settled, she'd miss a lot of it. The advice helped, but the whip was always lurking.

One Friday afternoon, Minty was sitting at the supper table, positioned in the corner of the cabin. She sat close to the hearth, where a fire was burning. A big black kettle hung over the flames. She was waiting for Miss Susan to hand over the baby so she could watch the little girl. Miss Susan had the baby propped on her hip, when she suddenly started screaming at her husband, Mister Jack. He had an empty whiskey bottle in his hand, and another empty bottle was propped on the fireplace mantle.

"Couldn't you at least wait until your work was done to get drunk?" Miss Susan shouted.

Minty had seen her share of grown men who drank themselves blind; her Mama would say they were trying to forget their woes. If that's the case, all she could think was that with a wife like Miss Susan, she was surprised Mister Jack wasn't drunk all day long.

While Miss Susan tore into Mister Jack, Minty kept her eyes on a bowl sitting in the middle of the table. It contained lumps of sugar, tantalizing white chunks that had been picked apart by the nippers. The one time she had eaten a piece she'd been in heaven. She never got anything good to eat, and that sugar, so close, looked so tasty. She thought about reaching out and snagging a lump, but that would be mighty dangerous with Miss Susan and her husband so close by.

Shooting a sideways glance, Minty saw that Miss Susan had her back to her, and Mister Jack was staring at his shoes. So she slowly, carefully reached out her right hand toward the sugar bowl. They would never notice.

SMASH!

Minty yanked her hand back and nearly leaped two feet out of her chair.

Miss Susan had suddenly grabbed the empty whiskey bottle from the fireplace mantle and shattered it. She was threatening Mister Jack with the jagged half of the bottle. It was the strangest sight. Her mistress had her baby propped up on her left hip, and she held out the sharp end of the bottle in her right hand as she continued to tongue-lash her husband.

"Where'd you hide the other bottles?" Miss Susan bellowed.

"Ain't none of your business!" Mister Jack fired back.

Quick now, before they turn and look! Minty's hand shot out and filched a lump of sugar, as quick as a frog's tongue. Then she popped the sugar in her mouth and leaned back in her chair, acting all innocent.

"Give me the other bottles or I'll cut you!"

"Just try."

Sometimes, Miss Susan tongue-lashed her husband so severely that he would finally snap back and slap her. Minty wondered if it would happen this day, but she shoved those thoughts away, trying to concentrate on the sugar as it melted on her tongue, giving her a blast of flavor.

She craved more. Just one more lump of sugar. A small piece.

Glancing over at the bickering couple, she saw her chance. Her hand shot out, grabbed a piece, and popped it in her mouth, all in one swift motion. *So good, so good, so good.*

Minty was afraid to take any more. Even if she could snag another lump of sugar without being seen, surely Miss Susan would notice that some of the lumps were missing. But still…there was a heap of heaven just sitting there for the taking.

Just one more piece of sugar. Miss Susan wouldn't notice.

"You stay back, Jack!" Miss Susan hollered.

Minty glanced over and saw that Mister Jack had his right hand raised, about to strike his wife. But Miss Susan shoved the jagged glass at his face, and he backpedaled two quick steps.

This was her chance. Minty's hand shot out again, but this time it caught the end of the dish. The plate rattled. A clink sound.

Looking up, Minty found Miss Susan and Mister Jack both glaring at her. They had caught her in the act! Her mistress, with the baby settled in her left arm, snatched the bullwhip down from the mantle. Minty leaped down from the dining table chair, and the rawhide snapped at empty air, wrapping around the back of the chair. As Miss Susan untangled the whip, cursing wildly, Minty saw her chance to dash out the back door. Yet, just as she started, Mister Jack suddenly appeared on the threshold, blocking her escape. Minty quickly changed course, spry and speedy.

Miss Susan, giving up on the tangled whip, tried to corner her by the fireplace, coming at her from the right, while her husband came from the left. But the man was drunk, and he was in no condition to snag a fast-moving little girl.

He didn't even come close when he tried to grab Minty as she sprinted by him, as fast as a fox. He staggered forward, grabbing at empty air, and nearly fell right into the fireplace.

A whipstitch later, Minty was out the door and sprinting into the woods. Barefoot, she didn't even notice when she ran across a scattering of pinecones and acorns. She just flew, sprinting all the way through the forest, moving faster than her legs had ever carried her. She blasted through the forest, past a neighbor's house, and she never looked back to see if the crazed pair was close behind. She moved so fast that she thought if she started flapping her arms, she might take off like a bird.

Reaching the Johnson place, she dashed past the barn, aiming to plunge into the woods beyond. But when she heard the bang of a door at the farmhouse up ahead, she made a sharp left turn, her eyes darting for any sign of a hiding place. If Mister Johnson spotted her, he might beat her for running through his property. If she was running, she was up to no good, he'd figure.

The only hiding place was the pigpen, so she vaulted the rickety, wooden fence and landed ankle deep in muck. She heard man-sounds coming toward her, so she scrambled on all fours to the hog house, the mud splashing. Mama always warned her never to enter a hog house, but today she had no choice. She shoved open the swinging door and scrambled in on hands and knees, moving swiftly through the darkness to the back wall of the hog house. There, she finally came to a stop, turned, and pressed her back against the rough wood. Her chest heaved as she sucked in air. The stench was awful, and she tried to keep from coughing and choking. She was clear tuckered out.

Minty heard Mister Johnson moving about just outside, talking to himself. He must not have spotted her ducking into the hog house or he would have come straight for her. It sounded like he was feeding his chickens and talking to them like they were people. Mister Johnson was strange that way.

Then the darkness suddenly came alive. On the opposite side of the hog house, she saw the blackness shift and snort. She was not alone. She was in the hog house with a big old sow, which started snorting and rooting at the floor. The sow was huge. Minty watched the hulking shadow lumber in her direction, still grunting. She pressed harder against the wall behind her, trying to shrink in size.

In moments, the huge sow was upon her, but not acting mean. Not yet at least. That nasty boy, Tom Carroway, once told her about how a bunch of pigs had gobbled up a farmer whole, and the only thing left of him was his straw hat. Why she ever talked to Tom Carroway about anything was beyond her.

The pig's bulk pushed against her, but not like it was trying to crush her or anything. It was almost acting friendly—maybe too friendly because for a moment she thought it might crush her to death. Then Mister Johnson suddenly called out from somewhere beyond her: "C'mon Sylvia, I got some good slop for ya!"

Sylvia must have known the word 'slop' by heart because she reacted instantly. The sow charged toward the hog house door faster than Minty had ever seen a pig move before. Sylvia banged through the swinging door, squealing in delight. While Mister Johnson fed slop to the pigs, Minty heard more voices and was horrified when she recognized Miss Susan and Mister Jack. She didn't dare move. Miss Susan's voice was the loudest of all, and Minty heard her name shouted amidst a tumble of curse words. Then she heard Miss Susan and Mister Jack's voices fade into the distance as they went on their way, but the tension still had Minty by the throat. Soon, she heard Mister Johnson talking to Sylvia, saying something about "Miss Susan, that grumpy old sow, no offense intended."

Following her escape from Miss Susan's house, Minty lived near the Johnson place for four days. Sometimes she would hide out in the woods and sometimes in the barn, where she hunted for scraps of food. She even found herself chatting with Sylvia whenever she was absolutely sure Mister Johnson wasn't around. But hunger eventually got the best of her, and she reluctantly trudged back to Miss Susan and Mister Jack's cabin. She was all covered in slop and stinking like hog heaven when Miss Susan saw her emerge from the woods.

"Where've you been, you little imp?"

Miss Susan grabbed her by the ear and dragged her into the cabin, filling her other ear with curses. And when Minty entered the dim interior, she saw Mister Jack waiting for her. He had the bullwhip in his right hand.

4

Benjamin Ross woke to rough shoving. Someone draped in shadow had both of their hands on his right shoulder and was pushing him back and forth, like he was a hunk of bread dough on a wooden board.

"Wake up, Benjamin, wake up," the person whispered. He should have guessed it would be his sister, Minty. Who else would haul him out of a nice slumber for whatever crazy idea had just popped into her head?

"Whatya want?" Benjamin mumbled, rolling over to go back to sleep.

"I wanna go see Mama," Minty said.

"Then see her." Benjamin closed his eyes and started to drop back down into his dreams. But then came the shoving again.

"Wake up. I need y'all to stand guard for me."

By this time, Minty was pushing on his back, trying to shove him off of his wooden pallet. He tried to resist her, but there was no fighting Minty. He knew his sister, and she would never give up.

"Why now?" He sat up on the edge of the pallet with his eyes closed. He nearly fell back asleep in the sitting position, but Minty poked him in the side until his eyes reopened.

"I couldn't sleep, so I figured I'd steal out and see Mama."

Didn't it occur to her that just because she couldn't sleep, that didn't mean he should be wide awake too?

"We can't go to Mama's in the middle of the night," Benjamin said. "Y'all wanna get us killed?"

"That's why I need you. For a lookout."

Six months ago, their Mama, along with their brothers Moses and Henry and their big sister Linah, had been whisked away to work on a neighboring place called the Polish Mills Farm. The farm was just a short hike through the woods, but with all of the rules about slave movements, they didn't see each other all that much. By now, the Ross family had nine children, with one of them long gone, sold south, leaving Linah, Soph, Robert, Rachel, Minty, Henry, baby Moses, and Benjamin himself. It was bad enough that Benjamin's father worked on the Thompson place, ten miles away, but now he didn't have Mama, either.

Yawning, Benjamin noticed that his sister had already taken hold of his feet, slipped his shoes on for him, and tossed a raggedy coat in his lap. It was fall, so it was a little nippy outside. Benjamin let Minty take one of his arms and yank him into a standing position. Even then, she had to stand directly behind him and shove to get his legs started. He was nine years old, two years younger than Minty, and although he already stood a head taller than her, she knew how to order him around like a soldier.

It was no use arguing with his older sister.

Blurry with sleep, he staggered out of the cabin. He looked up to see that the night sky was clear, a bluish black. Minty hushed him when he stepped on a branch, snapping it loudly.

Normally, Minty barreled along wherever she went. She was always moving fast, always powering forward, figuring that anything in her path would just have to get out of her way. But on this night, he noticed she moved carefully because what they were up to was extremely dangerous.

"You sure you wanna be doin' this?" Benjamin asked.

"Don't you wanna see Mama?"

"Course I do."

"Then keep shushed. Patrollers might be hearin' us."

That shut up Ben, and they continued through the dark woods in quiet. Ever since Nat Turner and his men wiped out a bunch of plantation folks in their beds, whites all across the South had gotten tougher on blacks moving around at night. They put out extra patrollers, so Minty and Benjamin needed to be extra careful.

Soon, the two of them came to a string of four slave cabins—one-room boxes lined up one after the other behind the Big House on the Mills Farm.

"You stay here," Minty ordered him as they approached the cabins. Big tree limbs hung over the houses, like giants reaching down to grab them. Mama's cabin was the second one in line, and there was still a little light burning through the window. Maybe Mama couldn't sleep either.

"I wanna go in and see Mama too," Benjamin said.

"You can see her when I'm done. We'll take turns standin' guard. Give me a bird whistle if you see or hear trouble."

"What kinda bird?"

"Can you do an owl?"

"What kinda owl?"

"I don't care. Any kinda owl."

"How 'bout a screech owl? Like this." Then Benjamin let out a whinnying sound that he had perfected. He was very good at his bird calls.

"That's a horse, not an owl. Patrollers gonna wonder what a horse is doin' wanderin' 'round at night."

Benjamin snorted at Minty's ignorance of bird life. "But that's how they really sound when they're defendin' territory. Don't you know nothin'?"

"I know the patrollers are gonna wonder what a horse is doin' wanderin' 'round at night if you do that call."

"Then how 'bout this?"

Benjamin demonstrated another call, this one a trill sound that was clearly bird-like. Screech owls use this song to communicate with other owls in the family. If Minty didn't like this birdcall, he was going home.

"What kinda bird is that?"

"A screech owl I said."

"That a screech owl, too? Why didn't you do that one in the first place? That'll do."

"Here, let me try out another." Once Benjamin started in on his bird calls, he had a hard time stopping.

"I said that'll do," Minty snapped with a wave of her hand, cutting him off just when he was about to try out a different owl sound. She told him to keep a lookout, and he watched through sleepy eyes as she marched off in the direction of the cabin. Benjamin sat down on a tree stump, and he let out the sound of a screech owl, just for the fun of it. Minty came dashing back, her hands fluttering.

"What was that for? You see something?"

"Oh. Sorry. I forgot I'm only supposed to do that when I see trouble."

Minty slugged him in the shoulder. "Next time there really better be trouble, or I'll give you trouble of my own."

As Minty returned to the cabin, Benjamin rubbed his right shoulder. Lordy, Minty packed a hard punch.

■■■

Minty had felt so lonely the past six months without her Mama. The day that Mama, Moses, Henry, and Linah were shipped away to the Mills Farm, Minty had been out working in the woods for Master Brodess. He had given up on Minty ever being much use hired out as a domestic, so she was put to work with manual labor: hoeing, plowing, wood-cutting, and doing all manner of boy-chores. Outdoors, she could breathe in God's good air, and she didn't have to stare at a whip hanging over a mantle. She also noticed she was becoming as strong as some of her brothers. They started to notice too, especially Benjamin.

When she had returned home at the end of this particular work-day, she found her Mama clean gone, like she had been raptured away. Minty never even got a chance to say goodbye. She learned not to trust that anything or anyone would ever remain where it should be, especially if she took her eyes off of them. Everyone she loved was being moved about, like furniture.

So Minty came up with this plan to see Mama, knowing she could always get Benjamin to do her bidding. Ever since Benjamin was a sprout, she ruled over him. Minty used to watch him while Mama was off working in the Big House, and she would frolic with him, hanging him upside down in his sleeping dress and swinging him around like a pig in a poke, his head almost hitting the floor.

She still laughed about the time she stuck a chunk of pork in his mouth to keep him quiet. When Mama got home and saw him sleeping with that hunk of pork hanging out of his mouth, she thought it was his tongue and that Minty had killed him. It wasn't funny at the time, because Mama whacked her good, but she could laugh about it now.

Even Mama could chuckle about it, and just the thought made Minty miss her something fierce. It's why Minty was beside herself with excitement as she slipped up to the cabin and eased open the squeaky door, which had no latch.

"Mama?" she whispered.

A gasp came from the shadowy corner, where Mama sat near a dwindling fire in a rocker, smoking on her pipe. Lord, Mama loved that corncob pipe. Beside her, sprawled out on pallets, were her brothers Henry and Moses, and her sister, Linah. All sound asleep.

"That you, Minty?"

"Yes, Mama."

Minty heard the rustle of hurried movement, and her Mama yanked her across the threshold and into the cabin.

"Minty, what y'all think you're doin' comin' over here in the middle of the night?"

"Come to see you. I miss you, Mama."

Mama wrapped her in an all-enveloping embrace, pulling her into the softness of her body. Her Mama was short, like Minty, with a round face and short-cropped hair, with a small, square patch of gray at the forefront of her hairline, on the right side. It was like she had spilled a little bit of flour on her head.

"I miss you too, baby daughter, but I'd miss ya even more if y'all got caught and taken away from me. Don't you be doin' dangerous things like this."

"I'm fine. Benjamin's keepin' watch for patrollers."

In the candlelight, Minty could see the fear glowing in Mama's eyes.

"You brought your little brother with you? Whatta you thinkin', Minty?"

"Just bein' safe like you said, havin' him stand guard."

"Safe would be stayin' back at the Brodess place."

Mama let go of Minty and made a move toward the door. But that's when they heard the long trill of an owl, coming from close by. Minty never thought about how realistic Benjamin's calls could be, and she wasn't sure whether it was his warning or whether it was a real bird.

But when Mama opened the door, there was Benjamin standing at the threshold, all out of breath. He must have seen trouble.

"Mama, y'all gotta see this," he said, grabbing her by the hand and pulling her through the door.

By this time, Minty's big sister Linah had awakened. She was staggering toward the door, rubbing the dreams out of her eyes.

"What's goin' on?"

But Mama didn't answer. Like Minty and Benjamin, Mama had her eyes raised to the heavens. It was the most amazing sight Minty ever laid eyes on. The sky was on fire. Stars dropped from the night canopy, like it was snowing flames. Stars were shooting all which way.

"Is this the end of the world, Mama?" asked Benjamin.

"Benjamin?" Linah said. "What's Benjamin doin' here?"

Again, Mama didn't answer. She was struck stone still.

"Mama, is Jesus comin' back?" Benjamin asked. "Is it Judgment Day?"

"Let's hope so," Minty said. She had been praying for the day Jesus would separate the goats from the sheep; she'd love to see the look on Brodess's face when he was heaped in with all of the goats.

"I don't know if this is the end, but we gotta pray," said Mama, and she dropped to her knees right then and there. Minty, Linah, and Benjamin did the same, all of them falling down like they were shot.

"We're gonna hold steady on to you, Lord," Mama said. "We're gonna hold steady on to you, and you hold steady on to us. We ask this, Lord. We know you gonna hold on to us, even when the sky is fallin' down on our heads."

Hold steady, hold steady. Harriet repeated the words over and over in her head, until it became like a bell ringing in her skull. Then she lifted her head and looked up at the sky with those bright streaks against the blackness, looking like someone up there was throwing balls of fire down on the earth. So beautiful.

In the months to come, people everywhere talked about this heavenly display, which went on for close to an hour. Some people insisted it was a sign of the End of Days, but others said the streaks were falling stars. They called them meteors, whatever those were. But even if the world didn't end that night, some incredible things happened. When certain masters saw the sky on fire, they called out all of their slaves in the middle of the night. The masters started telling the slaves who their mamas and papas were, even informing them where their parents had been sold. The masters must've thought God was coming to judge them, and they wanted to get in some last-second good deeds.

Minty sure wished the world had actually ended that night, but at least it gave the masters a scare, and that was almost as good. Problem was, the masters returned to being masters two days later. Isn't that always the way?

5

Bucktown, Maryland
1835: Two Years Later

M inty took her anger out on the flax.

Perched on her lap was a flax break, a kind of miniature bench with blades. As she crouched in the field, she laid a bundle of cured flax across the long blades on the bottom of the bench. She then slammed down the upper blade, again and again, all along the length of the flax stalks. This broke the flax skin and freed up the fibers trapped inside the stalks, creating a tangle of them like long, stiff hairs.

It was hard work, and Harriet came away with little cuts on her hands, but the man who had hired her out to do the job was even harder—the worst man in the area. It was autumn, but the day was unseasonably warm. Minty was a sticky mess, all covered in yellow flax dust. Her hair poked up all over the place, like a bushel basket, and it caught pieces of plant material in it. When she got home, she would do as she always did; she would wipe some of the grease from her evening meal onto her hair, to get some control over her rebellious strands.

That was the plan, anyway. Minty was alarmed at day's end when she returned to the plantation only to have the cook, a slave by the name of Miss Amelia, tell her they had to go to the general store to pick up supplies.

"With me lookin' like this?" Minty was now thirteen years of age, more conscious than ever of her appearance.

Miss Amelia just laughed. She was a tall, skinny woman, with a mouth too large for her thin face. A lot of the time, it appeared as if she couldn't stop smiling.

"You think y'all gonna meet your future husband at the general store or something?" Miss Amelia asked. "C'mon, nobody cares what ya look like. Get a move on, Minty."

Miss Amelia swatted Minty on the behind with a spoon, like she was still a child. At five feet tall, Minty wasn't much taller than the children on the property, but she was beginning to grow in womanly ways.

"At least give me something to cover my hair," Minty said.

Miss Amelia sighed and tossed her a shoulder shawl. "Take this," she said. "You do look a mess."

On the way out, Minty stopped at the horse trough to splash water on her face, trying to wash away some of the flax dust. Miss Amelia had to give a hard yank on her arm to pull her away.

They went on down to the general store at the Bucktown crossroads, where three roads met like an unholy trinity—Bucktown Road, Bestpitch Ferry Road, and Greenbrier Road. Benjamin told her the devil shows up at crossroads, and with these three roads meeting together like the end of a pitchfork, Minty could believe it.

The yellow building had a peaked roof pointing skyward. Barrels sat on the front porch on either side of a tattered door that swung loose and was slightly open. When they stepped onto the store's porch, Minty heard loud voices coming from inside. One sounded like the voice of a young black man, and she was determined not to let any young man see her in such a state.

"I can't go in," Minty said, folding her arms in front of her chest. Miss Amelia snagged Minty's collar and gave it a tug.

"You get inside, fool girl!"

"I ain't steppin' inside lookin' like this."

Being short, Minty didn't topple easily, and Miss Amelia must've realized that any amount of yanking on her collar wasn't going to dislodge her. Her dress would tear before she was ripped off of her spot.

Another sigh from Miss Amelia, a big heavy one this time. "All right, you don't hafta go in, but don't you go nowheres. I brought you here to help me lug back supplies."

Minty responded with a grunt and a nod.

But as Miss Amelia entered the store, Minty heard angry voices erupt from inside. Something strange was happening, so Minty decided that, messy hair or not, she was going to at least take a peek. Peering through the door, she was shocked to see a young black man, Thomas, vault over the counter. Meanwhile, a man named Hopkins, an overseer from the nearby Barrett place, tried to corner him.

The countertop was U-shaped, running all along the back and side walls of the store. It formed a barrier between the slave and overseer. Thomas stood on one side of the counter, near the back wall, and the overseer, Hopkins, was on the customer side of the counter. The storeowner, an elderly gentleman, had retreated to a far corner, timidly watching it all unfold.

"You stay right there, boy, or I'll tear you limb from limb!" Hopkins bellowed, jabbing a fat finger at the air. He carried a coil of rope in his other hand.

As Miss Amelia went running out of the store, she gave a tug on Minty's collar. But once again, Minty wouldn't be moved. She knew she should probably steer clear of this trouble, but she was mesmerized by what was unfolding before her eyes, and she wondered if she could do anything to help the slave.

As she edged inside the store, she considered throwing herself at Mister Hopkins' legs and getting him all tangled up. But if she did anything like that, she would feel the whip from the overseer—or worse.

Thomas made a move to run down the side of one wall, toward the front door, but Hopkins ran parallel to him, on the opposite side of the counter, trying to head him off. Then the slave, young and nimble, reversed directions, heading back toward the rear of the store. Hopkins nearly tripped, trying to reverse directions and keep up.

Thomas faked left, and Hopkins started to move to his right, and then the slave faked right, drawing another mirrored response. Minty continued to just stand there staring. She was rattled back to life when the overseer suddenly turned toward her and shouted, "You cut him off from one side, girl, and I'll come at him from the other!"

Hopkins wanted her to help him catch Thomas?

Minty didn't budge.

"Do it!" Hopkins shouted. "I gotta hog-tie this one and take him back where he belongs!"

The man, standing on the far side of the room, shook his coil of rope at Minty, but she still didn't lift a hand to help.

Meanwhile, Thomas must've realized he had to make his move now, if he had any hope of escape. So he darted back along the wall, leaping the counter and heading directly for the door, where Minty still stood, her feet anchored, her mouth hanging open. Minty watched him race by; she wasn't about to do anything to stop him. The big overseer probably knew he wasn't fast enough to catch the slave. So, as Thomas made for the front door, the overseer turned and grabbed something off of the counter. Minty never saw what it was.

The man whirled around and hurled the object at the escaping slave. Problem was, Minty stood directly in the path of the missile. To this day, she could not remember the thing hitting her. The last thing she saw was the white man's angry face, and his arm coming down in an arc as he hurled the object. She remembered seeing a gray blur coming straight for her like a meteor.

The next thing she knew, sparks flared in her mind, like shooting stars. Then it was all darkness.

...

Minty was flying. She soared high above an intricate river system, moving slow and easy through the air, her arms outstretched like a bird. On both sides of the river, the trees were height-of-summer green, and the water reflected the rich blue sky. Just ahead, a bridge spanned across the river. A man crossing on a wagon looked up and waved his hat at her. A train track hugged one side of the river, and a locomotive spewed a cloud of white and black smoke, puffing rhythmically.

She dipped lower, flying at a faster speed, nearly touching the tiptops of trees. The evergreens and oaks became a green blur, until she pulled up and rose higher. Further ahead, in a clearing in the forest, stood three large white crosses, like Calvary trees. A second river branched in from the left, and a plume of sediment pointed a finger of brown-shaded water across the body of the main river.

Next, she passed over a small town, where four white men on horses stopped to stare up at her. Minty was flying north. She could sense it. Looking down, she also saw three black men moving through the trees and running for cover when they spotted her fly overhead. Not until they saw who she was did two of the men step out from behind the trees, and one of them waved his floppy hat at her. Even from far away, she heard him let out a whoop.

Then she saw the line. It was as if someone had taken a pot of paint and ran a big black line across the land. The thick line ran right across the tops of the trees, down along the red-dirt field, and across the river. She could even see the rippling black line painted on the water.

This was the line separating South from North.

Just beyond the line, Minty spotted a large farmhouse, with a big barn and lots of sheep and cattle chewing on grass. Standing on the front porch of the house were four white women. Two of them waved their bonnets while the other two held out their arms and shouted, "Come to us! Come to us!"

But before she could cross over the line, Minty found herself falling, losing control, like a bird shot from the sky, and she tumbled and somersaulted in mid-air, seeing the trees of the forest shoot up at her like spears.

...

For two days, Minty came in and out of this otherworldly place, seeing visions from God. Not until the third day was she able to ease herself off of the loom bench where she had been laid, her head throbbing and still trickling blood. She learned that she had been struck by a two-pound hunk of lead, used for weighing out goods.

On the third day, she went back into the fields to work, the sweat and blood rolling down her face until she couldn't see.

6

Minty was strangely fascinated by what was unfolding before her eyes. Her sister Linah and brother Robert had the good sense to run out of the cabin when Master Brodess showed up, but Minty remained fixed in the corner, watching. Meanwhile, her Papa had dragged her brother Benjamin into the cabin and set him up in front of Master Brodess. There was a lot of anger boiling over in the room, with Papa mad at Benjamin, and Mama furious at Papa.

Strangely, Master Brodess was the calm one. It was an eerie calmness, with him sitting in a rocker in the center of the room, sipping coffee that Mama had given him. Mama stood off to the side, glaring at her husband, while Minty watched from the far corner of the room. She hoped that Mama and Papa wouldn't take notice of her, because she wanted to see what Master Brodess was going to do to her younger brother, Benjamin.

Master Brodess was a young man, with a very trim beard and ears placed much too low on his head, like they had slid down from where they were supposed to be. His eyes had a blank meanness in them that made Minty quiver just looking into them. Brodess was the master for Mama, Minty, and all of her brothers and sisters, but he had no claim on Papa. Up until about three months ago, Brodess's stepfather, Anthony Thompson, was Papa's master. But Master Thompson up and died three months ago, and now Papa's master was the son, Dr. A.C. Thompson.

Most amazing, the elder Thompson's will stated that "my man, Ben" would go free four years after he died, so Papa was well on the road to freedom. Why, the elder Thompson's will even said that four years from now, Papa would be given ten acres of his own land in the Poplar Neck area, just east of the Choptank River. *Ten acres, all his own.* Papa was going to be rich! It made her proud to know how much white men respected her father, but there was something a little strange about it, like a picture on a wall that was just a bit tilted.

And now this: Her Papa was fixing to wallop her brother Benjamin, and it scared Minty. Mama sometimes smacked them for doing wrong, but her Papa loomed larger, and his deep voice filled a room. Minty hadn't been around her Papa much because he lived on the Thompson place, about ten miles away. He was basically a stranger to her, so she couldn't guess what he was going to do to her little brother—although "little" wasn't the right word. At twelve years of age, Benjamin was quite a bit taller than Minty, who was fourteen.

"Scat," said Mama, yanking Minty to her feet and swatting her on the behind.

Minty reluctantly left the cabin, but she remained within earshot. She plopped down on the ground, just to the side of the cabin door, where she could hear what was being said inside.

"My boy has something to tell you," she heard Papa say to Master Brodess.

Then silence. An awful quiet. She could imagine poor Benjamin, shaking in his britches, unable to speak. Earlier that morning, Papa discovered that Benjamin had taken one of the chickens from Master Brodess's coop, snapped its neck, and sneaked it back home for a meal. He had done it before, but the other time Mama had cooked the chicken on the sly, and no one was the wiser. Today, Benjamin made the mistake of stealing it when Papa was around. Papa was furious, and he immediately told Master Brodess what his son had done.

He told on his own son!

"Talk, boy!" she heard Papa bellow, and then she heard Benjamin's voice—more of a mousy squeak, really. She couldn't make out his words, but he was probably admitting to the theft of the chicken. Papa had caught him red-handed, with blood from the chicken still smeared on his palms.

"He will be punished." That was her Papa speaking. He had a deep voice, like God almost.

"I trust that you will make sure the punishment is strong, fittin' the crime," said Master Brodess.

"My punishment will be stronger than that," her father said.

Then another silence. Was Benjamin talking again, and she just couldn't hear him? Minty, still sitting on the ground, leaned over and tried to peer through the narrow crack where the door didn't close completely. She could make out the back of Master Brodess.

"You were good in tellin' me 'bout the chicken, Ben," said Master Brodess, rising from the rocker. Ben was her father's name, the same as her brother Benjamin. "If it were anyone else's son, I'd see to the beatin' myself. But seein' as it's your son, Ben, I'll leave y'all to it."

Then Master Brodess turned around to head for the door, and there were those dead eyes of his, looking straight at Minty. With a gasp, Minty pulled away from the door and darted around the side of the cabin. Holding her breath, she pressed her back against the outside wall. She could hear the door squeak open, and for a moment she thought Master Brodess was coming around the corner to grab her by the hair and drag her before Papa—another child who needed a beating. But she soon heard his footsteps moving off in another direction, and when she finally had the courage to peek, the man and his horse were both gone.

Inside the cabin, she could hear loud voices. Her Mama and Papa were squabbling.

"How could you snitch on your own son?" Mama shouted. "Who are you to do such a thing?"

"I'm your husband, and my word is my word. I don't lie to no one."

"But no one asked y'all to lie! I just asked you to keep what your son did a secret!"

"But it's still a deception, and the master don't tolerate a deception."

Minty slipped up to the front door, which was open wide. Master Brodess had slammed it on the way out, but the door must have bounced back open. She could see Benjamin hiding behind Mama, which disappointed Minty. What was a twelve-year-old boy doing hiding behind his mother's skirt? Benjamin was pretty good-sized, almost as tall as Papa. He should be standing up for himself.

"Don't you be touchin' a hair on my boy," Mama said, blocking her husband's advance.

"I gave my word that I would punish him. Would y'all rather I let Master Brodess do the punishin'? I can tell you, Benjamin Junior wouldn't like that none."

"But if you hadn't told on your son, there wouldn't a been any punishin' to be done by anyone in the first place," said Mama, continuing to block Papa. It was like they were doing a strange dance, the three of them shuffling in a circle as Papa tried to get at his boy. "You shouldn't a told what he done."

Papa shot a finger in Mama's direction. "I'm gonna be a free man 'cause Master Thompson trusted me. *All* the folks 'round here trust me 'cause my word is gold."

"Fool's gold, Ben Ross!"

This time, when Mama tried to block her husband's path to her son, young Benjamin stepped out from behind her skirts.

When Mama made a move to jump in front of Benjamin again, Minty's brother put up a hand to stop her. "Papa's right, Mama. It's better he beats me than Master Brodess."

Mama's eyes flitted from Benjamin to the older Ben and back again. Her anger flowed from her like fire from an oven.

"I'm raisin' me an honest boy," said Papa, yanking Benjamin by the arm.

"How can you raise an honest boy when you don't even live here to do any raisin'?" said Mama. That stopped Papa in his tracks, and Minty was afraid he might wallop Mama. She could see in Mama's pained expression that she felt bad about saying what she did. Mama knew Papa had no choice about where he lived.

Mama's words took a little of the sap out of Papa. You could see it in his face, as his eyes went down and his whole body seemed to sag. He even let go of Benjamin, but Minty's brother didn't run. He walked to the door on his own free will.

"I'm ready for my punishment, Papa."

Minty was proud of her brother. She had never seen him stronger. She stepped aside as Benjamin walked boldly out of the cabin. He fixed his gaze straight ahead, although she could see his surprise when he caught a glimpse of her in the corner of his eye.

When Papa emerged from the cabin, Minty backpedaled two quick steps. Her eyes went immediately to what Papa carried in his right hand. It was a switch, not a whip, but it was going to hurt all the same.

7

Cambridge, Maryland
1842: Six Years Later

Whater a miserable Christmas Eve.

Benjamin Ross paced back and forth in the cold corner of a jail cell, hugging himself for warmth. Christmas was one of those rare occasions when masters sometimes served their slaves a small slice of freedom—a few days off to be with family. But not this Christmas. He had been tossed into the Dorchester County Jail, a tiny space with just three cells, and a corridor running in front of them. On this festive night, he was the only occupant of the jail, residing in Cell Number Two. A small, dingy cot had been shoved in the corner, and he had a bucket for a toilet.

But at least they had put him in the cell that had a single, barred window looking out at the courthouse. The jailhouse was dark, but the window allowed in a meager stream of moonlight.

Standing six feet tall, eighteen-year-old Benjamin was the tallest of the four Ross boys. But he sure wished he had a small portion of the confidence that was packed into the compact body of his five-foot-tall sister. Minty had enough confidence for ten tall people, with some left over. Benjamin also didn't have the same faith that Minty brandished. He prayed, but she *believed*.

Since being locked behind bars, he had done little more than pace the cell and occasionally stand on tiptoes to peek at the courthouse through the north-facing window. He fretted about his master's money problems, but not because he had any real concern for Edward Brodess. It's just that Brodess's woes usually turned into Benjamin's. Master Brodess had been selling off property like a sailor trying to pitch things from a sinking ship. He was in a bad way for money, and in a place like Dorchester County, news travels fast. Even the slaves heard that Brodess was being sued for his debts.

Benjamin had been out in the back, cutting wood, when three officers came up and shackled his hands, taking control of the master's property until he settled his debts. Then Benjamin was led off, along with Brodess's ox. The ox was an aging old thing named Leviticus, after the book of the Bible. Benjamin was a worrier, and he found himself fretting about the fate of Leviticus, a once-strong ox with which he had spent many seasons. Leviticus was getting on in age, so Benjamin figured the ox wasn't going to fetch much of a price to help Brodess out of his troubles. That's why Brodess was getting set to start selling off his people-stock as well.

He was preparing to sell Benjamin.

Benjamin sat down on a wobbly stool, put his head in his hands, and tried to squash his growing panic. He dreaded the idea of being sold to the Deep South. Maryland was positioned so close to freedom, but if he got sold down to Georgia or Alabama, it would be like being buried in a deep, dark mineshaft. No air. No light. There would be so much rock above his head that he would be crushed by misery and futility.

It wasn't fair. Benjamin wished he could be a "term slave," to be set free at a certain age, just like his Papa had been two years back. Why, Papa was even given ten acres of land of his own that he could use for timber—just as Master Thompson's will had promised. But Benjamin was stuck with Brodess as a master, and if he were sold south, he would never see a day of freedom.

It was late at night when the deputies brought in another prisoner. The door at the end of the corridor swung open with a bang, and two men dragged what sounded like a woman across the threshold.

"You can't take me from my children!" the woman shrieked. To Benjamin's horror, the voice in the dark was familiar. It took two men on either side to drag the woman along because her body had given out and gone completely limp. She was moaning and crying, calling out to God for help.

A third deputy carried a candle, and the small glow confirmed his fears. His sister Linah was being caged in one of the adjoining cells. Linah was the oldest of the nine Ross children, thirty-four years old, and she had always been frail and sickly. He saw her slump onto the cold floor of the cell as the deputies extinguished the candle and gave the jailhouse back to the darkness.

Benjamin got up and moved to the outer limits of his cell, crouching down and putting his face to the cold bars. Linah was curled up in a far corner, and in the dark she looked like a pile of old clothes. Her moan, low and continuous, was the only clue there was a living person in the midst of that pile.

"Linah. It's me. Benjamin."

The lump didn't move, just continued to sob. Was Brodess aiming to sell her as well?

"Linah! It's me, Benjamin."

Finally, the lump in the corner began to stir, and he saw the shadow of his sister as she crawled on all fours across the cold prison floor. She put her face to the bars that separated her cell from his, and Benjamin could make out her face, all wet with tears. He put his hand to her cheek and wiped away one of the tears, like a parent wiping away a smudge.

"What's gonna happen to my children?" she moaned.

Linah had two daughters, but for the past few years she hadn't given birth to any more children. That's probably why she was seen as expendable by Master Brodess. She brought in fifty dollars a year, being hired out, but that obviously wasn't enough in Brodess's mind to justify keeping a woman who couldn't give him any more slaves.

"We don't know for sure we gonna be sold away," Benjamin said.

"Course we gonna be sold," Linah said. "The master needs money bad."

Benjamin didn't know what to say. He wished he had his sister Minty with him, telling him what to do. But she was off working for a string of timber men. Brodess had hired Minty out to Dr. Thompson, and she had convinced Thompson to let her be her own agent. This allowed her to find her own work, bringing in an extra bundle for him and even getting to keep some for herself.

Benjamin didn't know how Minty pulled off things like that, but she did. If she were here, she would know what to say and do to keep them in Maryland.

"We gotta pray," Benjamin said, because praying would be the first thing Minty would do. His sister always said the Lord was a prayer-hearing God.

Interlocking fingers through the bars, Linah continued to cry, while Benjamin struggled for the right words.

"Satan is busy, Lord," he said, remembering snatches of Minty's prayers. "Satan is prowling our roads, Satan is forging shackles tonight in the fires of hell. But you, Lord, you're stronger than any devil. So reach on down and deliver us from evil! Deliver us, Lord! Deliver us!"

"Deliver us," Linah muttered, but her voice was barely audible.

8

Minty hefted the large ax above her head, taking aim. But before she could split a hunk of wood right down its center, she heard the sound of horses. She turned and stared way down the hill, where she could see an army of horses thundering in her direction, churning up the earth and kicking up a storm of dust. There must've been a hundred horses moving up the hill, plowing through the tall grass. As they neared, she could hear the screaming of women mixed in with the thunder of hooves. Women were crying out in pain.

When Minty blinked her eyes, she saw there were now riders on all of the horses, although she couldn't see their faces. But she knew what they were. Minty had heard of the Four Horsemen of the Apocalypse—Pestilence, Famine, War, and Death—but this was *One Hundred Horsemen* with hundreds of names. Too many evils to count. Some carried bows, and they began to unleash arrows tipped with fire, and others carried spears with the heads of their victims mounted on them. One fiery arrow whizzed right by Minty's left ear.

"I can't die but once!" she shouted at the horsemen, to show she wasn't afraid. "I can't die but once!"

Still, the horses kept coming, and they were almost upon her now, and yet she still couldn't make out the faces of the riders. Their faces were all a gray smear.

"I can't die but once!" she shouted, as two more arrows passed by her head. She held out her hand, as if to stop this infernal army single-handedly. The horses loomed close, and the cloud of dirt rose to such a height that it blotted out the sun; the smell was awful, like rotting bodies, and she bellowed even louder: "I can't die but once!"

Then the horses ran right over and through her, like ghosts, and as they did, they evaporated, one by one, turning to ash.

"Minty! Wake up, Sister Minty!"

When she opened her eyes, she was back in the work yard, sitting on a tree stump with her ax leaning up against her side. The ground was coated with a thin layer of snow, and her fingers were stiff with the cold.

"You havin' a bad dream," came the voice from only a few feet in front of her face. When she finally emerged from the fog, she saw John Tubman standing there, looking all concerned. He had a hand on her right shoulder, lightly jostling her.

"Y'all right, Sister Minty? Y'all kept shoutin' 'bout only dying once. I thought maybe you were dyin' right there in front of my eyes."

Minty let slip a smile. "Y'all know me, Brother John. God takes me on these short trips to another world, but I don't think I'm leavin' for good any time soon."

"You sure you ain't just dreamin'?"

"I know the difference between a dream and a vision sent by God, Brother John."

"All right, all right. Just askin'. That's all."

Most people in the camp knew about Minty's visions. It happened often enough. She'd just be working away, normal as can be, and then she'd fall off to sleep, as simple as stepping off a cliff. It had been that way ever since the day she got whacked in the head by the chunk of lead flung at the Bucktown store. The lead had struck her so hard that it drove a piece of her headscarf right into her skull. Today, the only reminders of that strange day were the visions and the V-shaped scar she displayed in the middle of her forehead.

Minty rose to her feet because there was still work to be done. She aimed to cut a half cord of wood this day, so she better get back at it.

Minty wasn't sure what to make of John Tubman. Her Mama said it was long past time she should be finding a husband because she was twenty-one years old. But she wasn't in any hurry to marry. Tubman was a good-looking man, dark skinned for a mixed-race man. He had a youthful look, despite being in his thirties, a full ten years older than Minty. You could see some of the Caucasian features he got from his white father on the Tubman family side. John was a free black man, so she was a little puzzled why he was showing attention to a slave girl like her. Surely, he couldn't have matrimony with a slave in mind.

"Stay and sit a spell," he said, putting both hands on Minty's shoulders. "I got some news 'bout your brother and sister."

Minty felt her heart flutter, but she remained standing. Her brother and sister were in jail, awaiting sale to the South, so she braced for bad news.

"What's happened?"

"Benjamin is outta jail."

Instantly, Minty felt a weight come off of her back, like a large black crow lifting off and rising into the air. "Praise God, praise His Holy Name. So he ain't bein' sold?"

"I don't know how Brodess done it, but he's wiggled out of his debt somehow."

"I don't care how he done it. That's good news."

"Brodess didn't have to sell Benjamin or even that old ox."

"Leviticus?"

"That's the one."

Minty let the good news soak into her bones. She felt a lightness, but it was only fleeting. She suddenly wondered: Why didn't Brother Tubman say that *both* Benjamin and Linah had been released from jail? If they had both been freed, wouldn't that be the natural thing to say? The silence between them scared her. The air was filled with evil.

"There's bad news with the good, ain't there?" she said.

Brother Tubman wouldn't keep eye contact. Another bad sign. He seemed afraid to speak.

"Tell me!"

"Linah's been sold, Sister Minty."

It was like Minty had been struck behind the eyes by another chunk of lead.

"But couldn't Dr. Thompson save her?" she said.

"He said he would help out, but he didn't lift a finger to keep your sister from bein' sold."

"Oh." Minty went quiet and stared at the ground. First Mariah, then Linah.

John Tubman wouldn't look her in the eyes. He said softly, "I'm sorry, Minty."

"Has she been sold to someone close by?"

Minty was met by another wall of silence from Brother Tubman. Didn't the man realize that his silence was more painful than his words?

"Where was she sold? Tell me!"

"Linah went to a man from Georgia. I'm sorry, Sister Minty."

Brother Tubman made a move to wrap his arms around her for comfort, but Minty gave a hard shove to his chest. She took hold of the ax and raised it high—an incredible sight because the ax handle was nearly as long as she was tall. From the look on Brother Tubman's eyes, he probably thought she was aiming to split his skull. But she still had a piece of wood standing upright on a stump, and she brought the ax down with a force beyond her powers. The ax cut through the wood, smooth and straight.

Brother Tubman stood to his feet and took a couple of steps back as Minty set up another chunk of wood and let the ax fall again. She didn't blame him for moving a safe distance away, based on the rage she was feeling, but he should know by now that her aim was as sharp as this blade. She dispatched four more pieces of wood, cutting them cleanly and helping to get some of her anger out.

Her mind was storming, and her arms were strong with rage, but her legs began to go wobbly as she set up another piece of wood to be split. Then she found herself crying, something she didn't do too often; the ax fell from her hand, and she dropped backward onto the ground, bringing her knees to her chest and weeping so hard she could barely breathe. Her entire body convulsed. She thought about how she was never going to see her sister ever again. Linah, being the oldest, was like a mother to her whenever Mama wasn't around. She remembered sharing a bed with her, and how Linah comforted her whenever she was scared of storms—or terrified that Mama was going to be sold away. Linah would snuggle up to her, keeping her warm and safe. But now she was gone.

Minty felt as if she were a block of wood, set up on a tree stump, and the devil had just sliced her clean through with one swipe of his blade. Once again, Brother Tubman approached, and once again he put his hands on her shoulder. And this time, when he wrapped her in an embrace, Minty let him.

...

Benjamin felt the furies when he learned that Linah went for just four hundred dollars, and that Master Brodess used the money to buy more land. But that was only the beginning. Next to go was Soph, the third oldest daughter. Brodess bragged that Soph went for top dollar because she was a "slave for life." She wouldn't be freed at a certain age. In righteous anger, Benjamin felt the strong wind of the Lord's judgment words: *Let his days be few. Let his children be fatherless, and his wife a widow. Let the extortioner catch all that he hath; and let the strangers spoil his labor.*

Next to be offered up for sale was Moses—Benjamin's baby brother, only eleven years old. Talk had been swirling around like a dust devil, and rumor had it that Master Brodess was fixing to sell Moses. Benjamin's world was falling to pieces. First his sisters, now his little brother.

"Moses!" hollered Master Brodess from the Big House.

Benjamin was out hoeing in the garden, not too far away. He was getting the soil good and ready for spring planting when he heard Brodess shout. He looked up and spotted Edward Brodess on the porch, cupping his hands around his mouth and bellowing. Standing next to him was a strange man that folks said came from Georgia. He was a fine-dressed man, middle-aged with a gold cane, tight waist-coat, and high top hat.

Brodess was no longer the young man who threatened to beat Benjamin for stealing that chicken so long ago. He had a middle-aged paunch, and his hair had receded, revealing a high forehead, like a white tower. To match the high forehead, Brodess also had a long beard extending in the opposite direction. Put them together, and they made for one long, horsey face.

"Moses!" he shouted again. "Fetch this gentleman's horse!"

Benjamin looked around. Still no sign of Moses anywhere. Brodess could've been talking to a ghost.

"What's the matter, Brodess?" said the Georgia gentleman in the top hat. "Your slaves don't obey when you call?"

"They obey. Don't you worry nothing 'bout that."

Benjamin suspected the man had come looking for slave flesh to buy and haul farther south. He was afraid the man would want to buy him, but the word was that he wanted younger slaves like Moses. As soon as Mama had heard that Brodess was fixing to sell her youngest son to this Georgia fellow, she had hustled Moses out to the Green-brier swamp, where he was well hidden in the maze of marshes. No way were they going to be able to find him.

Just then, Mama came barreling around the side of the house.

"What you want with my boy?" she demanded, right there in front of the man from Georgia. The stranger chuckled, seeming to delight in Brodess's obvious embarrassment over Mama's impudence. Master Brodess went as red as a tomato.

"Ain't none of your business," Brodess blasted back. "Just fetch me a pitcher of water!"

Mama paused, and for a moment Benjamin thought she was going to refuse a direct order. But Mama must have realized that fetching a pitcher of water was not worth squabbling over. She should save her ammunition for the battles that really counted—like protecting Moses. So Mama obeyed and disappeared into the house while

Benjamin went on hoeing. He worked over the same soil twice so he could hang around long enough to see what happened next.

After Mama brought out the pitcher of water and two glasses, she disappeared back into the house while Brodess and the Georgia man sat on the porch, rocking and talking business. Benjamin couldn't hear what they were talking about, but when he spotted money passing from the Georgia man to Brodess, he knew it was serious. Benjamin stared at the end of the hoe in his hands, thinking how its sharp blade could till the master's scalp right off, as cleanly as removing a thin layer of soil.

He had just lost two more sisters. He couldn't lose a little brother.

Benjamin felt the sweat plastering the back of his work shirt to his skin, despite it being a pleasant spring day. The tension and fear created a heat all their own. He pounded the soil with more force, churning up the dirt. A little time went by, and Master Brodess stood to his feet once again, cupped his hands around his mouth, and hollered. "Moses!"

The master had drilled into them the Brodess golden rule: Come running straightaway when you hear his call. But instead of Moses answering, Mama came tearing out of the house and planted herself in front of the two men. She had her hands on her hips, so Benjamin knew she meant business. Whenever Mama's hands went to her hips, Benjamin ran for cover.

He poked at the soil, pretending to work, but his ears were wide open.

"What did you come for?" Brodess asked, looking down on Mama. "I hollered for the boy, not you."

At that instant, Mama ripped out an oath that would make any man blush. Benjamin's jaw dropped. Mama was about the only one who could intimidate Master Brodess, but had she gone too far? Embarrassing the master in front of a potential buyer from Georgia was crossing a line of some sort. He feared for Mama.

"I expect Moses to come here this minute to hitch the horses to my guest's carriage," Brodess said, trying to sound strong. But the fact that he had to explain himself to a female slave made him appear weak, almost pitiful.

"Oh no, you ain't wantin' my Moses to hitch any horses," said Mama. "You're only wantin' Moses so you can sell him to this lurkin' Georgia man."

Up until this point, the Georgia man had been grinning like a baboon, obviously taking pleasure over Brodess's impudent slave. But now, all of a sudden, Mama had shoveled a load of anger onto him too; based on the look on his face, you'd think she had dropped a load of manure on his shoes. He rose to his feet, his face reddening.

Benjamin's hands tightened around the wooden handle of the hoe. He knew Brodess, and he was pretty certain he wouldn't do anything to hurt Mama. But the Georgia man was a stranger. Insult him, and Mama could wind up hanging from a tree.

The two white men loomed over Mama, who didn't back down, not a single step. Then Master Brodess cast a glance over at Benjamin, who had paused in his hoeing to stare. The moment the master's eyes hit him, he started hoeing once again.

When he had the nerve to glance back up, he noticed that Brodess had vanished. Only the Georgia man and Mama remained on the porch, and Mama still had her hands on her hips. Soon, Brodess reemerged from the house, and Mama let rip with another oath when she saw that the master carried a bullwhip in his right hand.

"What you think you're doin' with that thing?" she shouted.

"Fetchin' your boy!"

Master Brodess descended the porch steps two at a time and marched toward the woods. Benjamin could hear him spouting curses every step of the way. When Benjamin sensed a presence at his side, he turned and was startled to see that Mama had slipped up next to him. Together, they watched Master Brodess storm off toward the forest.

"Don't you worry none, Benjamin," Mama said quietly. "Ain't no way he's gonna find your baby brother."

And she was right. Looking for a slave in the swamp was about as easy as finding a lone mouse hiding in a wide field of grain. Master

Brodess never did find Moses, even after one of his house slaves gave away Moses's hiding place. As soon as Mama had the chance, she went running off to track down Moses and move him to a new hiding spot. Even more remarkable, when Brodess and a neighbor came to Mama's cabin to talk about the sale of Moses, she met them at the door and let loose, shouting: "The first man who steps into my house will have his head split open!" Brodess knew better than to test whether she'd back up this threat, and they slinked away.

Eventually, the Georgia man gave up and left town without adding Moses to his batch of newly bought slaves, and Benjamin could breathe again. The tension had been suffocating.

The strange thing was that Master Brodess started acting like he was *glad* Mama had hid Moses, but he supposed that that was just the master's way of saving face. Or maybe Brodess was trying to win Mama to his side and make her better-behaved.

But that would never happen. When it came to her children, Mama was a Mother Bear. Benjamin would never forget that for as long as he lived.

9

Dorchester County
February 1844

Minty rode the log with nimble ability. Being so short, she had great balance, as the massive log, cut down to sixteen feet long, skidded along the snow-covered path. Four strong oxen pulled the log behind them like a crucifix, while Minty stood on the log and snapped the whip to keep them moving. The temperature had warmed on this winter's day, and steam rose from the animals' hide as if the oxen were smoldering. Yesterday had been much colder, and her hands nearly froze because she didn't have gloves—only strips of cloth wrapped around her frigid fingers. Today, however, she was feeling fine, riding the log like she was standing up on a sled.

Then Minty felt the shudder of somebody else leaping aboard, and she twisted around to see that John Tubman had jumped on the moving log.

"Mornin', Minty!"

"Mornin', John. You tryin' to add to these oxen's woes by piling your weight on to their load?"

"Don't worry, they're plenty strong. Almost as strong as you."

Minty took that as a compliment, even though most women wouldn't see it that way. There wasn't much call for being lady-like when working in timber. She was one woman in a world of men, cutting and hauling wood from the forest down to the river. She even earned some money of her own and had almost saved up enough to buy a pair of steers. John Tubman seemed smitten by her ability to work hard. Sometimes he would have her show off for his friends and demonstrate how she could lift a huge barrel of produce all by herself.

She had to admit...it gave her pleasure.

Minty knew she wasn't a great beauty, so she wondered if John had his eyes on her because she was the only lady in the camp. Or maybe he just saw her as a novelty—a five-foot woman dwarfed by monstrous trees and strong men.

"Don't fall!" John said, putting both hands on Minty's waist.

She jabbed his right hand with the butt end of her whip, and he yelled out, yanking his hand back and shaking it like he had been snake bit.

"What y'all do that for?" he said, rubbing the sore spot where she whacked him.

"You don't need to be grabbin' me, Brother John. I can keep my balance all by myself. And why ain't you off fellin' trees, anyway?"

"I saw you skiddin' by and thought I'd hitch a ride."

"Don't let the overseer see you shirkin' your work."

"He's off fillin' his mouth with beans."

Minty turned around on the moving log to face John squarely—and to make sure he didn't get fresh with her. But as she turned, the oxen reached a sharp right bend in the path and came to a jolting stop. The next thing Minty knew, she was backpedaling to keep her balance. She tumbled off the side of the log, landing on her backside, and her whip went flying, landing straight up in the deep snow.

Laughing, John leaped from the log, reached down, and scooped her up in his arms like she didn't weigh anything at all.

"I thought you didn't need no help balancin', Minty!"

"I wouldn't a fallen if you hadn't been bouncin' around like a grasshopper on my log! Now put me down!"

"Not without a kiss."

"I'll kiss you with my whip if you don't let go!"

John obeyed instantly, removing his hands from beneath her. It felt like the floor had disappeared under her. She fell straight down, once again landing on her rear end. Fortunately, the snow was deep enough to cushion her crash, although the sloppy wetness seeped all through her clothing.

She glared up at John, who plucked her whip from the snow. He grinned from ear to ear.

"You didn't need to drop me," she muttered, climbing out of the snow and wiping the soggy clumps from her dress.

"You said let go. And here's your whip, Minty—although I'm not sure I should be puttin' this in your hands, seein' that fire in your eyes."

She was tempted to give his legs a snap of the whip, but she had experienced the lash enough in her life that she wouldn't dare use it in jest.

"You better get back to work, John Tubman. The overseer's gotta be close to finishin' his feedin' time, and he's gonna be wonderin' where y'all are."

Minty leaped back onto the log, and she snapped her whip at the unhappy oxen, which were still struggling with the sharp turn. When the whip wouldn't get them moving, John helped out by smacking one of the ox in the rear with the flat of his hand. He nearly caught a hoof in the shin as the big animal kicked backward.

Minty hopped down from the log so she could apply the whip to the two oxen in front, and that finally got them moving. But then the big animals stopped again, straining under the enormous wooden yoke. Minty and John worked together to eventually get the oxen around the sharp bend.

With a straight path ahead, Minty hopped back on the log, and then John followed suit.

"I'm serious, John. You better get on back to work. I don't wanna hear of you gettin' whipped by the overseer, like one of these ox."

"So you care for me?" John grinned big.

"I care enough to not want you gettin' whipped."

"Do you care enough to marry me, Minty?"

Stunned, Minty very nearly fell off the log once again. This time, she caught her balance, as the log slid along with a little more speed now that the oxen were on a straight path through the woods.

"What did y'all say?"

She knew exactly what he had said, but that didn't stop her from asking him to repeat himself.

"I wanna marry you, Minty."

Minty knew Brother John was sweet on her; she'd have to be blind to miss it. But she never really thought he would ask for her hand. What free black man would want to marry a slave woman? Surely, she didn't have to remind him that any children they had would be slaves because the children always followed the mother.

"I'm a slave, Brother John. Don't you know what y'all are askin'?"

"Slave or no slave, you don't *act* like one."

"Don't matter how I act. It matters what the law says I am."

"But you cut your own deals with the masters. I like that."

They both stood on the moving log, just staring at each other. She looked at his same silly grin as she scratched her head, trying to puzzle out this man. John Tubman was thirty-two years old—ten years older than her. Was he desperate to settle down, and she happened to be the only one handy in this logging camp? Then again, most reasonable people would say it was time for her to settle down. At twenty-two, she was getting beyond the point when most women marry and start firing out children.

"So will ya marry me?"

"You caught me by surprise, Brother John. I'm gonna have to give this some thinkin'."

"What's there to think about?"

"The rest of my life, for starters."

"But why think so far ahead? You could be dead tomorrow."

"You're not convincin' me with those words, Brother John Tubman." Still, she hated to admit it, but she had always been strangely drawn by his carefree ways. He was a bit of a rascal and didn't take too much in life seriously. Maybe he would be good for her.

"Give me the night to think on it."

"Okay, but I don't know why we can't get hitched together like those oxen right this day."

Minty looked over her shoulder at the four animals, grunting and straining to move their legs one step at a time. "I sure hope that ain't your idea of marriage, Brother John."

John laughed so hard that he nearly lost his balance. "No, nothing like that, Minty. My yoke is easy. And bein' married to you would be a lark."

A lark? She wondered if he really knew her.

"All right then, I'll think on it. Now get on back before the overseer whips you so hard you won't be in any shape to marry."

Once again, his face brightened.

"I expect your answer tomorrow." John took a soaring leap off the log, landing on both feet in the snow. "But we all know what your answer will be! We're gettin' married, Minty!"

She watched as John went running back through the woods to fell trees. Then she turned, saw that the oxen were barely slogging along, and snapped the whip. The rawhide cracked the winter stillness.

...

Minty's clothes smelled of smoke as she trudged into Master Brodess's tiny office, with its one small bookshelf partially filled with about a dozen books that he probably hadn't read. Brodess was not a book man, but he liked to think he was. The Brodess house was not nearly as grand as the Thompson place. It was a compact, one-and-a-half-story structure with three bedrooms overrun by their eight children. She could hear several of them screaming upstairs and thumping around.

Minty had been delivering firewood to the Brodess house when she was told the master wanted to see her. Brodess leaned back in his chair and sized her up and down, even though there wasn't much "up and down" at five feet tall. There was no chair for her to take, but he wouldn't have asked her to sit anyway, and not just because she was a slave. He would probably be afraid that if she sat down she'd drop off asleep, as she did multiple times a day.

Master Brodess stared at her for a good ten seconds, and Minty stared right on back. She was not one to give masters the expected "down look" of a slave.

"I hear that John Tubman asked for your hand, Minty," said Master Brodess. This shocked her. Apparently, word got around pretty quickly. "Is that true? Did John Tubman ask to marry you?"

"Yes, sir, you heard right."

"What answer are you planning to give him?"

No gentleman would dare ask a white woman such a question. Minty shrugged. "Haven't come up with an answer just yet."

"You're over twenty years old, Minty." He said it as if she had one foot in her grave.

"Sounds 'bout right."

"I expect children from all my wenches."

Minty fixed him with a hard gaze. She tried to show him her steel, but she felt herself going sick on the inside. All she could think about was her oldest sister, Linah, who had given birth to two children. When Linah dried up, Master Brodess sold her to Georgia. Minty couldn't let that happen to herself.

"Do you understand, Minty? I need breeders. Good breeders."

She wished so much she could grab the whip she used on the oxen and turn it on Master Brodess. In her mind's eye, she saw herself striking him right across the face. She continued to look him straight in the eye because that was as close to using the whip on him as she could get.

"I understand clearly," she said.

"You work alongside many men. Strong bucks, most of them. So if John Tubman is not suitable, perhaps one of those would do."

"Ain't none of the others looked my way."

That wasn't entirely true. She did catch the admiring glance from some of the men from time to time. But she knew that none of the others were interested in marriage. Maybe other things, but not marriage.

"Think about it," Master Brodess said. "Think long and hard."

She knew what that meant. Breed or be sold.

"I will, sir."

...

The wedding was a simple one—just a few of the men from camp were in attendance. One of them was a preacher, and he did the officiating. A slave wedding wasn't legal in the eyes of the law, but it was holy in God's eyes—and Minty's, as well.

In the end, Minty had taken two weeks to finally give John Tubman the answer he wanted. He had demanded that she answer him in one day, but she decided that that was reason enough to delay her response. After one week, she decided she would marry him, but she hemmed and hawed an extra week just to see him sweat. She wasn't going to let him start ordering her around from the get-go.

Minty married John Tubman because she had no way of knowing when the next offer might come along. She wanted so badly to spite Master Brodess by refusing to get married, but she couldn't get her sister Linah out of her mind. Sold off to Georgia because she couldn't have any more children.

But did she love John Tubman?

Time will tell, she decided. He was a light-hearted man, and Minty could use somebody like that. She had seen too much sorrow, and she was certain John had too. But he had a way of covering it up with his horsing around.

Being a free man, John kept a small, tumbledown cabin in the middle of the woods straight west of Bucktown near Harrisville Road. As they hiked through the trees on their first night as man and wife, John came up with the bright idea of carrying her in his arms the last mile or so to the cabin. She was intrigued to see if he could really do it.

"Most fellas just carry their wives across the threshold. I can do better than that," he said proudly.

"Are you sure you know what you're doin'? There ain't no snow on the ground if you drop me."

"Don't worry, I ain't droppin' you. You're a little thing."

But he wasn't very far into his march before Minty could see him beginning to drag along, sweating and panting. All of the snow had melted, leaving the cold ground slick and slippery. He started out smiling, but now the strain was showing. He bit his lip, and a vein popped out from his neck. His breath was visible, puffing from his mouth like a steam engine. The going got especially hard when he hit an upward slope.

"I can walk a spell to give you a rest," she said. Truth be told, Minty was starting to get a little tired of this stunt. She also wanted to get to the cabin before nightfall.

"I said I'd do it. I'll do it."

"But y'all don't have to carry me the whole way."

"Yes, I do."

"Ain't no law sayin' a husband gotta carry his bride through the woods."

"It's John Tubman's law that says it!"

"Then John Tubman better elect himself some better lawmakers. Seems a fool law."

She said it in jest, but she could tell John didn't like it. What started out as a happy jaunt turned into an oppressive slog, John barely getting one foot in front of the other. At this rate, they might not ever get to the cabin.

A couple of times, his foot caught on a tree root, and Minty was sure they were going to hit the ground.

"Tell me one of your stories," she suggested. "That'll keep your mind off of your burden." John loved to spin a good tale, but he was breathing so heavily that he would probably have a difficult time getting out the words.

"Maybe when we get to the cabin," he gasped between huffs and puffs.

They weren't too far from the cabin when John suddenly dropped to his knees. He knelt there for a few moments, catching his breath with his bride still in his arms. She didn't know how in the world he was going to get back up.

"I can stand up, and then you can pick me up again," she suggested with uncharacteristic meekness. Normally, Minty wouldn't be so tactful. If this had been any other day, she would have told John he was acting like a fool, and that he should just put her down and walk to the cabin like any other newly married folk. But this was their wedding day. She decided she could control herself for one day at least.

"I ain't quitting this close to the cabin," he said.

John tried to bring himself back to a standing position without letting go of Minty. He failed on his first try. His groan carried through the trees.

"You can do it, John."

A little encouragement did the trick. With his kneecaps popping, he struggled back to a standing position and trudged on. When they finally reached the cabin, he nearly dropped her as he used one hand to open the door. They entered the dim interior—sparsely furnished and very cold. He lit a candle, revealing a pallet covered with straw: their wedding bed. The problem was that the bed was only big enough for one person. He saw her staring at it, and from the look on his face, it appeared he hadn't thought through the sleeping arrangements.

"I can sleep on the floor," he offered.

"You bet you are."

So Minty began her new life with a new name. But she didn't just take his last name of Tubman. She also decided to change her first name. She would no longer be Minty, the name of a little girl. She would have a woman's name—the same name as her mother. She would be Harriet.

She had crossed a new threshold, and from this day forward, she would be Harriet Tubman.

HARRIET

"There's two things I've got a right to, and these are, Death or Liberty—one or the other I mean to have. No one will take me back alive; I shall fight for my liberty, and when the time has come for me to go, the Lord will let them kill me."

— HARRIET TUBMAN

10

Poplar Neck, Maryland
February 1849: Five Years Later

The horses came, swifter than evening wolves. They came for violence, with the riders on the horses devouring everything before them; the land in front of the horses was an Eden and the land behind a desolate wilderness. Nothing escaped them, and they gathered captives like sand.

The walls of Harriet's cabin shook at the thunder of the horses streaming by on all sides, and she could hear the screams of women calling out for their children, mixed with the sound of stallions. The land quaked, and the swords of the riders drank their fill of the blood of the people.

"Snap out of it, Harriet!"

A hand pushed against her left shoulder, hard and impatient. It was her husband.

"You dropped off to sleep again!" John thundered. "Can't you keep your eyes open for ten minutes? The food is near burnin'!"

When Harriet and John first married, he'd find it amusing whenever she would suddenly drop off the edge of reality and fall into a vision. But after five years of marriage, it had been a long time since he found it funny. John made it clear in so many little ways that marriage had become a heavy burden for him. That made Harriet mad.

The end of winter was in sight, and it couldn't come soon enough for Harriet. This winter had been a terrible one. She had been sick for weeks, burning up with a fever, hacking cough, and bones aching like they were infested with termites. She and John lived in Poplar Neck, north of Cambridge, because Edward Brodess had hired out all of the remaining Ross siblings to Dr. A.C. Thompson. Harriet had been included in this transaction. They worked on Dr. Thompson's sprawling timber operation, and they all lived in small cabins on a bend of the Choptank River between the Marsh and Skeleton creeks.

"I dreamt of horses again," she said, rising from her chair by the fire where she had a pot of stew bubbling. She stirred the pot and could tell that some of the potatoes had burned to the bottom.

John sat in the corner, staring up at the low ceiling of their cabin, his hands folded across his belly. He just grunted. John didn't seem to care one whit about her visions from God. But Harriet was going to make him listen, whether he wanted to or not.

"The horses mean trouble," she said. "God's sendin' me a warning, John."

"Just a dream. Nothing more."

"I saw horses when Linah and Soph were sold away. The horses mean trouble is comin'. The master might be fixin' to sell *me* this time."

"December's when the tradin' season happens, and you weren't sold away. You'll be fine."

"Yeah, but Master Brodess did try to find a buyer for me in December, and that worries me. Every time I see a white man talking to him, I'm afraid of being carried away."

John let out a hoot. "Who'd wanna buy a sickly slave who can't work for more than an hour without falling into a vision? No one will give a sixpence for you."

"He sold Mariah Ritty first, then Linah and Soph. I'm the next daughter in line."

"But your sisters were more valuable. They could breed."

John found every chance to remind her that she couldn't have children. Five years and not a single child. Just another reason for Master Brodess to get rid of her.

Harriet muttered under her breath as she continued to stir the pot.

"I been prayin' that Master Brodess be converted," she said.

Again, John hooted. "Might as well pray that the devil convert while you're at it."

"There's been many masters findin' God these days, such as Mister Parks, and the Lord's been tellin' 'em to free their slaves. God can do anything."

"Anything but soften Brodess's heart."

"Don't you disrespect the Lord!" she shouted. "The Lord can do *anything!*"

"Then ask the Lord for a child, Minty." Sometimes John still called her Minty, just to get her riled. He didn't see her as a real woman because she didn't have children, so he called her Minty to remind her that she was still a girl when it came to childbearing.

Harriet wheeled around and waved the large spoon at him. "Don't you think I been askin' God to give us a child? Don't you think Sarah in the Bible asked God for a child, and He gave her one when the time was right? He'll give us a child when He's good and ready!"

She turned back to the pot. "Besides, you know any child born to us is property of Master Brodess. Maybe that's why God ain't lettin' us have any children."

John sat in the shadows, but Harriet could sense him looking her up and down. "Maybe you're too small to have a child."

Now it was Harriet's turn to hoot as she threw a glance over her shoulder. "You think givin' birth has to do with size? Don't be a fool, John."

That shut him up, and Harriet turned back to the pot. As she did, she thought about her older sisters and where they might be now. She had heard many horrors about the land down south.

"Stir my heart, Lord, stir my heart toward you," she said, as she continued to stir the pot. That's how she kept prayers in her head all the time. She connected what she was doing with her conversations with the Lord. When she washed her face in the horse trough, she asked God to wash away her sins and make her clean. When she wiped down the furniture, she asked Him to wipe away her iniquity. When she swept the floor, she asked God to sweep away all the evil from her heart.

Keeping the Lord in her head at all times was the only thing that kept her from losing her mind.

"If you hadn't caused such a fuss, maybe Brodess wouldn't be thinkin' of sellin' you," John said. "I told you not to make a fuss."

"'Bout time someone did."

John was referring to the lawyer that Harriet had hired. Against John's wishes, she spent five dollars to have a lawyer look into documents concerning her mother, Rit. After a good deal of digging, the lawyer discovered that her Mama's first owner, Atthow Pattison, said Rit was supposed to be set free at age forty-five, which meant she should have been freed a long time ago. Mama's current owners, the Brodesses, were furious and unwilling to cut her free.

"There ain't nothin' you can do with that information, except get Edward Brodess riled at you," John had told her. "You gotta stop pokin' the hornet's nest."

"It got the Pattison family interested, didn't it?"

"Starting a squabble between the Pattisons and the Brodesses does nothin' for us."

The Pattisons once owned Harriet's mother, but when Mary Pattison married Joseph Brodess—Edward's father—Mama suddenly became Brodess property. Then, when Joseph Brodess died, Harriet's Mama remained the property of Edward Brodess, just a baby at the time. Edward didn't take over the duties of being master until he reached twenty-one, the age of inheritance.

The families in this neck of the woods were just like the landscape, which was crisscrossed with streams and marshes—water everywhere, mixing and mingling. The families mixed and mingled as well, one clan spilling into the next. You couldn't walk very far without running into a stream or river or marsh of some sort, the same way you couldn't go very far without running into a Thompson or a Pattison or a Brodess.

What's more, the three families were always squabbling. Anthony Thompson once built a cabin for his stepson, Edward Brodess, and he expected Edward to pay him back. But Brodess being Brodess, he was always in some sort of money trouble, and he didn't pay his stepfather back. And now a squabble was starting between the Brodesses and Pattisons over a will a long time ago. It was all a confusing mess, tangled up with the three families.

"I had no choice but to dig into the law," Harriet told her husband. "The will said we're term slaves, and it's against the law to sell a term slave outta state. Brodess was breakin' the law when he sold my sisters outta state."

"Will you stop frettin' about your sisters?" John bellowed. "That was seven years ago when you lost Linah and Soph. It's time you forgot 'bout them."

"I ain't never gonna forget!"

"Then you ain't never gonna be happy!"

"Brodess broke the law when he sold my sisters!"

"But Brodess don't care nothin' 'bout breakin' the law, and he cares even less about breakin' your heart. You gotta get that through your thick head."

Harriet growled, but she was afraid there was truth to John's words. Her meddling did nothing to help her situation and probably made it worse.

The only thing that seemed to make any difference was praying. So she told the Lord regularly: "Make me strong and able to fight."

The way she saw it, prayer was the only stick with which she could beat Brodess.

...

March 1, 1849. That date would remain etched in Harriet's mind. It's when she first heard the rumors bubbling up all around her.

"Wake up! Wake up, John!" After a long day's work, her husband had fallen asleep in the rocker on the front porch, and she shoved at his shoulder. The night crickets were chattering away, intermixed with frog croaks and birdcalls.

"What now?" John said, emerging from his slumber.

"It's Brodess. People say he's aimin' to sell. This time for real."

"You been saying that for weeks. Let me go back to sleep."

"It's serious. People are sayin' Brodess is aimin' to sell me and my brothers and my sister, Rachel."

"Woman, you're like Old Cudjo, who didn't laugh at a joke until long after it was told. You worryin' 'bout bein' sold, long after the danger's past." Shaking his head, he closed his eyes again.

But Harriet would not be ignored so easily. She shoved him on the shoulder once again, this time nearly toppling him over backwards in the rocker. His eyes popped open as he caught his balance.

"Leave me be!" he shouted. "Go talk to your God! Ain't nothin' I can do."

John closed his eyes, and Harriet just stood there, glaring down at him. Her breath pumped in and out like a bellows, her chest heaving. She sensed the thundering horses coming for her, the riders aiming to swoop down and scoop her up.

They come and devour the land and all that fills it. For behold, I am sending among you serpents, adders which cannot be charmed, and they will bite you, says the Lord.

Harriet threw open the front door of the cabin, nearly yanking it off of its hinges. She stomped into the cabin and paced the room, beating her chest, as if that could stop the racing of her heart. She plopped down on her knees, hoping that prayer would calm her, bring her breathing under control. She felt the Old Testament coming over her like a strong wind, felt the call of a Justice God, ready to bring down his wrath on sinners like Brodess. *As a young lion growls over his prey, so the Lord of hosts will come down to fight upon Mount Zion and upon its hill.*

Then Harriet prayed the words that came out of her like hot steam.

"Oh, Lord, if you ain't never gonna change that man's heart, kill him, Lord, and take him out of the way."

Kill him, Lord. Kill Master Brodess.

It terrified her just to speak the words out loud.

Six days later, on March 7, Edward Brodess was dead.

11

The guilt grew inside Harriet like a fast-spreading weed. She had called down the Lord's wrath, and the man died within the week! Her prayers had killed him, making her every bit as guilty, as if she had walked into his room and shot him in the head. She was terrified that Brodess's widow, Eliza, would find out what she had done and send the authorities to rouse her in the middle of the night and drag her off to hang for murder. Harriet would give a world full of gold to bring that poor soul back from the dead.

"You should be *happy* the man's dead," John told her for the hundredth time, during an early morning meal of cornbread and sweet milk. "Stop your moanin'. You were afraid he was gonna sell you, and now you're afraid you're gonna be arrested for prayin' him to death. Is there no end to your frettin'?"

Harriet regretted ever telling her husband that she had prayed for Brodess's death. He found it funny at first, and she was afraid he was going to joke with the other men about it. She couldn't afford for the widow, Eliza Brodess, to find out what she had done.

"Besides," he said, "it weren't you who done the killin'. God struck Brodess down, and the Lord can't very well be hauled off to jail."

"They can jail his instrument, though."

"You're God's instrument?" John said, jamming a hunk of corn-bread into his mouth.

"I am."

He swallowed and chased the cornbread down with a sloppy mouthful of milk. The milk spilled down his chin, and he wiped it away with his forearm. "If you're that powerful, you ain't got nothin' to fear."

But she did have plenty to fear. With Brodess dead, she had to tangle with his widow, Eliza, and that was just as bad. That woman flew off the handle as a matter of routine, especially when the money woes got to be too much—which was always. Miss Eliza had eight children, five under the age of eighteen. So what was stopping her from selling off her slaves to get money to feed her brood? There were already stories going around that Eliza was fixing to sell off both a daughter and grandchild of Harriet's big sister, Linah.

Harriet feared the worst when Eliza Brodess called her to the house and told her to stand and wait for her in the main room. Miss Eliza ordered her not to budge and then bolted to another part of the house, leaving Harriet standing there for the longest time. Harriet eyed a nearby upholstered chair and was tempted to take a seat; her back had been giving her fits lately, and she could do with a way to take the pressure off of her spine. But she knew that Miss Eliza was probably watching and waiting for her to sit down, so she could swoop in and smack her for disobeying a clear command. Harriet wasn't going to give in to her games, so she remained standing and began to sing a song. Softly.

> *"Heaven bell a-ring, I know the road.*
> *Heaven bell a-ring, I know the road.*
> *Heaven bell a-ring, I know the road,*
> *Jesus sittin' on the water side.*
> *Do come along, do let us go.*
> *Do come along, do let us go.*
> *Do come along, do let us go.*

Jesus sittin' on the—"

"No singin'!" Miss Eliza shouted, as she came zipping back into the room. "This ain't a church, you know."

"Don't I know," Harriet muttered under her breath.

Miss Eliza gave her the evil eye, but then tore out of the room once again. Miss Eliza had ordered her to stop singing, but she said nothing about humming. So Harriet hummed the song quietly and spent the time praying, telling God she was standing in His presence, standing before the throne, standing in the glory, standing up for his Word. *Standing, standing, standing...*

If Miss Eliza was going to make her stand all day, then she was going to stand for God, not for some miserable mistress.

Finally, Miss Eliza ordered her into the office—the same tiny office where Master Brodess would sometimes give Harriet a talking to. Harriet noticed that the books on the shelf were gone, replaced by Miss Eliza's knickknacks.

The widow sat behind the master's old desk and glared. She looked to be in her thirties, with an oval-shaped face and puffy cheeks. Her eyes were sleepy-looking, with heavy lids, and she had a little dimple on her chin. Her auburn hair was parted cleanly down the middle and covered by a black bonnet. Her dress was all black, with white frills at the cuffs. She didn't cut a very frightening figure, but Harriet knew she had a way of going wild-eyed when she felt cornered. Before her husband died, most of her anger had been directed at him, but now that he was gone, Harriet wondered where her fury would be aimed.

She expected the mistress to start shouting, but instead she talked calmly.

"You know the trouble you started, don't you?" she said.

Harriet was sure Miss Eliza had discovered that she prayed for her husband's death and had turned her into a widow woman right like that.

"Trouble, ma'am?" Harriet acted dumb.

"You know perfectly well what trouble you started," Miss Eliza

67

said. "I've a good mind to sell you south for what you did, hiring that lawyer."

Lawyer? So Miss Eliza wasn't talking about how her prayers had killed Master Brodess. But she was talking about something almost as serious. Harriet stood up straighter and stiffened all over.

"The law won't allow for me to be sold outta state," Harriet said.

It was true. A judge had told Miss Eliza she couldn't sell any more of Rit's children until the legal mess could be untangled.

"Do you think I'm gonna let a judge stop me from sellin' off my property?" Miss Eliza asked.

"Ain't for me to say, ma'am."

"That's right! It ain't for you to shove your nose into my affairs! And it ain't for a judge to say neither! This Pattison mess is all your doin'!"

The "Pattison mess" was the lawsuit the Pattisons recently aimed at Miss Eliza. They claimed that when Harriet's mother turned forty-five, the Brodesses were supposed to return her to them. The Pattisons demanded that Miss Eliza pay the money that she and her late husband had made off of Rit for the past nineteen years. They also claimed that Linah and Soph had been sold away illegally, and they should be compensated for them as well. The Brodess family had enough money woes without these issues, too.

Miss Eliza rose to her feet, her wide dress swishing and crinkling. She stepped within a few feet of Harriet but couldn't get any closer because of the ample girth of her dress. Then she pointed a finger directly at Harriet's forehead, as if she were pointing at the mark left by the lump of lead that had smacked Harriet in the head when she was a girl.

"I'm fixin' to sell Kessiah, and I'll also sell you if I have the inclination!"

Harriet felt a hot anger rising at the mention of her niece's name; Kessiah was the daughter of Harriet's long-gone sister, Linah.

"Now get out of my sight!" Miss Eliza snapped. "And don't be surprised if I find a way to ship you off to Georgia or Alabama! Go!"

Harriet turned and made her way to the door, chin raised high and heart thumping crazily. She tried not to let on that she was afraid.

After the tongue-lashing from Miss Eliza, fresh visions started pouring into Harriet's head during her sleep. They were accompanied by the same old vision of her flying north, skimming the tops of the trees and looking down on freedom.

God was talking again, and it was time to make a move.

12

Poplar Neck, Maryland
September 15, 1849

W hen Benjamin spotted Harriet moving like a bullet in his direction, he thought about running and hiding. From the look on Harriet's face, she wasn't bringing good news.

It was a Saturday morning, and the sun had just risen on this September day. Benjamin sat on a tree stump in front of his cabin, nibbling on a biscuit and downing a tin of strong coffee before the work of the day began. Benjamin shared a cabin with his brother Robert and Robert's new wife, Mary Manokey. There was a chill in the air, and the trees all around the cabins were alive with birds.

But judging from the fierce light in his sister's eye, this was no social visit. She marched right up to him and spoke like a general snapping commands.

"Go get Robert and Henry. We gotta talk," she told Benjamin, snagging him by the sleeve. Harriet never asked Benjamin anything. She *told* him. She pulled him to his feet, and some of his coffee sloshed out of his tin and onto his shirtsleeve. He was always amazed at how strong she could be, despite her size.

"It's time," she said, yanking on his shirtsleeve like she was pulling on a fishing line, reeling him in.

He knew exactly what she was talking about.

"Hush," he said. "Keep your voice down. What makes you think it's time?"

"Kessiah is gonna be sold, and we will too if we don't do something. It's time we run."

That's exactly what Benjamin thought she was going to say. He had seen it coming from a mile away.

"Go get Robert and Henry," she added.

Of the three grown brothers, Robert was the oldest at thirty-three —quite a bit older than his seventeen-year-old bride, Mary. Benjamin was now twenty-five years old, and Henry was nineteen. Benjamin had an open, friendly face—almost gullible-looking—while Robert had a way of looking at people sideways, with arched eyebrows, as if he didn't believe a word he was being told. Henry was the shortest and stockiest, with a round face that separated him from Robert and Benjamin, who had long, narrow faces. Henry had intense eyes that stared at you and through you. He was also the only brother with facial hair, in the form of both a moustache and beard.

But even with all of their combined power of age and masculinity, none of them could stand up to their petite twenty-seven-year-old sister, Harriet. Obediently, Benjamin rounded up Robert and Henry, and Harriet led them all to the edge of the forest, away from the cabins.

As usual, she didn't beat around the bush. "We gotta run."

Robert scoffed. "In September? You know it's better to run in December with the nights bein' longer."

"By December, we might all be sold. First goes Kessiah. Then us."

"I don't think Miss Eliza will move that fast," said Benjamin. "She still has the courts to contend with. And I don't think—"

"Miss Eliza don't care 'bout no courts. She only cares 'bout gettin' her hands on some money and diggin' herself outta debt."

"But we got a new baby," said Robert. "How am I gonna run?"

"Take the baby with us."

"What if she makes a noise?"

"We'll give the baby somethin' to knock it asleep."

"Mary won't abide it."

"Then go without your wife and child if you gotta," Harriet told him. "We can come back and get them later."

"Leave my wife and baby? If you had a family of your own, you'd know not to ask me to do somethin' like that."

Benjamin shook his head, amazed that his brother had the nerve to say anything about Harriet's dearth of children. He thought Harriet was going to jump on Robert and start ripping out his hair, but she controlled her all-too-obvious rage.

"*You're* my family, and it's time we run," she said.

"But what I'm sayin' is why should I run off, only to come back later, grab my family, and run again?" Robert said. "It don't make no sense."

"What makes no sense is us stayin' here and gettin' sold south."

Henry had been fidgeting the whole time, shifting his weight from one foot to the other. Finally, he spoke up. "She might be right. Saturday is the best day for runnin'."

So much for putting up a united front to face their sister. Henry had given Harriet the opening she was looking for.

"Listen to Henry," she said. "He may be the youngest of us, but he's whip-smart. You oughta know we gotta run on a Saturday. We gotta run *tonight*."

Benjamin wouldn't admit it out loud, but Harriet and Henry were right that if you ran on a Saturday night, it gave you a day's head start before the escape notices go out on Monday. Thank the Lord for the Sabbath.

"There's a full moon out," said Robert, fumbling for any excuse he could find. "We can't run with a full moon shinin' down on us."

"It's so bright, we won't be able to see the North Star," Benjamin added.

"No worry, I'll still be able to see the stars," said Henry. Benjamin wondered why he was trying to shoot down all of their arguments.

Benjamin recalled how Harriet used to hold him upside down and swing him around when he was a baby. He was too young to remember it himself, but his sister Linah loved to tell that story. Today, he felt like Harriet had him by the heels again and was flinging him around like he had no power of his own.

"What about John?" Robert said.

Harriet wheeled around to face Robert, her nostrils flaring. "What about him?"

"Your husband's gonna give us away."

Harriet had no answer for that, just a wordless glare. Even Henry didn't jump in to shoot down this argument. The four siblings went completely quiet. Harriet bit her lower lip so hard that Benjamin thought it would begin to bleed.

"We gotta take our chances," Harriet finally said. "Even if John betrays us, that won't matter none. Notices don't go out till Monday. We'll be long gone."

In the past, Harriet had always been quick to defend John whenever the question of his loyalty came up. This was the first time Benjamin had heard her say out loud that her own husband couldn't be trusted. If anything, it showed how serious she was about escaping. She was willing to face the truth.

"Tonight, we meet here at this tree," Harriet commanded, pointing to a large oak that had been felled in a thunderstorm during the summer. "It's time we got outta this hell."

Harriet marched off without waiting to hear if there were any objections. Benjamin, Robert, and Henry were left standing there, speechless and gawking at each other. Benjamin sighed. Harriet never took no for answer; they were going to run, whether they liked it or not.

13

"Where's Robert?" Harriet said, when Benjamin showed up at the tree that night without him. Henry was already there, sitting on the fallen tree, swinging his legs in the air.

"He ain't comin'," said Benjamin.

"And why not?"

"He talked with his wife. He ain't comin'."

Harriet let out a grunt. "Imagine that. A grown man pushed around by a woman."

Imagine that, Benjamin thought. What were *they* doing, if not being pushed around by a woman? And a five-foot-tall woman at that.

"You want me to talk to Robert?" Henry asked.

"Ain't got time," said Benjamin. "We need to move."

Harriet nodded. For once, they agreed on something.

"When we get north, we can always come back and get 'em all out," she said.

Benjamin exchanged a glance with Henry. Was Harriet crazy? They were about to risk their necks to go north, and she was already talking about coming back to get out the rest of the family!

Clouds moved in, smothering everything in the sky and making it impossible to see the North Star. They planned to head east toward

Preston, a small town about five miles from the Thompson place in Poplar Neck. Harriet said they could stop off at the home of a widow, Hannah Leverton, a Quaker abolitionist. So the three siblings set off through the woods, surrounded by insect chatter, birdcalls, and other sounds of the night. The wind was strong, rattling the branches together like bones.

"You think the sky will clear?" Henry asked, peering up through the branches. "We can't do this without the North Star."

"Don't worry 'bout it. We know where we're goin'," said Harriet, moving at a quick clip through the forest.

They decided to travel alongside Choptank Road, keeping out of view in the woods. The road shot straight east toward Preston.

"John won't say nothin' to give us away, will he?" Benjamin asked.

"Not if he knows what's good for him," Harriet said.

That wasn't a very reassuring answer.

The Leverton house was outside of Preston, to the southeast of town. Harriet said she knew the way to the house through the trees, but could she guide them there in the dark? They didn't dare enter Preston proper; when they neared the town, they veered off to the right, plunging deeper into the woods and heading away from the road. But after a long stretch of hiking, then splashing across a narrow stream, they still hadn't come across the Leverton place.

"I think we musta overshot the house," said Henry.

"What do you know about anything?" Harriet asked.

"Just this mornin' you said Henry was the smart one," Benjamin pointed out.

"Then he musta hit his head on something since the mornin' 'cause he ain't smart no more."

"Sure wish we could see the stars," said Henry. "I'm not even sure what direction we're goin'."

"I know the way," said Harriet. "Their house is dead ahead."

"Can't be. We been walkin' forever and shoulda passed the house a long time ago."

"Just shut up and pray," Harriet said, marching onward.

Ever since they veered away from Choptank Road, Benjamin made sure he marked the trees as they went, in case they needed to follow the path back. He used his knife to mark right turns, left turns, and straight paths, each one getting a different kind of notch. But as time wore on, still no sign of the Leverton house.

"Stop," hissed Henry. The other two obeyed, even Harriet.

"What is it?" asked Benjamin.

"You hear that?"

They paused to listen, but all they could hear was the steady drone of insects, the occasional croaking frog, and an owl.

"Only owls," said Harriet.

"Not the owl. I thought I heard dogs."

"It can't be slave hunters. They wouldn't a been alerted this quickly."

"What if John went to Miss Eliza?" Benjamin asked.

"Why would he do that?"

"To report you missin'."

"What did you tell John about where you were goin'?" asked Henry.

"Told him I was gonna spend the night in Mama's cabin. He won't miss me till mornin'."

"Then he'll report you missin' come sunrise."

"No he won't. He'll think I went straight to church, and he won't suspect a thing till later."

"Don't he go to church, too?" said Henry. "Won't he not see you at church? And won't he start askin' questions?"

"He won't do nothin' of the kind. And even if he did, we'll be at the Quaker place by then."

"If we ever find it," said Benjamin.

"If we don't find the Leverton place, then we just keep goin' north."

"We don't even know where north is any longer," said Henry. "Sure wish we could see the North Star."

"Stop frettin'!" Harriet snapped. "We don't need no stars when we can look at the trees. The moss grows on the north side."

"You can't see moss in the dark!"

"Pffffff," said Harriet, continuing on.

When they reached a clearing, they peered up at the sky, hoping that the cloud cover had broken up to give them a view of the stars. But it began to drizzle, answering that question.

Then they heard it, clear as a bell. The sound of a dog barking. Two dogs, maybe three.

"Just some wild dogs," said Harriet, sounding awfully sure of herself. "They can't know we're gone this soon."

"This is foolish," said Benjamin. "We need to wait for another Saturday night when we can see the stars. We're lost. We could be heading direct south for all we know."

"We ain't lost, and y'all just gotta stop complainin' and start prayin'."

"I been prayin' for the last hour," said Benjamin.

"Then pray harder!"

"I agree with Benjamin," Henry said. "We need to head back, try this another time. You think you can see your tree marks in the dark?"

"Gonna be awfully hard, but we should work our way back regardless," Benjamin said. "Let's try another Saturday."

"There might not be another Saturday for us," said Harriet. "We can't turn around!"

Henry tried grabbing on to Harriet to slow her down, but she became a wildcat and bit his hand to break loose.

"Lordy, what did y'all do that for?" Henry bellowed.

"We're pushin' on," she said. "C'mon."

"We're lost, Harriet. You gotta know it. We shoulda been at the Leverton place a long time ago. We veered past it."

Harriet started kicking everything in sight. Kicking up leaves. Kicking at dead branches strewn on the ground. Kicking at the base of a tree, like she was trying to fell the tree with her foot. Benjamin and Henry just stood by watching, waiting for her to run out of steam.

When she was finally done, she dropped down on the ground and put her head between her knees. She sat there moaning and praying out loud, shaking her head. Benjamin and Henry each sat down on a fallen tree and watched her wear herself out. Before long, just as

Benjamin hoped might happen, she went out like a light. Fell asleep, like she always did.

Benjamin caught Henry's eyes in the darkness.

"You think she's asleep?" Henry whispered.

"She was due. She ain't dropped off all night."

"Shall we carry her?"

"Let's wait a short spell, make sure she's really out."

The brothers sat in silence, watching their sister's head droop lower and lower. They heard the sound of dogs again, but Benjamin had to agree with Harriet on one point: There wouldn't be dogs after them just yet.

Benjamin helped Henry to raise Harriet up and throw her over his shoulders like a sack of grain. As they began to work their way back, following the marked trees, it began to rain. Everything was against them this night. The stars, the clouds, and the rain.

They would wait for another day, if they even get another chance.

14

September 17, 1849

Harriet sat on a stool, pushing on the cow's udder, getting the big animal to relax so the cow could let her milk down. Harriet told Mama she would take care of the milking this afternoon, but she could tell that her Mama was suspicious. Mama had been on edge ever since the disastrous escape attempt the other night, and she had been watching Harriet like a hawk for the past two days. Milking the cow was a chance for Harriet to be alone and figure out her next move.

When Harriet regained consciousness on Saturday and discovered that Benjamin and Henry were carrying her back to the Thompson place, she was furious. But she was mostly discouraged that she had fallen asleep—so discouraged that she walked the rest of the way back without putting up a fight.

Last night she had another one of her flying dreams, and as always she dreamed that she fell from the sky just before crossing over to the North. Was God telling her she wasn't ever going to make it, no matter how many times she tried to go north? It was hard to believe; why give her such vivid dreams if they were nothing more than a warning to stop? It didn't make any sense, so Harriet decided she would try once again to escape, only this time on her own steam. No worrying brothers would join her.

Harriet clamped her hands at the top of one of the cow's teats, where it met the udder, and gave a gentle squeeze. She was rewarded with a thin stream of milk. Then she grabbed hold of a second teat and started up a rhythm, alternating teats and listening to the squirts as milk shot down into the bucket below. Occasionally, she would blast a squirt directly into her mouth, just to steal some refreshment.

She decided she would leave word about her next escape attempt with someone, but she certainly couldn't tell Mama her plan. Mama would raise an uproar and try to stop her from going, and that would give everything away. So she decided she would tell Mary, Robert's young wife. Mary was owned by Dr. A.C. Thompson and worked in the Big House. She could be trusted.

With the milking done, Harriet strode back to the Thompson house. When she marched into the kitchen and left the milk buckets, she found the place bustling with workers scurrying around and getting supper going.

"What's cookin'?" Harriet said, lifting the lid on a big pot and taking a whiff of the soup.

"Get your nose out of my pot!" commanded Dolly, the cook. "What you doin' in here anyway?"

"Just finished milkin' and come to see what's for supper."

"This ain't for you, and you know it, so skedaddle."

Harriet spotted Mary off to one side of the kitchen, scrubbing up some of the mess on a countertop. Dolly insisted on a tidy kitchen, even during the hubbub of preparations. Harriet called Mary a "crumb patroller," because she hunted down crumbs relentlessly, like a bloodhound. Dolly didn't tolerate crumbs or drips or anything messing up her kitchen.

Harriet had to figure out a way to give Mary the news of her leaving in private. To do this, she needed to get Mary out of the house, so she started to frolic with her, snagging the cleaning rag out of her hands and letting out a whoop.

"Give it back, Harriet!" Mary shouted, but Harriet was too quick, and she put the rag behind her back. Then she held it up in the air and Mary bounced up and down, trying to snag it from her hands. Mary had the height advantage, but Harriet kept switching the rag from hand to hand, foiling her every time. "You give that to me, Harriet!"

Mary wasn't really mad; she was always a good sport whenever Harriet teased her. Pretty soon they were both giggling and hooting and dashing around the kitchen.

"You two scat if you're gonna be silly fools!" Dolly snapped, and Harriet was happy to oblige. She darted out the back door, with Mary in hot pursuit. On the way out the door, Harriet snagged a biscuit to take on the road with her.

The two girls kept laughing and carrying on, as Harriet dodged Mary, waving the rag in front of her friend's face, and leading her on a chase around a weeping willow tree. Then Harriet sprinted back toward the house and ducked around the corner.

"You give that back to me!" Mary shouted, between blasts of laughter.

At last, Harriet came to a halt and tossed the rag back to Mary. They tumbled against each other, laughter bubbling out of them. This was Harriet's chance to tell her about the escape plans. Mary may be silly, but she could be trusted to tell Mama where she had gone—once she was far away.

But just as Harriet settled down and was about to spill her plans, Mary's laughter stopped as suddenly as a spigot being turned off. She stood still, staring at something directly behind Harriet, so Harriet spun around and was horrified to see Dr. Thompson, on horseback, coming down the path in their direction. Master Thompson didn't tolerate frolicking among his slaves, especially when there was work to be done. Mary turned and ran back to the kitchen, leaving Harriet to face the master alone.

What happened next seemed almost like one of her dreams. Harriet found her legs suddenly taking her down the pathway leading away from the Big House. She walked directly *toward* Dr. Thompson, who continued to approach on his horse. Dr. Thompson was a small man, dwarfed by his large steed. He concealed his bald head with a wig and had thick whiskers that stuck out sideways from his cheeks, like hooks you could hang a hat on. But behind his odd appearance was a sharp mind and sharper tongue. Slaves knew to hush when he went by.

But something inside told Harriet *not* to keep quiet. The Spirit told her she should start singing right in front of Dr. Thompson. So she did.

> *"I'm sorry I'm going to leave you,*
> *Farewell, oh farewell...*
> *But I'll meet you in the morning.*
> *Farewell, oh farewell!"*

Of all the songs to sing...she couldn't believe those words were spilling out of her mouth. *I'm going to leave you? Farewell, oh farewell?* How much more obvious could she be?

Dr. Thompson halted his horse and stared at Harriet with a look of utter disbelief. She walked right on by, smiling like she didn't have a care in the world. When she passed him, she could sense his eyes following her every step of the way, and she waited for him to say or do something. She kept on walking and singing.

> *"I'll meet you in the morning,*
> *Safe in the Promised Land,*
> *On the other side of Jordan*
> *Bound for the Promised Land!"*

Bound for the Promised Land? Could she be bolder than that? But she felt the Spirit in her bones, and the Spirit was urging her to sing even louder as she approached the gate at the end of the path. As if on an evening stroll, Harriet raised the latch on the gate, walked on through, and turned to calmly close the gate behind her. As she did, she looked up, and there was Dr. Thompson, still on his horse and still staring at her. What could be going through the man's head? He had turned his horse around partway and was leaning forward, stroking the tips of his side-whiskers.

Then Harriet gave a wave. Just a little wave of the hand and a smile. Strangely, she wasn't afraid. A calmness had settled down on her, as if the Lord was patting her gently on the back and saying, "It'll be all right. Everything will be all right, Harriet." Not one wave of trouble rolled across her peaceful breast.

After giving Dr. Thompson one last glance and a smile, Harriet turned back to the path leading away from the plantation. She picked up the song again.

> *"I'll meet you in the morning,*
> *Safe in the Promised Land,*
> *On the other side of Jordan*
> *Bound for the Promised Land."*

And just like that, Harriet Tubman was gone, on her way to a land flowing with milk and honey.

15

Benjamin wondered who in the world was pounding on the cabin door, like they were trying to hammer it down. When he swung open the door, there stood John Tubman, looking like he wanted to start hammering on Benjamin's forehead next.

"Where is she?" John demanded, stepping inside and glaring around the room. It was early evening, and most of the Ross family had gathered in the cabin. In addition to Benjamin, Robert was there with his wife, Mary, who sat in the rocker by the hearth, holding their baby boy. Henry and Rachel were also present, seated in chairs, while Moses sat on the floor with his back against the wall. In fact, only Mama and Papa were missing because Benjamin didn't want them to know what had happened to Harriet. If they did, Mama would raise a fuss, and Papa would tell the honest truth if someone asked him what had happened.

"What is this—a family meeting without me...and without Harriet?" John said.

Benjamin wasn't about to point out that they didn't view him as real family. As for Harriet, she was long gone, as far as they could tell.

"Where's Minty?" John demanded. "That's what I come to find out."

"Don't really know," said Robert, playing innocent. "I figured she was with you."

"Ain't she in your cabin?" asked Mary. She bounced her baby boy, Adam, on her knee.

"Course not! Do y'all think I'd be comin' here if she was? Minty's small, but not small enough to hide from me in a one-room cabin."

No one had a response for that.

Before John showed up, Mary told everyone that she and Harriet had been frolicking outside the Thompson Big House earlier in the day. According to Mary, she heard Harriet singing. *"I'll meet you in the morning, safe in the Promised Land, on the other side of the Jordan, bound for the Promised Land."* Mary said she went outside to look for Harriet and was shocked to see her just strolling on down the path, leading away from the house. But even more astounding, Mary said Dr. Thompson was simply sitting up on his horse, watching her go. No one had seen hide nor hair of Harriet since.

But they weren't about to tell John any of this. The man couldn't keep a secret if his life depended on it. He was even less reliable if Harriet's life depended on it.

"Do you think she's run?" John asked.

"Nah. You worryin' about nothin', John," Robert said. "She'll be along, don't you worry."

"Maybe Master Thompson knows where she is, if I ask him," said John.

Almost simultaneously, Benjamin, Robert, and Mary blurted "No" and "Don't," visibly startling John. He scoured the room with obvious suspicion.

"You ain't tellin' me somethin'," he said. "I'm her husband! I gotta know!"

Benjamin drew John back toward the door, with Robert and Henry close behind. He was afraid that if any overseers were passing by, they might hear John's overheated words.

"Now don't get so excited, John."

"I have a right to get excited! She's my wife! And if she's run, she has no right to do it without talkin' to me first!"

For a moment, Benjamin thought he was going to say, "I'm her master."

One more outburst, and Benjamin was going to have to clamp a hand over the man's mouth.

"Listen here, John," said Robert, leaning in close. "If you start talkin' 'bout Harriet bein' gone, and if it's a false alarm, the overseers are gonna take it out on you for gettin' them all riled up for nothin'."

"So keep your voice down," added Henry.

This seemed to do the trick. John continued to act agitated, his eyes flitting around the room, his feet all fidgety. But at least he quieted down.

"I think she's run," said John, this time much softer. "I can't let her run out on me. I won't tolerate it. I'm her husband."

"She ain't run," Benjamin lied. The three brothers moved in closer, clustering around John, forcing him into a corner.

"Tell you what," Henry added. "We'll go fetch her if you just agree to sit a spell and stay quiet."

John's eyes flitted from brother to brother. "You do that. You find her, and y'all tell her she belongs at home. She belongs to me."

"She knows that," said Benjamin, using a soothing tone. "She's probably just doin' some chore or other."

"This time a night?"

"We'll find out what happened. We'll talk to the house servants."

"Let me take you back to your cabin," said Robert, putting a gentle hand on John's right shoulder. "Benjamin and Henry'll scout around, tell us what happened."

Benjamin nodded. He thought Robert's idea was a good one. Someone needed to stay with John to make sure he didn't do anything foolish, while he and Henry would go out looking. He really didn't expect to find any sign of Harriet, but if they searched for her, it would keep John pacified. For now.

...

When Harriet emerged from a belt of trees, she spotted the house sitting directly in front of her across a long field—a two-story brick house with a gable roof and a front door facing south. A huge tree rose up behind the house, rising high above the roof. From her vantage point, it almost looked as if the big tree was busting right through the roof.

It was the Leverton house. This time Harriet had made no mistakes in finding it. The setting sun flared red, but there was still enough light left to see the place clearly. It was an ideal location for a safe house, tucked away in the middle of nowhere. Shooting a look in all directions and making sure there was no one about, she lifted the hem of her long, brown skirt with her left hand and hurried across the ragged field. In her right hand was a walking stick, which she had picked up along the way; it would be essential when the sun goes down because walking in the dark without a stick was like walking in the daylight without eyes.

She gave the agreed-upon signal, tapping a code on the front door. Hannah Leverton opened the door so quickly that Harriet thought she must have been lurking just on the other side, waiting for her. Perhaps she had seen her through the window.

"Welcome, Harriet," said Hannah, quickly drawing her across the threshold and closing the door. "I had expected thee two nights ago."

"Long story," said Harriet.

"Tonight, we must get thee prepared for the next stage of thy journey. There is no time to spare."

Like all Quaker women, Hannah wore a plain, floor-length dress with no frills such as buttons, scarves, or gaudy stomachers. The dress was moss green, and her modest bonnet was dove-white. The Quaker way was to avoid drawing attention to yourself. Hannah's face was equally plain, her eyes were bordered on all sides by wrinkles, and the hair sticking from beneath the bonnet was squirrel gray and thin and dry, like parched grass. Her smile was warm and welcoming.

"I have written a note for thee to carry," said Hannah, taking Harriet's right wrist. She placed the note in her palm and folded her fingers over the paper. Harriet could not read, so this note was for other eyes.

Harriet looked around the house, wondering where the Quaker woman's children, Mary Elizabeth and Arthur, might be. Hannah must have read her mind.

"Mary Elizabeth and Arthur are visiting Dr. Thompson," she said, her smile becoming mischievous.

Harriet was startled by the mention of Dr. Thompson, so Hannah quickly explained.

"Dost thou recall that our daughter is engaged to marry the son of Dr. Thompson in two month's time? Arthur is over there settling some of the financial arrangements."

Harriet nodded. She had heard that the Leverton girl was marrying into the Thompson family. It seemed like a strange match. A Quaker girl from an abolitionist family marrying into a slave-holding family? Again, Hannah Leverton seemed to sense her uneasiness. She put a hand on Harriet's.

"Our deepest prayer is for our daughter to plant seeds of abolitionism in the soil of the Thompson family. We will make the Thompson family freedom-lovers yet. Just you wait."

"God works wonders in the flintiest of hearts."

"That is the glory truth, Harriet. Now, thou hast not time to squander. Let us begin thy preparations."

Hannah proceeded to explain that there was a house along the way, ready to take her in. The family would provide her with sustenance, and send her on to the next station along the route north. She explained how to reach this house by following the Choptank River, and she made sure Harriet had the information memorized and burned into her mind.

"I will provide thee with victuals, but thou must leave soon, when darkness falls," Hannah said. "Thou must sleep by day."

As Miss Hannah bundled up some bread and fruit, Harriet cast a look at the quilt she had given the Quaker woman as a present one year earlier. When Harriet heard about what the Levertons were doing, smuggling slaves north, she felt God nudging her to express her thanks. Not knowing what kind of gift she could give out of her poverty, Harriet saw the image of a colorful quilt in one of her visions, and she decided that was the answer. Harriet wasn't much for women's work, but she had done the best she could on the quilt, and Miss Hannah had displayed the handiwork on the back of a bench—a place of honor. Quilts seemed to be the one area of Quaker life where color was splashed, standing out like tropical birds in a plain, gray world.

Noticing where her eyes had settled, Miss Hannah said, "Thy quilt is a treasure. Thank you." The woman took both of Harriet's hands in hers and gave them a squeeze.

"Thank you," said Harriet, feeling embarrassed because Miss Hannah's hands were soft and hers were like leather.

Miss Hannah gave her hands one last squeeze before opening the front door. It was now dark, and Harriet had the note in her pocket, and her walking stick in hand.

She stepped over the threshold and into the night.

■■■

"You think Harriet's really gone?" Henry asked Benjamin as they moved off into the dark woods.

"I'm sure of it," said Benjamin. "Ain't you?"

Henry nodded. They came upon Choptank Road, the same path they had taken with Harriet just two nights earlier. Keeping to the woods, they followed the road east toward Preston. The two brothers had set off with the pretense of acting as if they were looking for Harriet, even though they were both certain that she was long gone. But if they reported to John that they couldn't find Harriet, there's no telling what her foolish husband might do. So, almost unconsciously, their feet kept moving east.

"Get down," Benjamin hissed when he heard the snort of a horse. The two brothers ducked behind a tree, keeping still as they crouched about thirty feet from Choptank Road. It was two days past a full moon, but the clear night sky still shed a generous amount of light on the road. Benjamin prayed the moonlight didn't spill too far into the woods and give them away. He heard the voices of men—two men from the sound of it. They might be patrollers, looking for the movement of blacks at night.

Through the screen of trees, Benjamin could see the hulking shadows of two horses, plodding along slowly. He could also smell smoke as it wafted in their direction. Soon, he spotted a dot of red-lit ash as one of the men drew on his cigar. The men continued to talk in low tones, but Benjamin could not make out the words. If these patrollers had caught Harriet, they would have been behaving with greater urgency. Their lackadaisical manner was a good sign that all was quiet.

Benjamin and Henry waited a long time after the men had passed before they dared to move. Benjamin's knees ached as he stretched into a standing position.

"Should we keep going?" Henry asked.

"We keep going," Benjamin said.

So they continued to move through the woods. They remained a safe distance from the road, but not so far that they lost track of the path east. They didn't say a word for quite a spell until Henry spoke in a whisper.

"Robert said he heard that all the black people up north are starving," Henry said.

"Robert's gotta stop listening to overseers," Benjamin scoffed.

"But what if it's true? What if white people in the North steal our food and starve us? At least we get food at the Thompson place."

"Freedom is food for the soul," Benjamin said.

"But freedom don't fill a belly."

They continued in silence until they neared the outskirts of Preston. Neither of them had said a word about when they should turn around and go back to the Thompson house—or even if they *should* turn around. So they just kept on walking. But now that they reached Preston, they were forced to make a decision. Should they turn around and follow the road back, or should they veer left and continue north, in Harriet's wake?

"The sky is clear," Henry said to his older brother, pointing up at the Little Dipper, where the North Star twinkled at the end of the handle. "It's a good night for runnin'."

Benjamin and Henry stood still, staring ahead at the edge of Preston, where they could see a scattering of flickering lights. Something suddenly rustled in the brush off to their left, and Benjamin's heart did a flip. But it was probably just a small rodent.

Henry moved first, turning left, away from Preston, and plunging deeper into the woods. After a momentary pause, Benjamin followed. Without a word between them, they both moved north. They had no idea how far the free border of Pennsylvania lay, but if they kept on walking, they would reach it eventually.

16

Night moved into day, and Harriet continued to follow the Choptank River, which ran along on her left side, pointing her toward Denton, Maryland. The soft sound of moving water provided a subtle cover for the crack and rustle of her movements. She had walked all night, and the call of sleep became overwhelming. When she had set off she was energized by suspense, but now she was dead on her feet. It was Tuesday morning, and by now a lot of people would know she was gone. She wondered if Dr. Thompson had already alerted the Brodesses about her disappearance, and if there would be slave hunters out in hot pursuit.

She considered curling up somewhere and catching a few winks, but she realized it would be wiser to postpone sleep until she reached the safe house that Hannah Leverton had steered her toward. Hannah said she would not reach the house until daylight, so there was no chance she could have overshot the mark during the night.

Harriet trudged on, her legs heavy, her eyes drooping. She knew she shouldn't even stop for a moment, shouldn't sit down, because sleep would consume her in an instant. But it was so tempting, just to sit down for a short spell. Sleep seemed so delicious, as tantalizing as the sugar she snatched from Miss Susan's table so long ago

—or the sweet milk she turned away when she lived with the Cooks.

Then she heard music. It was an otherworldly sound, mostly strings at first, but then she heard voices as well. There were no words to the song, just a rising tone, a pulsing chorus that grew louder and more inescapable. This wordless chorus filled the forest all around her, and she spun around, looking for the source.

The music was beautiful—more enchanting than anything she could imagine—and it lit up every leaf, every branch with God Almighty. The music pulsated in expanding waves, going soft, then rising in volume. Harriet found herself staggering away from the river, in search of the singers. But when she moved right, the sound suddenly seemed to be coming from behind. She spun around and stumbled in the opposite direction, only to hear the sound coming from another angle. It was like the games of tag she played with Mary Manokey, only this time she was chasing an elusive song that darted and flitted on all sides.

As she staggered through the forest, looking for the singers, she saw a long-bearded man on horseback just up ahead and peering around. Surely, word of her escape hadn't traveled this far, this fast, so maybe the hunter wasn't looking for slaves; maybe he, too, was looking for the source of the song. The man swiveled in his saddle, and his eyes landed on Harriet. Like looking down the sights of a rifle, he had her in his view, but that's when the music rose into a crescendo, and she could almost see the man being buffeted by sound. His entire body vibrated violently and suddenly the man splintered into a thousand pieces right in front of Harriet's eyes, like a glass goblet shattered by music.

One moment later, the song was over, and Harriet found herself back in the waking world, sitting on the hard ground. The music was gone, replaced by the sound of birds, and she noticed that the river was still within sight. Then she heard the crash of underbrush, and her head snapped to the right, and she saw at a distance, a horse and rider moving slowly through the trees. Just as in the vision, the man was looking right and left.

It was the very same man! Was she still in a dream? Or was the threat real and near?

Peering at the sky, she noticed that the sun had risen higher than she remembered, and she wondered if she had been asleep for a long time. Carefully, quietly, Harriet lowered herself to the ground, until her body was completely blocked by a massive tree that had fallen on its side. She closed her eyes, breathed in, breathed out, and prayed. She knew the Lord does not slumber or sleep. The Lord was the shade upon her right hand, her rod and staff, her refuge, her shield, her defender, her fortress, her secret place, her armor, her strong tower.

Her enemy was close. She heard the horse's hooves crackling across dead leaves, and the man spitting and muttering to himself. But the sound was becoming fainter, as the man and the horse moved off through the forest, slowly but surely.

Harriet waited for the sounds of the hunter to fade into oblivion before she rose to her feet and continued on, pushing north.

...

Harriet's mother, Rit, was furious with her children. All morning, she had been searching for Harriet everywhere on the Thompson place, but she couldn't find any trace of her, and she also hadn't seen Henry, Benjamin, and Robert. In fact, the only son she could track down was Moses, her youngest.

Rit found Moses back behind one of the slave cabins, talking with her husband, Ben.

"What you doin' here?" she asked Ben, like she was hurling an accusation.

Her husband grinned. "Don't sound like you're too pleased to see your old man."

"I thought y'all were at the sawmill, leavin' me here with all the worries of life."

"What'd Harriet do now?" Ben asked.

Rit was afraid to answer. If she told her husband she suspected that Harriet and the boys had all run off, what was stopping him from telling Master Thompson or Miss Eliza what they did? Ben wouldn't volunteer such information, but to this day he still had this uncompromising conviction about his word being his word. He didn't lie to *anyone*, including white folks. If someone asked him if his children had run off, he would feel obliged to tell the truth. So it was best he didn't know.

Rit just shrugged.

Ben stared hard at her for a few moments. "Maybe you're right not to tell me," he said. "Moses, I'll leave you and your Mama to talk."

If Ben didn't know his children were on the run, he could honestly deny he knew anything. Sometimes, Rit wanted to slap some sense into her husband. When someone asks if your children have escaped, you lie, and you lie big. Rit was weary of her husband's incurable honesty, but at least he had the sense to know when he should be kept in the dark.

"You seen your brothers?" she said to Moses after Ben had wandered off.

"Robert's in John Tubman's cabin," Moses added.

"What in heaven's name is Robert doin' at John's cabin?"

"Makin' sure that man don't make a fuss 'bout Harriet bein' missing."

So it was true. Harriet, Henry, and Benjamin were at it again. They were on the run, and heaven help them if they got caught. Also, heaven help John Tubman if he ever tells the master about it.

Rit didn't know who she was most angry at. Was it her husband, whose honesty could get them all killed? Was it Harriet, whose escape plans could get herself and her brothers killed? Or was it John Tubman, whose orneriness could get Harriet killed?

She decided there was plenty of wrath to go around.

...

Robert kept his arms wrapped in a bear hug around John, as the man thrashed and squirmed.

"Let me go!" John shouted, trying to peel Robert's arms away. But

Robert drove him forward like a locomotive. He lifted John off of his feet, slamming him against the back wall of the cabin.

Robert had stayed in John's cabin all night, just to make sure the stupid man didn't do anything to give his wife away. He also made sure he stayed awake until John had safely drifted off to sleep. But come morning, John had awakened in a rage, rousing Robert from his fitful sleep. Robert hurled aside the blanket, which he had been clutching as he slept in a rocker, and he threw himself at John before the man could barge outside. With John pinned against the cabin's back wall and seeming to calm down a bit, Robert let go and stepped back. His arms smarted after being pinched between Robert's back and the wall.

"Where's Harriet? You said she was just off doin' an errand," John said.

"I never said I knew for sure." Robert slid sideways to cut off John's path to the cabin door.

"Then where is she? She never come back last night."

"Maybe she's at the Brodess place." Robert didn't really believe it, but he hoped John would.

"Don't lie. You know she's run."

"I don't know nothin' of the kind."

"She's my wife. She ain't got a right to leave me."

Robert saw that it was no longer any use trying to cover for Harriet. She was far away by now, and the overseers were going to soon discover she was gone, even without John giving her away.

"If she's run, then you gotta keep quiet about it. Be loyal to your wife," Robert said.

"*Be loyal*? She ain't been loyal to me! Why should I be loyal to her?"

"'Cause she's your wife."

"She shoulda told me she was leavin'. Now get out of my way."

"Only if you agree you won't give her away."

John took a swing, but Robert ducked out of its path with ease. He shoved John in the chest, putting him off balance.

"She shouldn't a left without tellin' me so," John insisted.

"Why would Harriet tell you she's leavin'? You'd just stop her."

"You're right, I woulda. You know how dangerous it is to go north. You know how dangerous it is to *live* up north."

Robert couldn't argue with that. He was terrified by the stories he heard of slaves escaping north, only to be forced to work in huge factories, where they were starved and beaten every day. On the Thompson place, they didn't face the whip, and they were fed every day. Robert knew what he had to deal with in Maryland, but not in the North. He had heard that abolitionists were just tricksters, luring blacks north to feed the factories with more workers.

This time, Robert didn't stop John from leaving as the man strode right past him, throwing open the cabin door. After a moment, Robert followed. It was a bracing autumn day, and his breath was visible in the cold. He could also see smoke curling from the top of his own cabin, so Mary must have the fire stoked and breakfast cooking. He watched as John went from cabin to cabin, looking for Harriet. He appeared to get angrier by the moment.

Robert had had enough of John Tubman. He had done all he could to stop the man from blabbing the news that Harriet was gone, but he couldn't stifle him all day long. Exhausted, Robert rubbed the crick in his neck, which had come from sleeping all night in the rocker. Then he wandered into his cabin, where Mary had the food cooking. The place smelled strong of smoke, and baby Adam was squalling.

Robert's Mama was there too, along with his youngest brother, Moses, who looked worried. Moses was seventeen years old, but sometimes he acted even younger. That's why Harriet hadn't included him on their first escape attempt; she had not trusted that Moses would keep his wits about him.

"Benjamin ain't come back," Moses said. "Henry ain't come back either."

Robert suspected as much. Seemed like everyone was on the run, except for him.

17

Benjamin felt like he was in hell. It was their second night on the road, and what had started out with cautious optimism, even excitement, had become a misery. Cold rain came down in sheets, forcing him and Henry to hunker down beneath a massive fallen tree. The tree angled down from its shattered base, leaving plenty of space to sit beneath. Benjamin and Henry cut up small, leafy branches and put them down on the ground beneath the tree like a blanket. But the leafy bedding wasn't enough to keep out the water, which puddled all around and streamed in rills through their makeshift shelter.

"You think we're doin' the right thing?" asked Henry. He and Benjamin sat facing each other. Benjamin had his back squarely against the tree's base, and the top of his head scraped against the tree-trunk roof.

"I think so. What do you think?"

"I'm torn. I wanna get free, but I'm afraid of what we'll find in the North. Ain't you afraid of that?"

"I ain't afraid," Benjamin lied.

Henry scooted a little to the left, to avoid a trickle of water squiggling through the mud. He leaned back and closed his eyes.

"I met me a nice gal runnin' errands in town a month ago," Henry said.

"You did?" This was the first that Benjamin had heard any such thing. "Why didn't you say so?"

"I'm sayin' so now."

"Where's she live?"

"On the Ellis place. A ladies maid."

"The *Ellis* place?"

Ellis was a tough man, eager to use the whip and other devices. Benjamin had even heard of an Ellis servant being half-hanged for thieving. Hung from a tree with his toes just barely touching the ground, so that he was choking but not dying.

"The Ellises are demons," Henry said. "I hate to leave her in that place."

This was a fine time for Henry to be bringing this up, Benjamin thought.

"It's like I'm a fox with its leg caught in a trap and the only way to get loose is to chew off my leg," Henry said. "Leavin' my girl to go north feels like losin' my leg. I'll be free, but I might bleed to death."

"Chewin' off your leg is still better than stayin' in the trap and bein' skinned alive by the hunter."

"You're right there, Benjamin."

The thunder rumbled overhead, and the whoosh of rain intensified so that it was almost too difficult to hear each other. Benjamin felt the water pooling beneath his britches, and he squirmed in the wetness.

"What's your girl's name?" Benjamin asked when the rain began to let up enough to hear themselves think.

"Harriet, believe it or not."

"*Harriet?*"

"That's right. Seems I'm surrounded by Harriets," Henry said. "But I wonder if I shoulda gotten her out of there before I ran."

"You can always come back to get her out once you're free."

Henry cracked off a stick and began drawing in the mud. "That's right. We can come back."

"But when we do come back, what we need is an army," Benjamin said.

Henry laughed. "And a general! Our sister Harriet would make a good general, wouldn't she?"

"Tougher than nails." Benjamin smiled as the night lit up with lightning, followed by a long, drawn-out thunder-rumble. "Good thing we're under this fallen tree. Lightning don't strike the same place twice."

"You think I should go back, get my woman before we go any farther?"

"So you already think of this woman as yours? Is she the marryin' kind?"

Henry shrugged. "And what about our sister Rachel—and Mama? All our women. Do you think we should go fetch 'em before we go any farther?"

Benjamin scratched his chin and said nothing. He always had trouble making big decisions. That's why he thought this escape would be easier; they'd never really made a decision to go. When they set off to hunt for Harriet, they just kept walking through the night and slept by day.

As the rain diminished to a sprinkle, Benjamin heard movement in the brush. He stared ahead and his night eyes made out a black bear, standing not more than fifteen feet away. The rain made it difficult for the bear to sniff out humans, so the animal probably didn't even know they sat so close by.

The bear was busily gorging on berries, in preparation for hibernation, but Benjamin had no fear. Black bears are timid creatures, and this one would probably run if Benjamin showed himself. He and Henry had had their fill of berries along the way, and seeing this bear made Benjamin hungry for meat—specifically, bear meat. Bears that fill themselves with berries make the best-tasting meat. He would sometimes go out hunting for bear with Dr. Thompson, loading the master's gun and carrying his gear; and if he had a gun right now, this animal would be dead.

As the bear snapped away at the clusters of small fruit, its tongue darting out, Henry suddenly sneezed. The bear was gone in an instant, as if it had never been there.

"He sure is jumpy," Henry observed.

"We all are," Benjamin said.

When the rain finally stopped, Benjamin and Henry crawled out from under the tree and just stood there, not saying a word. Benjamin was still torn by the choices set before them. Then, almost simultaneously, the two brothers began to walk again, side-by-side in the direction from which they had just come. They walked back south. For a good ten minutes, neither said a word until Henry finally spoke up.

"We're headin' back, ain't we?"

"That's right," said Benjamin. "We're headin' back."

Benjamin wasn't exactly sure how to feel. He didn't think Eliza Brodess would have them shot for running away for a couple of days, but you can never be sure.

...

Harriet studied the Quaker gentleman, who looked to be in his forties. "Climb on in," said Samuel. He was a thin man wearing a black coat with sleeves a few inches too short for his long arms. He motioned toward the back of his wagon, which was occupied by a large dog. A Golden Retriever.

"He friendly?" Harriet asked.

"Thou hast nothing to fear, Harriet," said Samuel. "Gabriel will guard thee. His name is that of an angel."

"As long as he's not a fallen angel." Harriet associated dogs with slave hunters, but she told herself she could trust a Quaker dog. She climbed into the back of the wagon, and then Samuel went into the house, leaving her and Gabriel alone together, sizing each other up.

She ran her hand down his soft coat, and he gave her a lick on her chin. "Now, now, that's enough, Gabriel."

Samuel soon emerged from the house carrying a large blanket.

"This is to hide thee," he said, flapping the blanket and spreading it wide.

"You wanna cover me?"

"That is the idea, Sister Harriet. The darkness is not enough to hide thee."

"All right then." As Harriet lay on her right side, Gabriel licked her again, this time a slobbery kiss on the cheek. Then Samuel raised the blanket in the air above her, and it came gently down on Harriet like a sheltering wing.

Harriet had spent the entire day at the home of Samuel Morris and his wife, Edith—another station on the route north. When Harriet had arrived at the break of dawn, Edith brought her into the house, as friendly as could be, and led her to a back room, where she slept away her exhaustion. It was still light when Harriet awoke, so Edith put her to work sweeping the yard. Harriet was shocked to be treated as this woman's servant, but Edith explained that no one would suspect a black woman sweeping as being an escaped slave. They would assume she was simply their servant. Made sense, putting it that way.

As darkness fell, Edith's husband returned from the fields. After they had all shared steaming bowls of broth, Samuel took her to his wagon and asked her to climb aboard. Once Harriet was settled, cloaked by the blanket, the wagon took off, rattling along the uneven road, and he drove her to the edge of a town. Then Samuel made his farewells, and Gabriel did too with another friendly lick to the face. Samuel gave her directions to the next station on the route north and told her he would be praying for her. Lightning flashed to the south, but judging by the thunder, the storm was distant. Hopefully she'd stay dry this night.

At the next house, the family there sent Harriet off with a warning: the final stretch to Pennsylvania was the most hazardous, the woods swarming with slave hunters, patrolling the border. What's more, the land was not as swampy, so there were fewer hiding spots. They gave Harriet detailed directions of the safest route and said that if she was careful, she might just make it.

She was forced into hiding three times after encountering patrollers in the woods. But another worry was how she would even know when she had crossed the line and reached the North. The

Israelites had their Jordan River to cross, with dreams of the Promised Land calling them on. But where was her Jordan River? Where was the magic line she had seen in her visions?

Early in the morning, when the sun was just rising and fog hung low on the land, Harriet reached a wide, open field of tall grass, swaying in the cool breeze. The sky was slate gray, but she didn't smell rain in the air. She stood at the edge of a hedgerow, staring across the field leading to another batch of woods on the other side, and she contemplated whether it was safe to cross in daylight. Her short stature worked to her advantage because she could stay below the tops of the tall grass.. She moved at a quick clip, staying low and trying not to rustle the grass. But she worried that anyone observing the field would see a fast-moving ripple through the meadow, like a wave across the water.

Just when she was about halfway across the field and starting to feel a sense of safety, she heard a noise coming from the woods at her back. She turned and didn't see anything, but she heard something moving through the shadowed trees, rushing in her direction. Instantly, she dropped to the ground and pressed against the earth. She lay there quietly and heard something rushing through the grass. Whatever it was, it was coming directly for her, and it was moving swiftly. She couldn't tell if it was human or animal. Either could be trouble.

Closing her eyes, Harriet dove deep into prayer. This would not be a good time for her to go off on one of her visions, leaving her help-less for slave catchers to stumble across. But as she called out to the Lord, her worst fear was realized.

She heard the bark of a dog, and the rush of animal movement.

"Whatya smell, boy?" came a woman's voice.

Harriet was pretty certain this dog wasn't coming to lick her face. This breed probably contained more Lucifer than Gabriel. In fact, if the dog was a Cuban bloodhound, a favorite among slave hunters, it might take a whole hunk out of her hide. Harriet wasn't going to let that happen, so she rose back into a crouch and rushed forward. The dog, however, was gaining on her quickly. She couldn't outrun it, so she whirled around to face the animal. It suddenly broke through the curtain of grass and appeared before her with its teeth bared and ears flattened back. Harriet straightened up completely and raised her walking stick, ready to use it as a club. Just behind the animal appeared a woman, carrying a rifle sideways in the crook of her arm. Fortunately, the weapon wasn't pointed at Harriet's face.

"Back!" Harriet shouted at the dog. It was best to show the dog who was boss, and it seemed to do the trick. The dog stopped barking, and it backed up a couple of steps, still letting out a growl through clenched yellow teeth.

"Don't mind Gus," the woman said, tipping her floppy hat. What kind of white person took her hat off to an escaped slave? And what kind of a woman hiked around lugging a gun and wearing a man's kind of hat? She was a tall woman, close to six feet, and she wore a dress made of heavy, navy-blue fabric.

"Where ya bound for, ma'am?" the lady asked Harriet.

Ma'am?

Harriet figured it was a trick, this politeness. She didn't answer and continued to glare at the dog, Gus.

"I guess you're wise not to say where y'all are heading, but I reckon you're wantin' to know where you're at."

"I know where I'm at," Harriet lied. She wanted to make it clear she belonged here—wherever "here" might be.

"Then you must know you're in Pennsylvania."

Harriet couldn't hide her shock, and the woman broke into a big grin.

"I assumed as much. You don't know you reached a free state, do you?"

"Sure I do," said Harriet. "I'm a free-born."

"Well you certainly are free now," she said. "Don't worry, I ain't a slave hunter. I hunt rabbit, and I hunt souls for the Lord. But I ain't no slave hunter. The name's Donnalynn Locke, ma'am. Me and my late husband, bless his soul, are former slave owners."

Just knowing she was a slave owner, former or not, set Harriet's heart to racing. But the woman kept smiling from ear to ear, as if Harriet had no cause to fear.

"My husband and I heard Jarena Lee preach at a camp meeting one day. And yes, white folks like us sometimes wander into her camp meetings, to see what's what. We came out changed creatures and freed our slaves that very month. We only had three of 'em, but we set 'em free indeed."

As Miss Donnalynn spoke, she and Harriet began to walk side by side in the direction of the woods, as if a black woman and white woman walking together were as natural as rain. Gus trotted alongside, his tail wagging back and forth as if he had no memory of snarling at Harriet just minutes before.

"Christ has made us free and not to be entangled in the yoke of bondage," Miss Donnalynn continued. "That's what the Lord put in my heart. I felt like Jesus took a branding iron and stuck the word 'freedom' right on my heart."

Harriet could not believe her ears. What white person spoke like this? It had to be a ruse.

When they reached the edge of the forest, the woman stopped, and so did Harriet. Harriet hadn't said a word the entire time—too afraid to speak. She kept thinking Miss Donnalynn was luring her into a false sense of safety; she was going to point that gun at her at any moment and shoot her down or claim her as property.

"You be careful now as you keep going north," the lady said, talking to her like kin. "There's slave hunters who cross over into Pennsylvania, so keep a watch on strangers."

Then Miss Donnalynn Locke tipped her hat once again, and Harriet just nodded back. She was dumbstruck.

"Godspeed," said the lady, in a final parting word.

Harriet turned and strode into the forest, looking back every so often to make sure she wasn't being followed. But the woman just stood there at the edge of the field, watching her go. Miss Donnalynn gave a final wave, turned, and strolled into the tall grass.

"Lordy," said Harriet. "Lordy." She didn't know what else to say.

She was in Pennsylvania! For the first time in her life, Harriet was standing on free soil. Taking it all in with dazed amazement, she passed through another cluster of trees and came across another narrow field of grass. She stopped, overwhelmed by the moment. Crouching down, she dug out a handful of cool, crumbly soil and stared at it intently, trying to see any difference in free soil. She let the dirt filter through her fingers and watched as it caught in the breeze and streamed away.

Then Harriet held up her right arm and examined it. Her skin didn't look any different this side of freedom. She studied her hands, just to see if she was the same person. She saw the same old hands, and she was the same old Harriet. She inhaled deeply and laughed for the first time since leaving the Thompson place. There was such a glory over everything. The sun shone like gold through the trees and over the fields, and she felt like she was in heaven.

18

"They're calling it a stampede," said William Still, a free black man and abolitionist. William and his friends had found Harriet a cleaning job in a Philly hotel. On the way back from that job, she had stopped in to see William at the Pennsylvania Anti-Slavery Society office. She had heard folks talking about a big slave escape in Maryland, and she hoped her family might have been part of it.

"How many got out?" she asked.

"The papers say two dozen, but we can't be sure."

Two dozen? That truly was a stampede.

"Where'd they escape from?"

"Talbot County."

"You sure? Not Caroline or Dorchester counties?"

"No, Talbot," said William. "I'm sorry, Harriet. But they did pass through Caroline County on their way out, so maybe..."

"Maybe my family joined up with them," she said. "Maybe they picked up slaves on the stampede to the border. Do you think that could be?"

"Let's pray it's so."

When Harriet had first heard folks at the hotel talking about the big escape, she ran all the way to the Anti-Slavery office, with the good news nearly lifting her off of her feet. Now, Harriet stared aimlessly into the corner of the office and nodded, feeling the hope punched out of her.

She sat across from William Still, leaning on the green tablecloth. She studied the enormous, black pipe shooting out of the wall and forming a right angle, extending down to the sturdy, black-iron stove. A copper tea kettle sat on the stovetop, giving out the perfume of jasmine. She was surrounded by heavy, walnut furnishings, including an entire wall of books. Papers were strewn everywhere. She brought her eyes back to William, who looked like he was trying to think of something comforting to say.

Harriet had felt so alone since coming to Philadelphia a month ago, and she yearned for family—Mama and Papa, and all her brothers, and her one remaining sister, Rachel. Despite all of the troubles she had with John, she even craved the company of her husband. She knew he could be callous and selfish, but she still loved him. Her brothers didn't like him much, but they didn't see his softer side.

Yes, she was free. But she was also alone.

Coming to Philadelphia, a huge city sprawling with strangers, she felt like someone who had just been released from prison after a twenty-five-year sentence. After a spell in jail, a released prisoner finds that everything has changed; his family and friends are gone, and his house pulled down. In the same way, she found there was nothing familiar in the North. Nothing felt like home. Nothing felt safe. She was a stranger in a strange land.

Harriet had always seen herself as a bit of a loner, but this heightened level of loneliness made her body and spirit ache. She clutched her walking stick in her right hand because she had a hard time letting go of her only connection to home—a hunk of wood from the Maryland forests.

"How'd they get out in this stampede?" she asked William.

William was a handsome black man, about thirty years old from what she could tell. He dressed real fine, with a cravat and coat. His short-cropped hair was parted cleanly on the left side, with a line running through it, like the line separating North from South.

"They fled southeast, through Preston, to the Delaware border. Things are happening, Harriet. Things are beginning to happen with increasing speed."

William was one of the chief leaders in an organized effort to get slaves out of the South. The Anti-Slavery office in Philadelphia was the beating heart of the movement, and it had been beating rapidly as of late. William even told Harriet that earlier in the year, a slave from Richmond, Virginia, had shipped himself in a box to Philadelphia, and they'd all been certain he was going to arrive dead on delivery. But when they opened the box, right here in this very office where they sat, Henry Brown emerged bloody and half-dead, but resurrected like Lazarus. A few months before that, a light-skinned slave named Ellen escaped from Georgia by posing as a white man, while her husband pretended to be her slave.

Stories like that got Harriet's mind buzzing with possibilities. If slaves could get out from Deep South places like Georgia, then surely she could do something to help her family just over the border in Maryland.

"You with me, Sister Harriet?" asked William, waving a hand in front of her face.

She snapped out of it. "Sorry, just thinking 'bout my family."

"I thought you were reveling in one of your visions," he said, smiling. Folks in Philadelphia already knew all about her tendency to drop away from this world, into a Spirit-filled state. Since coming to Philadelphia, she stopped having the vision of flying north, but she continued to have visions about the horse riders attacking, and the slave women screaming for their children.

"The Lord made a vow to me," she told William. "He told me He was going to hold steady on to me. He said He'd see me through this."

"That He has, Sister Harriet."

"But I, too, made a vow to God to give my life to brave deeds. I vowed I'd go back, get my family out. I am free, but *they* should be free, too!"

William leaned back in his chair, lacing his fingers together on his stomach. He chewed his lip.

"You're talking about doing this yourself? Going back to Maryland?"

"They're my family. I know the way out, and I got God. What more you need?"

William looked at her carefully, and she knew what he was thinking. What could a five-foot-tall woman do to lead a whole group of slaves north?

"I'm strong enough to do this," she said defensively. "I cut wood with men, I hauled wood with men, and I can probably lift you over my head if you wanna see."

William laughed and held up his hands in surrender. "No need to prove anything, Harriet. I've heard stories about you."

People have been talking about me? She wasn't sure she liked that.

"I'm just thinking about *how* this can be done—not *whether* it can be done," William said. "Something like this takes planning."

"It takes the Spirit. The Lord's the one doin' the plannin'."

"I don't deny the Lord has His hand in this. But you can't just go barging back there if you don't have a plan."

"Don't need a plan in my head when I got the Lord in my heart. He's my plan."

This got William scratching his head and furrowing his brow. "So has God shown you this plan and put it in your heart yet?"

He had her on that one. She looked down at her scuffed shoes and noticed that the right one was beginning to split up the side. "I'm still waitin' on instructions," she said softly.

Harriet looked up and thought she could actually see him let out a breath of relief. He had probably thought she was just going to charge out of the office at this very second and storm on down to Maryland and start yanking her family out of slavery and carrying them all to Philadelphia on her back.

She knew William was right. She had to wait on the Lord. She had to wait on His instructions before she could make her move. God Almighty would show her when the time was right.

...

Benjamin and Henry sidled into the Brodess house, hats in their hands. They had been back now for about a month since their disappearance—their lying out time. This morning, one of Eliza Brodess's sons, John, had plucked them from the fields and told them his mother wanted to see them—*again*. She had been doing this to them once a week since the day they came back.

The day they first straggled back to the Thompson place, Dr. Thompson had given them an earful, but surprisingly he didn't strike them with either a hand or a whip. Benjamin wondered if Thompson's new daughter-in-law, a Quaker abolitionist, had softened his touch.

However, Thompson wasn't their actual master, so they still feared the lash from Eliza Brodess. And when they showed up at her place, Benjamin was sure she would have them whipped half to death.

Shockingly, Miss Eliza didn't go near the bullwhip. She brought them to her house, had them stand in the main room, and spent about an hour screaming about how she should sell them both down south. At one point, she even picked up a candlestick and hurled it at Benjamin, but it whizzed right by his head and crashed against the back wall, gouging the wood.

From that point on, Miss Eliza would regularly order Benjamin and Henry to the Big House. And each time she would behave in some odd and unpredictable way. Once, she had Benjamin and Henry stand in the main room for a good hour while she just circled them, not saying a word. Just kept circling them like a vulture and muttering to herself. The next time she called them to the house, she sat in the rocker with the whip across her lap, occasionally shouting at them about their disloyalty. But she never did use the lash. The last time she called them to the house, she sat in the rocker sobbing. That's when Benjamin started to wonder if she was losing her mind.

All of the white folks looked down on the Brodesses. People always had. But at least Miss Eliza and her husband always had each other—until he died the week Harriet prayed for his death. (Benjamin thanked the Lord that Miss Eliza still didn't know about that prayer.) When Master Brodess died, everything else seemed to die around the place. It also didn't help that the Pattisons were suing her, and Dr. Thompson despised her as well. Except for her children, Miss Eliza was all alone, surrounded by enemies. Benjamin was tempted to feel sorry for her, but he knew better. The moment you start feeling sorry for a rattlesnake, it'll up and bite you.

Now, Miss Eliza had called for them again. The house was dark because Miss Eliza kept the shutters closed, maybe so she wouldn't see all of the dust—a reminder that her life and her house were falling to pieces all around her. Something smelled foul. A dead rat beneath the floorboards maybe? Or perhaps just spoiled food?

They expected to see Missus Brodess waiting for them in the rocker in the main room, as she always greeted them. But there was no sign of the lady.

"Missus Brodess?" Benjamin called out softly.

"That you, Ben?" came a muffled voice from the first-floor bedroom. "What took you so long, boy?"

Benjamin and Henry exchanged glances. Should they enter the bedroom? They wouldn't dare.

"It's me," Benjamin said. "And Henry. We came right away."

Benjamin and Henry just stood there, continuing to look around at the mess that was the Brodess house. The mistress had hired out all of her slaves for extra money, so there was no one left to keep her place tidy—or even reasonably clean.

"What you waiting for?" the mistress shouted, her voice no longer muffled. "Get in here!"

Benjamin was afraid to move. Walking into a white woman's bedroom could lead to a lot of trouble.

"Get in here, you two!" she hollered.

"We better," Henry whispered.

Benjamin led the way, a little afraid of what they might find on the other side of the door. When they entered the bedroom, they found Miss Eliza covered up in quilts, her head propped against a pillow. She looked half dead.

"You feelin' all right, ma'am?" Henry asked.

"Of course I'm feelin' fine, you fool. You two come here."

It sounded like she still had life inside of her.

Benjamin and Henry inched closer to her bedside, but they maintained a safe distance, about six feet away. The bedcovers smelled like they hadn't been washed in months.

"Closer! Where I can see ya."

She stared at them through watery eyes. Her skin was splotched red on her cheeks.

"You ain't planning on running again, are you?"

"No, ma'am," said Benjamin, looking down at the hat in his hands.

"No, ma'am," echoed Henry.

"You wouldn't go off on one of these stampedes, would ya?"

"Course not, ma'am," said Henry.

"Never," added Benjamin.

Miss Eliza drew her right hand from under the covers and pointed at the Bible sitting on the nightstand. If she were expecting them to read to her, she would be waiting a long time, as neither of them could read.

"Pick up that there Bible and put your hands on it. Both of you."

Benjamin knew where this was going. Henry picked up the Bible and carefully wiped dust from the cover.

"Put your right hands on it. Both of you!"

Benjamin and Henry did as ordered.

"Now swear on the Bible that you're never gonna run on me again."

Benjamin hesitated. They couldn't swear such a thing! He had no problem lying to Miss Eliza, but they couldn't lie to the Lord.

"Do it! Swear you ain't gonna run or I'll have you both halfhung!"

Benjamin noticed that Henry kept his right hand hovering about an inch above the cover of the Bible. He probably figured that if it wasn't actually touching the Bible, then swearing before the Lord wouldn't count.

Unfortunately, Missus Brodess noticed it too.

"Get your hand down on that cover! Touch it, Henry!"

After a moment's hesitation, Henry did so.

"Swear you ain't gonna run!"

Benjamin pictured himself being half-hung out by the old oak tree, struggling for breath and trying to keep his feet on the ground so he didn't choke to death.

"I swear I won't run from your land, Miss Eliza," Henry said quietly. Benjamin glared at him. He couldn't believe his brother had given in so quickly. But then he noticed Henry giving him a wink and the hint of a smile, and he wondered what his brother had up his sleeve. Henry gave him a slight nod of the head, leaned in close, and whispered, "Speak the same *exact* words."

So Benjamin did just that. "I swear I won't run from your land, Miss Eliza."

Miss Eliza gave them a haughty look, like she was standing over them with her foot on their necks.

"Fine. Now you remember that, boys. If you run from my land again, the Lord will hunt you down and kill you dead. Remember your vow to God!"

"We will, ma'am," said Henry, ducking his head down, real submissive like. Benjamin thought he might have been overacting.

"Now git!" she blasted. "And leave me in peace!"

Benjamin and Henry were happy to oblige. The woman was clearly touched in the head. Once safely outside, Benjamin took out a handkerchief and mopped his brow.

"So, what was that all about?" he asked Henry when they were a safe distance from the Brodess house. "Why'd you give in so easily?"

Henry laughed. "We swore we wouldn't run from her land."

"Yeah, that's right…"

"Well, she's got us hired out to start workin' on Thompson land next week! And we didn't swear we won't run from Thompson's land."

Benjamin laughed lightly. He hoped such a loophole would be acceptable to the Lord.

"But what if she brings us back to live and work on her land? What then? We vowed we wouldn't run from her land."

Another big grin from Henry. "Then we won't run from her land. We'll *walk* off of her land."

Smiling widely and clearly pleased with himself, Henry marched back to work, and Benjamin followed after a moment of amazement. If his brother Henry had been white, he probably would have become a lawyer.

19

Baltimore
December 1850: One Year Later

Head lowered against the wind, Harriet barreled down the wide Baltimore streets, making her way toward the docks. She kept a hand in her right coat pocket, touching her freedom papers to ensure they were still there. Her forged freedom papers were her only means of defending herself now that she was back in slave territory for the first time in over a year.

Harriet had been in Baltimore for a couple of days now, staying with her brother-in-law, Tom Tubman. John had always talked about the brother who lived in Baltimore, and Tom was pleased when she showed up on his doorstep. Tom didn't seem to know anything about the troubles she'd been having with John, and Harriet kept it that way.

She still couldn't get over the fact that she was walking once again on slave soil. Returning to Maryland made her feel like she was Daniel strolling back into that lion's den for a second go at the big cats. Sometimes, she wondered if she was out of her mind.

The neighborhood near the docks smelled strongly of fish, and she was surrounded by the sounds of street vendors. One such vendor was old Moses, a redheaded black man whom she had met the day before. He sang out in praise of the oysters he was peddling.

"Oysh, oysh, shock-oy-sh! Oh, my charmin' oysters! My deeeeee-lightful fresh oysters! My oysters are fresh, an' just from the shell. I can't tell the reason my oysters won't sell!"

It was early morning, and the sun was just rising on a crisp, breezy day, as she pounded on the door to the tenement where her niece's husband, John Bowley, lived. It was a ramshackle, one-room place around the corner from the docks, where he plied his trade as a waterman. Bowley was free, but his wife, Kessiah, still lived as a slave to Eliza Brodess back in Bucktown. Notices had recently gone out announcing the auction of Kessiah and their two children: James and Araminta (or Minty), with the girl being named after Harriet. Bowley needed to know what was happening, and Harriet aimed to tell him.

"Mornin' Harriet," Bowley said, opening the door. She whooshed inside, rushing through the opening like a gust of wind.

"We gotta talk," she said, spinning around to face him.

"You want somethin' to eat?" Bowley said. From the setting on the table, she could see that he was just sitting down to eggs. Bowley was a silent soul—a large man with big ears sticking out and flapping like flags. He seemed older than his twenty-seven years—almost elderly in his slow, methodical ways. He took what came at him with a quiet calmness that boggled Harriet's mind.

Bowley slid his plate of eggs across the table toward Harriet, who remained standing. "Y'all can have mine," he said. "I'll cook some more."

"I can't talk and eat at the same time, but thanks."

"Suit yourself. You wanna take a seat?" He pulled out a chair for her.

"Oh, all right," she said.

He didn't seem to be in any hurry to hear her news, but that wasn't surprising. He was rarely in a rush about anything. But if sitting down would get his attention, then she would sit. He slid the chair in behind her like a gentleman, and then he took a seat across from her, care-fully tucking a napkin beneath his chin.

"We gotta act soon," Harriet said. "Kessiah's goin' up for auction."

Bowley winced at the news. For him, this was the equivalent of letting out a scream.

"Miss Eliza's at it again," she said, charging ahead. "She already sold off a slave named Dawes Keene, and notices have gone out announcing she's gonna auction off Kessiah and your children."

Bowley stared back at Harriet, quietly chewing on his first mouthful of egg. His mind was whirring, Harriet could tell.

"How much time we got?" he asked.

"One week until the auction in Cambridge. So we gotta make our move."

Bowley set down his fork, careful like, and then wiped his mouth with his handkerchief. He did everything so slowly that it drove Harriet mad.

"But we ain't got enough money saved to buy my family's freedom," he said. As a free black, Bowley would have the right to bid on his family at the auction, but he was correct in noting that they still didn't have enough funds raised. Over the past year in Philadelphia, Harriet had been pestering her rich abolitionist friends for donations. She had some of the money gathered for just this kind of situation, but she didn't have nearly enough to buy a mother and two children.

"We ain't gonna need money for this plan to work," Harriet said.

"No money? You mean I'm not gonna buy their freedom? You want me to go down there and just snatch them?"

"You're gonna do both."

Bowley scratched the back of his head. Then he leaned forward and gave her a hard stare. "I'm gonna buy their freedom *and* snatch them? That don't make no sense."

So Harriet dove in excitedly, telling him exactly how this plan was going to unfold. Her blood rose just talking about it, and she nearly jumped out of her chair. She leaned over the table while Bowley kept on eating, calmly and methodically. When she started using the silverware and the cup to help him visualize the plan, he had to temporarily suspend his meal. She maneuvered the silverware and cup around the table as if she were some great army general drawing up battle plans, explaining what was going to happen. When she was finally done talking, she noticed him eyeing the fork.

"Yes, y'all can use your fork again, if that's what you're thinkin'!"

"Thank you, Miss Harriet."

Harriet watched as he shoveled the last two forkfuls of egg into his mouth, then wiped the fork clean with his handkerchief. He lined up his fork to the left of his plate, all very carefully.

Harriet felt like she was going to explode, waiting for the man to speak.

"So what is it, John? You think this will work?"

Bowley continued to stare at the plate, then readjusted his fork again. *Say something!*

At last, he said: "I think I can do it."

"*We* can do it," Harriet said. "I'm goin' with you."

Bowley shook his head. "No. If you come with me, you might be seen, and that'd bring the whole plan crashing down. It's gotta be only me. The people there know me as a free man. They like me."

It was true. Most white folks in and around Cambridge respected John Bowley and were sorry to see him move to Baltimore to work the waterways. He had a way of hiding his rebellious streak with his calm, seemingly subservient manner. But he always managed to get his way by making it seem like the master was getting his way. Harriet didn't know how he did it.

She hated to admit it, but Bowley was right. If she went with him and were spotted, she might give the plan away.

Bowley eyed the tin cup on his table, the same one Harriet had been using to represent a safe house in her plan.

"You done usin' that?" he asked.

"Yes, go on now."

Smiling, John Bowley raised the cup and downed the milk in one gulp. Then he set the cup back down, careful to place it to the upper right of his plate. Just so.

20

Cambridge, Maryland
One Week Later

B enjamin pushed through the crowd that had gathered in front of the Cambridge courthouse, where the slave auction was set to begin. The courthouse stood on a slight rise, with a flight of stairs leading up to a massive, wooden front door with a coat of arms centered above it. The auctioneer stood at the top of the stairs before this intimidating, castle-like door, while a crowd of several hundred had gathered out front, most of them clustered beneath two large trees. The day was cool, in the mid-forties, but the sun was out. Benjamin's niece, Kessiah, stood off to the side of the front steps. She stood in a cluster of about a dozen slaves up for auction this morning. Looking forlorn and frightened, she held her baby, Araminta, in her arms while her younger boy, James, clutched her long, heavy dress.

Araminta was named after Harriet, whom Benjamin missed dearly, despite her pushy ways. He sometimes had dreams that Harriet had come to him in the middle of the night, shoving him out of bed just as she did on the night of the shooting stars. But he would wake to find himself in the cabin with other family members sleeping quietly around him—and Harriet long gone.

Word was travelling back and forth between Bucktown and Philadelphia through a network of slaves and free blacks. Through this, he had heard that his sister was forming a new life in the North, and not a week went by without Benjamin rebuking himself for failing to escape with her. He had sent word to Harriet about the impending auction, and he wondered if she received the news.

Miss Eliza had been threatening to sell Kessiah for a couple of years, but now the dreaded day had actually arrived. Benjamin ran his eyes across the crowd, sizing up the white men to see how many were strangers—possible buyers from another state. When his eyes landed on John Bowley, he nearly gasped out loud. Bowley, Kessiah's husband, had come down from Baltimore, which meant that word of the sale had at least spread that far. Benjamin hadn't seen Bowley for years now, not since the man left the Cambridge area to earn a better living in Baltimore. Benjamin looked around for Harriet, thinking he might spot his sister somewhere in the crowd, dressed up in a disguise.

Benjamin could see that Bowley's presence had caught the eyes of many people, but Bowley was a free man. He had a right to be there, although he was taking a big risk standing in the midst of this crowd. Slave hunters had a knack for ignoring a man's freedom papers.

The auction started with the sale of a young man named Bebb. The auctioneer, Mister Collins, was a short-waisted man in an ill-fitting coat and a top hat. With his hooked nose, long arms, and spindly legs, he looked downright spidery.

"This boy, twenty-five years old, is bein' sold for no fault of his own," Mister Collins announced. "The owner wants money, and three hundred dollars is where I'm starting."

"Does he have marks?" a man shouted from the crowd.

"Boy, pull off your shirt and roll up your pants to show you ain't been whipped."

Bebb did just that, and the man in the crowd seemed satisfied.

Soon, the bids began rolling in until the sale was finally made for five hundred and fifty dollars.

Kessiah was up next, along with her two young children. Benjamin could see John Bowley move closer to the courthouse steps, threading his way through the crowd.

"This here is a fruitful girl, only twenty-one years old and already with two children. At this age, she could deliver another ten or more children in no time. We're selling them as a family. Let me start the bidding at five hundred."

"Five hundred!"

All eyes moved to the man who had spoken up: John Bowley. As Benjamin knew full well, a free black could buy his own family, but that didn't always mean the auctioneer took the bid. Mister Collins stared at Bowley for a few heartbeats, before turning to Miss Eliza's son, John Brodess. Mister Brodess gave the auctioneer a slight nod of approval, and Collins turned back to the crowd.

"I have five hundred dollars! Do I hear five hundred and fifty?"

"Five fifty!"

This came from a man named Mister Wilkes. Benjamin didn't believe Wilkes was really looking to add slaves to his plantation, and he wondered if the man was just running up the price on Bowley—or trying to deny him out of spite. However, Bowley was well liked, even among plantation owners. Benjamin would be surprised if Wilkes would do it to be ornery.

"Six hundred!" shouted Bowley, and Wilkes was hot on his heels with a quick follow-up bid: "Six hundred and fifty!"

John Brodess looked pleased as the price topped seven hundred, then seven hundred and fifty. Wilkes seemed to be having a grand old time hurling out his bids, but if he was trying to fluster Bowley, it wasn't working. Bowley was rarely flustered by anything. He was the type who would calmly finish his cup of coffee in the midst of a burning building with a tornado bearing down on him at the same time.

"Eight hundred and fifty!" Bowley said, almost matter-of-factly, and every eye shifted in Wilkes' direction to see if he would respond in kind to this sudden leap in price.

Wilkes leaned on his cane and put a finger to his lips, as if seriously contemplating a rival bid. But if Wilkes was simply trying to inflate the price and not serious about buying the family, he had already done his job. Why go any higher and risk getting stuck with a sizable bill?

Finally, Wilkes shook his head in silence, throwing in the towel.

"Sold to John Bowley!" the auctioneer declared.

As the next slave was brought to the stairs, Benjamin noticed Bowley hanging back in the crowd—not approaching his family. At least not right away. The bidding began on the next slave, and Bowley slowly worked his way in the direction of his family, moving at a glacial pace. Finally, when he reached Kessiah, he leaned over and kissed her on the side of the face. He might have whispered something in her ear; Benjamin couldn't tell for sure. He then kissed baby Araminta's head—a baby he had probably not set eyes on for a year. Little James continued to hang on his Mama's dress, eyeing his father like he would a stranger.

All Benjamin could think was that Bowley must have been working like a crazy man on the Baltimore docks to be able to afford such a price. Or was Harriet behind this? Had she raised money from northern abolitionists? He wouldn't put it past her.

"So Bowley's gone and done it, eh Benjamin?"

Benjamin wheeled around to find his brother Henry ambling up, all smiles.

"Where do y'all think he got that kind of money? Rob a bank?"

"I wouldn't joke about those kinds of things," Benjamin said. "Probably some wealthy abolitionist."

"Let's go congratulate him," said Henry. "To buy your family out of slavery is a mighty big deal."

"Leave them be for now," said Benjamin, putting a hand on Henry's shoulder. Benjamin had a growing suspicion about what was happening, and he didn't want to do anything that might bring attention to the Bowley family.

"Why can't I just congratulate him?" asked Henry, but Benjamin didn't respond. His only answer was a glare. Henry got the message, and he shut up.

When the lunch break ended, the auctioneer climbed back up the courthouse stairs and called out to the men who had purchased slaves. It was time they handed over the payment in full. But from the looks of it, only white men approached the auctioneer.

The auctioneer, suddenly on high alert, began to scan the crowd, which had gathered once again for more sales.

"John Bowley!" he shouted.

No one responded. The crowd went as quiet as death.

"John Bowley!"

Then people began to glance around, hunting for Bowley. It shouldn't be too hard to pick out a black face among so many whites. The white folks stared at Benjamin and Henry, as if trying to figure out if one of them was Bowley.

Benjamin suddenly realized that hanging around at this auction might be a bit dangerous. But it would be even worse if they suddenly fled the scene. So he stayed put, feeling the heat of people's eyes.

"Has anyone seen John Bowley?"

The auctioneer stared directly at Benjamin and Henry, but Benjamin just shrugged. He honestly had no idea where the man had gone.

21

If there was ever a time to move fast, this was it.

Normally, John Bowley went through life in slow motion. He often moved like he was underwater because he felt it gave him more ownership of his time. But today, as soon as they were around the corner of the courthouse, he took James by the hand and used his other hand to give Kessiah a strong tug.

Immediately, they all began to run.

"Where we goin'?" Kessiah asked.

"Don't speak. Just move."

John directed his family through the string of backyards that led down High Street, away from the courthouse and toward the wharf on the Choptank River. He was eternally grateful he didn't encounter anyone smoking a cigar or dilly-dallying out back of any of the homes. They cut through the yards, following a path that John had already scouted out. That's how he knew there were no dogs lurking between the courthouse and the Trout house. High Street was lined with large, prosperous houses, lounging along the street like kings, and the yards were a riot of trees and bushes—although with it being winter, the trees didn't have leaves to provide cover.

They stopped in one of the back yards. "Good morning!" said their contact, one of the three Trout siblings who met them in the back-yard of one of the homes. She was a curly-haired blonde white lady, with a big red ribbon in her hair to match her white dress with red frills.

John hadn't yet met the three Trouts, but based on Harriet's description, this one must be Miss Jenny Anne, the writer. Miss Jenny was followed close behind by her sister Michelle and her brother Dave.

"Good afternoon, John and Kessiah, I trust your escape went well," said Miss Michelle. She spoke so calmly, as if their sudden appearance in the yard was as ordinary as a visit from country relatives.

John Bowley stood rooted in place, overwhelmed by the three white folks smiling at them. Four dogs, all of them Scottish terriers, danced around Miss Jenny's legs. Young James was immediately drawn to them.

"What's their names?" James asked. He broke into a smile as he crouched down and the dogs leaped up at him, licking his face from all angles.

"Max," said Miss Jenny.

"Max? Which one's Max?" James asked.

"They all are. Named after my late husband. It was hard to keep them sorted in my mind, so one name suits them all."

It sounded strange, but Benjamin recalled that Harriet warned him the siblings were a bit on the eccentric side. He wondered if she had understated the case.

According to Harriet, Miss Jenny was an Atlanta transplant, while her sister Michelle came from North Carolina, and Dave came down from Canada. After losing their spouses, all three had moved to be together in neutral territory—Cambridge, Maryland.

The three siblings were not accepted in town—being newcomers and on the odd side, Harriet had said. John Bowley worried that the Trouts' outsider status might make them the first to be suspected of harboring escaped slaves. But there was really no other option. John and his family had to hide somewhere during the hours of daylight and wait for darkness before moving on.

"Did anyone spot you?" asked Dave, who had a ruddy, good-natured face.

"Not a soul," said John.

John's voice came out a little shaky because he was still rattled by the auction. In some ways, it had gone smoother than he'd expected. On the other hand, he never thought the bid would go so high. *Eight hundred and fifty dollars!* John could not believe that Wilkes had fought him so hard, pushing up the auction price to a nearly a thousand. Any higher and there was no way people would have believed he had that kind of money at his disposal.

"Into the house," said Miss Jenny, leading them into the sprawling old home. Inside, it was meticulously maintained and furnished with rich cherry furniture. As they entered, each of the siblings introduced themselves; John had guessed correctly who was who.

"Sandwiches?" Miss Michelle said, picking up a tray and passing it beneath their noses. "You need to build your strength."

"Don't mind if I do," said Dave, reaching for a sandwich.

"But I do mind. These are for our guests," said Miss Michelle, slapping away Dave's hand.

"Thank ya," said John, picking off one of the small delicacies. It all seemed so strange, being served by a white woman. Kessiah shook her head "no" to the offer of food, but James dug in and snagged three of the crustless sandwiches.

"Tea?" Miss Michelle asked.

"No time for tea," said Dave, drawing John toward the staircase, leading up to the second floor. On the way, Dave picked off one of the finger sandwiches from the tray when Michelle wasn't looking.

"Wait! Before you head upstairs, there's this," said Miss Jenny. She approached with a bottle in one hand and a spoon in the other.

"Medicine?" said John.

"For the baby. Paregoric. It'll knock your baby out cold."

John looked over at Kessiah, who slowly shook her head. He had heard about the medicine's power to put people to sleep, and he also knew that Miss Jenny was right. If the baby started squalling while the house was being searched, they were all dead.

"It must be done," John Bowley said. When he gently lifted the baby out of his wife's arms, Araminta immediately began squawking.

After giving the baby a dose of paregoric, the siblings led John and his family up the ornate staircase to the second floor, where they directed them into a bedchamber. From the looks of it, the bedchamber likely belonged to one of the sisters. There were flowers everywhere. Flowers adorned the gleaming dresser, and the floral theme was repeated on the bedspreads and paintings on the wall. Also, the bed was an odd one—a canopy bed with end posts and testers carved to look like bamboo.

John noticed that Miss Jenny had found a perch on a floral window seat and was busily taking notes. Was she writing about their escape?

"Over here. Quickly now," said Dave. He threw open the wardrobe doors and announced, "There's your hiding spot."

John gave him a look of disbelief. "In here? Don't you think a wardrobe might be the first place they look?"

Not only did the wardrobe seem an obvious hiding spot, but it was on the small side. They expected them to spend the entire day hiding inside this thing?

The siblings were certainly eccentric, but John was beginning to wonder if they were crazy to boot. Or were they *trying* to get them found? Was this their strange way of getting into the town's good graces—by helping to trap escaped slaves?

John was at a loss for what to say or do.

...

Harriet felt so useless, hanging back in Baltimore and knowing there was nothing she could do except fret about what was unfolding down in Cambridge. The auction had been held late that morning. If John Bowley pulled it off, he should be hiding right now in the Trout house.

Harriet met the three Trouts a year ago when they were visiting Philadelphia, and she had immediately taken to them. Miss Jenny told

Harriet that if they could ever be of service, just let them know. Harriet knew straight off that "be of service" meant helping to hide a slave or two.

Harriet decided she had to get out and stretch her legs on the streets before she went stir crazy. Now that she was back in the slave state of Maryland, she had to keep reminding herself to be careful on the streets. This wasn't Philadelphia, after all. But still, she had to get outside for air.

The city was abuzz with talk about the Swedish Nightingale, the famous soprano. The circus man, P.T. Barnum, had brought her to America for a string of concerts, and when Harriet found her way down to the Front Street Theatre, she came across a massive crowd. What she saw was an eerie parallel to what had been going on in Cambridge only a few hours earlier. They were conducting an auction in front of the theatre, only in this case a man from the firm of Gibson and Company was auctioning off tickets to the soprano's concert.

"What's the bid for the first choice?" the auctioneer said, getting the spectacle going.

A hush fell over the crowd, and Harriet noticed she was probably the only black person in a sea of white faces. The women were dressed in stunning gowns, prepared for an evening gala, with the most colorful, feather-filled hats she had ever seen. Whenever someone stared at her, Harriet glared back until they diverted their eyes. In staring contests, there was none better than her.

"Ten dollars!" someone finally shouted, a modest bid. But the price steadily rose from twenty to thirty to forty dollars before one bold soul suddenly skyrocketed the bid up to seventy-five. Harriet was astounded that anyone would bid so much for a night at the theatre.

"One hundred dollars!" a man finally bellowed, raising his top hat as he shouted.

The seat was knocked down to that bidder, a Mister Whitehurst. Harriet knew this because several in the crowd suddenly erupted with, "Three cheers for Whitehurst!"

As Harriet wandered off, she shook her head in amazement at the ways of people who could spend a hundred dollars to sit in a seat and hear someone sing when you could just as easily head on down to a revival meeting and hear someone sing for nothing.

It also made her sad thinking about a different sort of auction down in Cambridge, and just knowing that if they caught John Bowley and his family, there would be a different kind of price to pay.

Harriet rarely doubted herself, but this was one of those times.

22

Baby Araminta was out like a light. John Bowley was happy that his wife had succumbed and allowed the Trouts to give their baby a dose of paregoric. Infants can erupt in crying at any moment, so it would be like holding an explosive in their arms if she were awake. Every so often, Kessiah would put a hand in front of baby Araminta's nose, just to make sure she was still breathing.

John thought about giving the medicine to James as well, just to be on the safe side. But their little boy seemed to understand the danger and the need for quiet. So far, he had been as silent as a soft breeze. The family huddled together in the darkness, waiting and listening for the inevitable arrival of the slave hunters.

It seemed like a long time coming, sitting in darkness and saying nothing, but the slave hunters eventually came. John heard a commotion erupt downstairs. It didn't sound like a social visit.

...

Jenny was surprised it had taken so long for the slave hunters to arrive. She thought their house might be the first place they would check in the hunt for the Bowleys. After all, people had been spreading all sorts of rumors about them in Cambridge—including stories about them being abolitionist rascals.

"I apologize, but we need to check your property," said John Brodess as he politely removed his hat while the three siblings welcomed them inside. Jenny had once felt a little bit of sympathy for the Brodesses, who were treated as outsiders despite being lifelong residents of the region. She could relate to their outsider status, but the day she met Eliza Brodess was the day she stopped feeling sorry for them. Jenny was modelling the villainess in her latest story after Miss Eliza.

John Brodess was accompanied by another man—a deputy—plus his mother, Miss Eliza.

"What seems to be the trouble, Mister Brodess?" Dave asked.

"I'm sure you heard by now. A slave family ran off from the auction block today."

"Oh my, we did hear the tragic news," said Jenny. "And you want to check our house? Do you think they could have snuck inside and found a hiding spot without our knowing?"

Her brother Dave shot her a look—raised eyebrows and wide eyes —as if to signal that she was overacting. But what did Dave know about acting?

"Tea and sandwiches?" asked Michelle, passing the tray beneath their noses. The deputy took two sandwiches, but John Brodess and Miss Eliza waved off the tray like it was a fly.

As the invaders moved deeper into the house, Miss Eliza cast an evil eye at the three siblings, one by one. Jenny just smiled back, as innocent as a dove.

"Be our guest and be thorough in your search," said Dave. He waved them into the parlor, where the two men immediately began looking for any possible hiding spots. There weren't many places to hide in this room, other than behind the curtains, so the group moved on. The Trouts kept suggesting places for them to search and pointing out spots they might have missed until Miss Eliza finally scowled, "We know our own business. So mind yours!"

The Brodesses spent considerable time hunting through the cellar, because that would be the most likely place to hide escaped slaves. Then, as they moved back to the first floor, Michelle said, "Did you check the closet beneath the stairs? I would hate to think that an escaped slave might be lurking in there, just waiting to pounce on us —and with us having no way to protect ourselves."

"I beg your pardon, sister," said Dave. You have *me* for protection."

Michelle rolled her eyes. "He doesn't even know how to shoot straight," she told Miss Eliza.

Miss Eliza just grunted. Jenny was pleased they were getting under her skin, as they all worked their way up to the second floor.

"I am sorry, ladies, but we must look in your bedchambers," said Brodess. "I brought along my mother for this very purpose, so that I would not intrude where gentlemen are not allowed."

"You are so kind and thoughtful," said Jenny, slathering her words with an extra helping of Georgia honey.

Jenny and Michelle followed Miss Eliza into the first bedchamber and stood back politely as the woman scoured the room, even getting down on her knees to peer under the bed.

"Don't forget the wardrobe," said Jenny, and Michelle shot her a look of warning. But she knew exactly what she was doing.

"You don't have to tell me my job," said Miss Eliza, groaning as she raised herself to a standing position. Then she made a move toward the wardrobe.

···

John was stunned when he heard Miss Jenny utter the words, "Don't forget the wardrobe." At that moment, he was certain the Trouts had betrayed them. Even in the dark, he could see Kessiah's eyes go as wide as an owl's.

Kessiah put her hand around James's mouth, to make sure he remained completely quiet, and then she buried her face in John's shoulder. Fortunately, baby Araminta remained as motionless as a rag doll. John held his breath as he heard the doors to the wardrobe open wide, squeaking on their hinges.

23

Tapping her right foot on the wooden floor, Jenny watched with arms crossed as Eliza Brodess threw open the wardrobe doors, revealing a neat row of coats and dresses. As the two sisters looked on, Eliza began to rifle through the clothing, first passing them through her hands from left to right and then going from right to left, just to be sure.

"I make my own dresses," said Michelle cheerily. "If you ever need some dressmaking done, just let me know."

"You think I am so rich that I can hire me a dressmaker?" Miss Eliza snapped, spinning around and glaring. "Today, I just had eight hundred dollars run off on me."

"Eight hundred and fifty I heard," Dave reminded her.

"That was truly unfortunate," said Jenny. "I have purchased only furniture at auction, not human beings, and even though furniture have legs, they are not likely to run off on you."

Miss Eliza shot her a look that could melt stone.

"I do hope you will find that slave family," Michelle continued, as they returned back down the stairs, the search completed. "I do not think I will be able to sleep safely in my bed knowing there are desperate slaves roaming the countryside."

"You keep forgetting you have a man in the house," Dave pointed out. "I know a thing or two about shooting a gun."

"Shooting is one thing," said Michelle. "Aiming is another."

"Do you suppose they could have gotten far?" Miss Jenny asked Mister Brodess as they approached the front door.

"They wouldn't dare move by day," Brodess said. "They'll wait until dark, but we'll be keeping an eagle eye out, watching roads and waterways."

"If we can be of any more service, please do not hesitate to let us know," said Michelle.

"And thank you for checking our premises," Jenny added. "We will feel much safer knowing that you made sure it is completely slave free."

John Brodess tipped his hat. "Mark my words, we will find them."

"I pray you do," added Michelle.

Miss Eliza nailed them each with one last glare before exiting, as if to say she wasn't fooled by their performance. Then the three Trout siblings clustered at the window. Jenny pulled the lace curtain to the side, giving them a clear view to watch and wait for the Brodesses to disappear.

Once the danger had passed and the search party was gone, Dave seemed irritated. "You didn't have to suggest they search the wardrobe," he told Jenny.

"Of course I had to," she said. "They were going to search it anyway, and it's all part of the performance. You need a better sense of the dramatic, David."

Back in the bedchamber, Dave made a beeline for the wardrobe. He pulled out an armload of gowns, handing them off to Michelle, who placed them neatly on the bed. Then he felt along the back wall of the wardrobe until his finger found a slight indention. Using this grip, he pulled out the back panel of the wardrobe, revealing a small door behind it. When he swung open the door, he found the Bowley family staring out at them, blinking at the blast of sudden light.

"The Brodesses are gone, and you are safe," Jenny declared with suitable drama.

"Thank you, sir and ma'ams," Bowley said. His forehead gleamed with a sheen of sweat.

"The Bowleys still have a ways to travel tonight before you can say they are truly safe," Dave reminded Jenny. "Tonight, we will have a boat ready."

"And I am sorry to say you have to stay inside the secret room until dark," added Michelle. "But take a moment to stretch your legs and feel the breeze."

Michelle offered them refreshments before Dave closed the door on them and put the false panel back in place. The Bowleys were entombed once again.

...

John Bowley's hands were stiff with cold as he and his family climbed into the rowboat, which awaited them at the wharf just a block from the Trout House on High Street. The Trout family had lavished them with a heap of blankets and hats and gloves all around, but the night's wind cut through the material with razor sharpness. The wind rippled the black water, which softly splashed against the large rocks all along the bank and shallows.

Another dose of paregoric had sent baby Araminta to a much warmer, sleepier place, but James complained of the cold almost constantly. The bank along the Choptank River appeared desolate, but John was well aware that patrollers could be near, moving up and down the bank, looking for the escaped family, so he tried to calm little James.

"Be safe," said Dave Trout, and then he and John shook hands.

"Thank you again," said John as the big man pushed them from shore and waved them off.

It was a typical December night, with temperatures near freezing. The waves cutting across the water were not high, but should their boat capsize for any reason, they would freeze to death—if they didn't drown first. The oars clunked wood against wood as John pulled hard on the handles. He knew enough to keep a loose grip on the oars because they had a long, cold journey ahead, and a tight grip would sprout blisters in no time. He sat up straight and drove back hard with his legs. He moved the boat a good distance from land on the wide river, hoping to be well out of view of any patrollers on shore. The moon slipped in and out of the clouds, so it was difficult to say just how much light would eventually come shining down on the river.

They cut a path northwest in the direction of Chesapeake Bay, which would take them north to Baltimore. John planned to row for the entire night. Then, come the first rays of sunlight, they would find safe haven on shore before venturing out again the next night. A second night of rowing would be necessary, assuming they were still alive.

From somewhere along the shore, John heard the sound of men's voices, and for a moment he thought they had been spotted. As he paused in his rowing, his eyes scanned the shore, afraid that a much faster boat might be pulling away at any moment and heading in their direction, loaded with armed slave hunters. Dave Trout had given him a pistol and hunting knife, and that was the extent of their weapons. But they were well stocked with food, thanks to the lavish preparations of Miss Michelle.

The sound of voices faded away, but just to be safe, John rowed the boat to the very center of the river—as far from the eyes of hunters as possible.

24

Baltimore
One Day Later

Harriet had never felt so useless, just sitting in the dark on the side of a hill near Baltimore's inner harbor, wrapped in a blanket and looking out on the black finger of water that was the Patapsco River. All types of tall-mast ships were outlined in the moonlight, and the water was mercifully calm. According to their plan, John Bowley would need two entire nights of rowing to progress up Chesapeake Bay and reach Baltimore. This was the second night, and Harriet was determined to remain awake until the Bowleys arrived—if they arrived.

By this time, John Bowley and his family could very well have been caught, whipped, and shipped South toward a misery-filled future. But it would be days before she'd know if anything bad had happened. News traveled like a snail, so Harriet was in the dark in more ways than one. The Bowleys might also have drowned or been run over by a steamboat. There were so many ways to die.

Harriet kept her kerchief pulled down over her ears, but the cold still found a way to sneak under and bite her on the earlobes. Her brother-in-law, Tom Tubman, had loaned her his great coat, which was so large that it swallowed her up. Tom was quiet and kind—very different than his brother. But Harriet still missed her husband's impish ways. He always had a way of finding levity in life, lifting her up in a world that weighed so heavy. Their marriage had lost much of this joy, but she still relished the first year or two when they would dance and sing and then tumble together onto the pallet that was their bed. She wondered if being apart would make him miss her. Maybe he, too, would want to recapture that early spirit. When they were reunited—and she vowed they would come back North together—it would be like starting fresh, like the day they rode the log together in the snow. If they did reunite, she prayed that a child might be the result. Even though she and John had been apart for so long, she kept asking God for a child, day after day. She figured if she kept firing prayers like bullets to heaven, one of them would hit their mark and she would be reunited with John. Then the children would start coming. God would make it happen.

Harriet stretched out her legs because her knees had cramped, and then she very nearly nodded off to sleep. She had done it three times during the night, but only one of her driftings had taken her into a vision. Her head jerked back as she pulled herself out of her dreams, like pulling herself back from the edge of a cliff.

"Be a wall of fire around me, Lord. Be the glory in my midst," she said under her breath.

Harriet listened to the hoot of an owl, and the sound brought her back to thoughts of her brother Benjamin, and all of her brothers. They too needed to be rescued from slavery, and she aimed to do it someday. She vowed she would lead her husband and brothers and sister Rachel and nephews and nieces all out of slavery. Next time she would go down there in person and do it herself. No more of this sitting around and waiting and praying. She had to *act*. She had to fight. She pictured those muskrats she'd captured as a child, their legs cinched in the steel trap as they dangled headfirst in the water at the end of a chain, fighting to reach the surface. She too wouldn't go out without a fight.

Then Harriet saw something move in the gloom. She sat up straight and peered into the blackness. Next: the thunk of wood hitting wood and the quiet splash of oars dipping into water. Her eyes caught the image of a rowboat, a different shade of black moving against the backdrop of the dark water. The rowboat headed for the bank, coming right at her.

Rising to her feet and drawing the great coat tightly around her shoulders, Harriet hurried down the slope, trying not to get her hopes up too high. There's no telling who might be landing a boat in the dark hours of early morning.

"Sister Harriet?"

It was John Bowley's voice. His glorious, ringing voice.

"John?" Harriet tried not to shout. "Are all of you there?"

"All of us." And then, as if on cue, baby Araminta, her namesake, began to cry.

Harriet also started to cry, while sprinting down the slope to the sandy landing, where the boat neared shore. She no longer noticed the cold or the aches in her legs, even as she waded through the frigid shallows to help pull the boat to land.

"Kessiah, you all right?" Harriet said, putting her arm around her niece and drawing her from the boat.

"Cold but happy."

"Brother Tom will have a fire burnin' for y'all. It's so wonderful to see you, safe and sound. Praise the Lord!"

"Praise the Lord," said Kessiah in a voice made shaky by the cold.

Before climbing out of the boat, Kessiah handed the baby off to Harriet. It felt so good to be carrying life in her arms. The child stared back at her with deep brown eyes and the softest, freshest skin Harriet had ever felt. She was proud to know that their actions this week would prevent this child from being forced to work the fields, turning that soft skin into leather just like her own.

Harriet felt like dancing right there on the bank, but with her husband still living down near Bucktown, she had no one with whom to dance. She would change all that. John would come home with her, and they would dance and sing whenever their free hearts desired.

John would be next. She made it her holy vow.

25

Cambridge, Maryland
Autumn 1851: Nine Months Later

B enjamin met her in the house of the dead. He first laid eyes on Jane Kane when they were cleaning a burial vault on the property of Dr. A.C. Thompson.

Always on the hunt to hire out Benjamin for extra cash, Miss Eliza had once again hired him out to Dr. Thompson. Thompson put him to work on the family's land in Cambridge—their Bellefield estate, fourteen and a half acres. Benjamin was told to clean and air out the family burial vault. It was discreet enough, located in a secluded spot, encircled by trees. A cousin of Dr. Thompson's had just passed away, but before he died he had asked to be buried in the family vault, which hadn't been opened for fifteen years.

He'd been paired with a hired maid that turned out to be Jane Kane. She was a tall, thin woman, with a long neck, like a queen. Her eyes were black, like smoke, her lips full and her head framed by close-cut hair. When she raised her chin up, emphasizing her long neck, she looked most regal.

Benjamin couldn't pull his eyes off of her. The only flaw on her face was a small scar along the left side of her jawline, but even the scar seemed perfectly placed.

"Mornin', ma'am," said Benjamin. He became suddenly aware that he hadn't scrubbed his hands and face this morning. He owned only three shirts, and wished he had picked his nicest one. Knowing he was going to be opening a burial vault, he had reached for the most raggedy shirt. He didn't know he would be in the presence of a queen.

"Mornin'," said the woman.

"My name is Benjamin," he said, standing in front of the vault. A brisk wind fluttered the heads of the flowers scattered throughout the graveyard.

"I know," she said. She carried a broom in one hand and a bucket of water and rags in the other.

Benjamin waited for her to introduce herself, but she said nothing. She looked over at the vault, as if signaling him to get on with his work.

"Right," said Benjamin. He wondered why she didn't set down the bucket to rest her arms while he went to work opening the vault with his pick, chipping away at the mortar between bricks on the front wall.

As he did, his stomach began to growl, and he hoped she didn't hear. His brother Robert told him to fast all day before he opened the tomb—to keep from being overwhelmed by evil spirits that had been cooped up inside the vault for the past fifteen years.

"What do they call you?" he finally said to the maid as he methodically chipped away at the mortar.

"Jane," she said.

"I ain't seen you before on the Thompson place."

"That's 'cause I don't live on the Thompson place."

Pausing in his work, Benjamin waited for her to explain where she did live. But once again her eyes went to the bricks, and she sighed, another signal for him to keep working.

"Where do you live?" he said, making sure he didn't let up in his work as he talked.

"My master is Horatio Jones. He hired me out to Master Thompson."

At the words "Horatio Jones," Benjamin couldn't help himself. He stopped working and stared directly at Jane. Everyone knew that Jones was the most vicious master in the region. He was free with the whip, and he took pleasure in making the lives of his slaves as miserable as possible. There were stories that he once caught a slave plotting to kill him, and he had the man burned alive.

Knowing that Jones controlled her life, Benjamin was surprised that Jane showed only the one small scar. But perhaps her other emblems of cruelty were hidden away beneath her clothes.

"Oh." That's all Benjamin could think to say. Then her eyes prodded him back into action, and he soon had enough mortar cleaned out that he could pull down three bricks, creating a small opening into the vault.

The smell nearly knocked him off his feet. If these were the spirits that Robert spoke about, then they must be the most evil of creatures. Benjamin put an arm to his nose and mouth and backed away. As the smell washed over him, he nearly vomited right there. Getting sick all over Jane's shoes would not be a good way to impress a young woman.

"Let's let it air out a bit," said Benjamin, continuing to back away.

Jane also backed away, but she didn't act as if the smell had overpowered her. And she still hadn't put down her bucket!

"Set down your bucket and rest," Benjamin said.

"I can't." Jane said it like she was afraid. Benjamin wondered if she had been beaten for setting down a bucket, but he didn't dare ask. Knowing Horatio Jones, it was possible.

Benjamin wanted to let the vault air out for a good long time, but he couldn't just leave Jane standing there with a heavy bucket in her hand, so he tied a handkerchief around his nose and mouth and went back to the task. With the first bricks removed, it was quick work to pull down the rest of the wall. A couple of times, the vomit rose to his mouth, but he willed it back down.

At last the vault was open, like an enormous gaping mouth. Benjamin stepped inside as the light flooded in.

"Here, let me carry that bucket of water for you," Benjamin said.

"No!" Jane's response was so fierce that he quickly drew his hand away, as if yanking it from an unfriendly dog.

"Sorry," he said.

"No. I'm sorry. It's just that Master Jones don't let people help other people with their work. If he sees it, he punishes."

"I understand." He suddenly felt an overwhelming desire to protect this woman. He fantasized about sneaking into the Joneses' house with a hunting knife and cutting the man's throat in his sleep.

All of the death in the vault gave him a chill. A dead stench still hung in the air, but fresh air had already driven away some of the smell of decay. Benjamin counted over a dozen bodies in the vault, about half of them in rotting coffins. The other skeletons were bodies laid out on stone slabs, covered by remnants of disintegrating clothing. At first, he thought he saw little clumps of weeds growing in among the skulls, until he realized it was hair.

"Looks like the masters wind up the same as all of us," Benjamin said, as he looked around the deathly hole.

In life, he thought, these skeletons once ordered around slaves. But in death, they were pitiful specimens. All of life streams into a vast sea of death, the masters and the slaves all mixed together and racing toward the judgment seat of God. All things are full of weariness.

Then Jane gave a little whimper. Benjamin saw her looking down into a coffin, its lid rotted away. Benjamin slid to her side and stared down into the coffin. Nestled in the box appeared to be a mother with a child in her arms. They had both been reduced to bones, but once again the hair was preserved. Tangled in among the mother's bones were gold chains, but her chest bones had collapsed inward, and a necklace dangled down into her chest cavity, touching her backbone.

Benjamin looked over at Jane, whose eyes seemed to be locked on the skeleton of the child. Her eyes pooled with tears, and Benjamin wondered how she could shed a tear for a dead slave-owning woman and her child.

Then Jane set down the bucket, freeing up her left hand. With her free hand, she took Benjamin's.

...

Harriet laid the suit jacket across the bed, with the coat's arms stretched to the sides. Then she tucked the matching pair of pants into the suit coat, making it appear as if there had been a man inside the flattened clothes just moments before he was raptured right out of his clothing.

When Harriet returned to Philadelphia, she had purchased the new clothes for her husband, John. She scrimped and saved from her cleaning job at a Philadelphia hotel until she had enough to give her husband suitable clothing in which to travel north. If he tried going north wearing his raggedy old clothes, no one would believe he was a free black, and he would be taken as an escaped slave, sure as rain. Hence, the new suit.

After a long time planning, Harriet was ready to go back home to Dorchester County. She was determined to keep her vow to bring back her husband. And despite the dangers, she was strangely excited. She missed her Maryland forests and streams, and she still felt boxed in by all of the big buildings in Philadelphia. The city didn't have the natural wonder of rural Maryland, but it possessed supernatural wonders for escaped slaves. After the Bowleys reached Baltimore, she had led them straightaway to Philadelphia, and from there they headed north to Canada.

With the passage of the Fugitive Slave Law—the Bloodhound Bill as Harriet called it—even Philadelphia had become a dangerous place for escaped slaves. This new bill smoothed the way for slave catchers to come north and recapture escaped slaves; therefore, many slaves had turned their eyes to Canada or even England.

But Harriet was not about to flee farther north, as so many were doing. She was going *south*, back into the jaws of slavery.

Harriet had been back to slave country twice before—once to plan the Bowley escape and the second time to plan the escape of her brother Moses and two other men. But in both of those cases, she had remained in Baltimore, from where she coordinated the rescue. This time would be much different. She would be venturing back to her hometown for this mission, deeper into the land of the Pharaohs, where one wrong move would slap her back in chains. But she was willing to take the risk for John. They had made a vow before the Lord, as man and wife, and they belonged together.

Harriet enjoyed her solitude, but only up to a certain point. She had God to keep her company, and she talked with Him every day, like she would her husband. But she still craved another soul in a material body—someone she could see and touch.

Running her hand down the arm of the new suit, Harriet tried to picture John filling out the new clothes. Then she carefully rolled up the suit, as gently as she would treat a relic, and slipped the clothes into a sack to be slung over her back. Next, she grabbed her wooden staff, the same one she had kept since the day she walked off of the Thompson plantation. She snatched it from the corner and set off for home.

26

It had been two years since Harriet had been in this neck of the Maryland woods, but it felt like yesterday. She set up camp in the heart of the forest, about eight miles from Bucktown, and she began to sketch out the plan in her head. She would begin by passing herself off as an old lady. Since she was short, virtually any man or woman would look down on her, and they would see nothing but her wide sunbonnet.

She didn't think it would be safe to approach her husband's cabin until she scoped out the situation. Her brothers had been keeping her informed about John and other matters through a secret network of messengers, but she couldn't be exactly sure where to find John's current cabin. So her first task was to contact someone she could trust in Bucktown and give him a coin to locate John and deliver a message.

On the way to Bucktown, she stopped at a small market, where she bought a couple of fowls to use as a distraction in a tight situation. She tied a string around the legs of the two chickens and set off with a bird in either hand. It was a pleasant enough day—a scattering of broken clouds but mostly blue sky. The temperature was warm for autumn, and the trees were just beginning to turn.

Bucktown was a long hike, but she was used to wearing out shoes.

In due time she was strolling down one of the roads leading toward the crossroads—the same place where she had been walloped with a piece of lead. As she neared the store, the door opened and out walked a white man. She nearly dropped the chickens right then and there. The man was Dr. A.C. Thompson—the very man who had watched her walk off of his plantation singing a song two years ago. She was tempted to spin around on her heels and take off in the opposite direction, but that would trigger instant suspicion. Black folks who blatantly avoided a white person raise alarms in the heads of men like Dr. Thompson. So, she kept on going, not missing a stride, and she kept her head down, hoping her bonnet brim was wide enough to keep her face concealed.

She could hear him get on his horse, but she sensed he was staring at her and through her—just like the day she walked off of his plantation. It's like no time had passed, and here they were, facing off on a dusty road once again, with him staring daggers at her. Did he notice her gait? Did he remember the way she moved?

She tottered along, like an old woman would, but she knew she would need to do more to cover her identity. She would need to put her chickens to good use. As she neared Dr. Thompson, she gave a yank on one of the strings in her hand—the string attached to the leg of one of her two chickens. Instantly, the chicken burst into life and started squawking and fluttering in her left hand like a bird possessed. Harriet held on tightly to the mass of moving feathers, keeping a grip on one of the chicken's legs as she tugged on the second string, connected to the leg of the second bird. Then that bird burst into action as well, fluttering and squawking and trying its best to peck at her leg. She prayed to the Lord Almighty that Dr. Thompson would put all of his eye power on these chickens and not pay any heed to the little lady trying to corral them. The chickens were screaming and making such a racket that Harriet finally had to stop and crouch down to get them settled—but that just gave her more reason to keep her head down, far below Dr. Thompson's eye level.

It seemed to do the trick because Harriet soon heard his horse clomping off in the opposite direction, from the sound of it. Still, she didn't venture a peek at where he had gone until she was certain it was safe. When she finally looked up and saw that Dr. Thompson had vanished, she sat down beside a tree and leaned against the bark, waiting for her heart to stop fluttering. It had been beating as wildly as the chickens' wings.

Eventually, the birds calmed down, and she returned to the business at hand—finding a courier to carry her freedom message to John. Glory be! The Lord had delivered her from the snare of the fowler, He had covered her with His pinions, and under His wings she found refuge. She needn't fear the pestilence that stalks in darkness, nor the destruction that wastes at noonday. The Lord was Harriet's habitation, and no scourge would come near her tent. Glory be!

...

Harriet hoped to find someone she knew to carry her message to John, and she had to settle for Sam Jenkins. Sam wasn't the most reliable man, but she didn't have time to be choosy. She gave him a coin for his troubles, and he took off running before she even had a chance to tell him where he might track down her husband. A few minutes passed before Sam realized his mistake and came running back.

Harriet gave him directions to where John used to live, and off he went again, leaving Harriet sitting in the bushes not far from the crossroads general store. From her hiding place, she watched folks coming and going, people laughing and carrying on. She spotted a young black girl and boy slip around back and start kissing like they were trying to swallow one another whole. John was the only man who kissed her that way, and she wondered what it would feel like to have his lips all over her again. She was just about thirty years old, so there was still time for her to have a child or two—or more.

A little later in the afternoon, she spotted a couple of black children chasing each other in the field, and she sat there, soaking up their energy and laughter. Before she even thought about what she was doing, Harriet tied her chickens to a thin tree, got down on her belly, and began to crawl through the tall grass like some animal on the prowl. From below the grass, she could no longer see the children, but she was guided by the sound, and she moved in the direction of the laughter. She was like a fox, hugging the ground, darting right, then left, following the ever-moving balls of laughter.

Suddenly the grass parted, and there stood the little boy, no more than seven years old. His eyes nearly popped out of his skull when he saw her in the grass. They locked eyes, and the boy's open-mouthed look of shock suddenly transformed into a smile. Harriet smiled back, got up on her knees, poked him on the shoulder, and said, "Tag, you're it!"

Then she turned and scurried back toward the edge of the woods, the boy laughing in her wake. She let him catch up with her and tag her on the back, and then she whirled around and chased him toward the general store, saying, "I'm gonna git you!"

The boy tumbled to the ground, and he began giggling crazily as Harriet gave him a tickle and said, "You're it." By this time, the little girl had joined in. The three of them frolicked in the tall grass, chasing each other in circles as if life held no danger or sorrow.

When Harriet heard the door of the store swing open with a groan, she dropped to the ground, and reality came back down on her like a stone. Staying low, she turned and slunk toward the forest. She returned to her hiding spot and watched the little boy and girl leap into the back of a wagon and head off down the road. The little boy waved in her direction, and Harriet gave a little wave back.

She sat there, at the edge of the woods, wondering what it must be like to carry a child like that in your belly—a human being growing inside, bigger every day. As the middle child, she had seen her share of brothers fill up her Mama's belly. She could remember putting her ear to Mama's stomach and listening for life and feeling the kick against her mother's skin. She wondered if giving birth was like the feeling she had when the Bowleys reached Baltimore, safe and secure. Was that what it was like when you pushed a new life out into the world?

Caught up in her imaginings, Harriet almost forgot the real world, and she didn't hear the crack of branches until someone was upon her. Her heart did a big jump, and then she spun around to see the flash of movement as a man rushed toward her.

Her sudden fear drained away when she saw that it was her brother, Benjamin! She was so happy to see him again, but he didn't look pleased to see her.

"Harriet, what on earth you doin' here?"

"How'd y'all know where to find me?"

"Sam Jenkins collared me, sayin' he had seen you. Said you wanted him to deliver a message to John. He said he had no idea where John was livin'."

Harriet growled her frustration. "Stupid man. I gave him exact directions, how to find my husband."

"Well, John ain't where he was before. But you need to get outta here before y'all get caught."

"I ain't goin' back without my husband. We gotta be together. It's the way the Lord meant it to be."

Then Benjamin stared at her with the strangest look in his eyes—a mournful kind of gaze. The kind of look you give a dog that got run over by a wagon. Harriet didn't like it one bit.

"What's wrong, Benjamin? Is John all right?"

Benjamin paused a couple of beats before answering. "Yes, of course, he's all right. John always knows how to take care of himself."

"Then what's wrong with you? You look like you got a heap of words stuck in your throat."

"You need to leave, Harriet. It ain't safe for you here."

"I told you I ain't leavin' without my husband. Did you even tell John I'm here? Did that stupid fellow deliver the message to my husband?"

"I told him not to," said Benjamin.

"Lookee here." Harriet unslung the sack from her back and dug into it, occasionally glancing up to scowl. She pulled out the rolled-up suit coat and unfurled it like a flag. "I saved a pretty penny to buy this new coat for my husband. I aim to put his living body inside this suit, and then we're gonna run back north. I know y'all don't like John much, but he's my husband, and the Lord put us together. We're goin' north together, and then we're gonna have enough children and grandchildren to populate all of Philadelphia."

"You can't, Harriet."

"I been prayin', and the Lord's gonna give me children."

"With John?"

"Course with John. Who else?"

"But John won't go."

"I'm his wife. We ain't seen each other for two years."

Then Benjamin started pacing back and forth, making Harriet awfully nervous.

"You tell me what's goin' on, Benjamin, or I'm gonna slap you with the thick end of my staff."

She would, too.

Finally, Benjamin stopped pacing, and he threw up his arms and stared at the tops of the trees.

"I said he won't go back with you," he insisted.

"I wanna hear those words from *him*, not you. You ain't God Almighty. You don't know what's in his head. Just 'cause you too afraid to go north, don't mean everyone is."

"He won't go back with you, Harriet."

"You keep sayin' that, but how do you know? Tell me!"

"He won't go with you 'cause he's got himself another woman."

Harriet stood there, stunned. Then, without warning, she delivered a punch squarely to her brother's stomach.

At that moment, she hated John more than she ever had before.

···

Harriet always could pack a wallop, and Benjamin felt like he couldn't breathe for what seemed like eternity. Then Harriet came around from behind and began beating on his back, like a crazed lady pounding on a back door. Benjamin just took it; he let her pour all of her wrath on him, although he hoped she'd save some of it for John Tubman. That man took up with a lady named Caroline only three months after Harriet disappeared.

When Benjamin and Henry had challenged John about his infidelity, Harriet's husband just shrugged and said, "What you expect me to do? Minty's probably dead, and I need a woman to keep me warm."

At the time, Henry had to restrain Benjamin to keep him from beating the man bloody.

Now, Harriet was beating on his back, but he knew the punches were meant for John. Finally, when Harriet had exhausted herself, she plopped down on the ground and stared at the forest floor, jabbing her walking stick into the soil.

She finally spoke. "How long this been goin' on?"

"Long time."

She raised her head, wiped away tears with her sleeve. "Why didn't y'all tell me? Why didn't you send word?"

"We were protectin' you."

"Lies don't protect nobody."

"We never lied. We…"

"Silence don't protect nobody neither."

"I'm sorry…We never could have imagined…"

"Imagined what?"

"Never could have imagined you'd be comin' back to get him."

"You shoulda told me, Benjamin. I risked life and limb comin' down here."

Benjamin hung his head. She was right. Then, to his alarm, he watched as Harriet reached deep into her tote bag and pulled out a knife.

"Where is he? I'm gonna skin him alive."

He had no doubt she would.

"Now hold on, Harriet. Don't go murderin' anyone."

"I don't care what happens to me. I'm goin' right into that cabin and make all the trouble I can. I'm determined to see my old man once more, and I'm gonna make all the mischief I can."

She sprang to her feet, and Benjamin stood in her path. She poked the air with the knife, and although she made no real attempt to stab at him, Benjamin scooted back several steps, hands extended. Just to be safe.

"Tell me where he's livin'," she demanded. When Benjamin didn't answer, she hollered, "Tell me!"

"He's at the Brodess place, doin' work for them."

"*She* with him?"

Benjamin nodded. "Just turn around and go back north, Harriet. You don't need a man like John."

"Don't tell me what to do. Watch these here chickens while I do what I gotta do."

As Harriet began marching through the woods, Benjamin untied the two chickens and ran after her with a bird under each arm.

...

There she was. That woman, Caroline, was out back hanging clothes on a line. Some of them were John's clothes—a worn-out old shirt and pair of trousers, frayed at the knees. But no sign of John.

Harriet didn't know this hussy. She was much taller than Harriet, with wide hips and strong arms. But she looked slow moving, and Harriet thought she could take her down, if she wanted.

Benjamin slipped up beside Harriet, crouching in the bushes like they were soldiers scouting out the enemy.

"Don't do what y'all are thinkin'," Benjamin said.

"You don't know what I'm thinkin'."

"I got a good idea what you're aimin' to do."

It wouldn't be difficult for anyone to read her mind.

Just then, one of the chickens that Benjamin was carrying gave out a squawk, and Harriet ducked low beneath the bushes.

"Whatya got those chickens for?" she hissed.

"You told me to watch 'em."

"Well get 'em outta here. They gonna give us away."

While Benjamin carried off the chickens, Harriet kept an eye on Caroline. The woman had stopped draping clothes on the line, and she glanced around, probably wondering about the sound of the bird. Wiping her hands on her apron, Caroline walked in the direction of the woods—straight toward Harriet. If the woman got within striking distance, Harriet didn't know if she could restrain herself. God might need to send an angel to stop her hand, but she couldn't get herself to ask Him to send one. She still had her knife drawn. Once again, her heart started racing, and her skin tingled.

Then the cabin door swung open.

"Hey Cinnamon, what y'all doin' there?"

Cinnamon? Is that what John was calling her? Was it some kind of joke? First Minty? Now Cinnamon? Was the fool trying to work his way through every spice in the cupboard? Oh, she wanted so badly to run out and start making a fuss.

Caroline, or Cinnamon, turned to face John, and she broke out in a big sloppy grin that Harriet wanted to smack off of her face.

"Thought I heard one of the chickens outta the coop."

When John and Caroline embraced, Harriet's heart thumped in her ears, and she began breathing rapidly. Her right hand tightened around the knife handle.

Then John gave that woman a kiss, swatted her on the behind, and told her, "Food's gonna boil over if you don't get in there."

Harriet was going to boil over was more like it.

Benjamin slipped back beside Harriet and whispered, "Don't do it."

Didn't her stupid brother realize that telling her not to do something was the surest way to get her to do it? But something stayed her hand, something began to calm her heart.

If John could do without her, then she could do without him.

That thought came to her as clear as day. It was so obvious. She didn't need a big vision from God to show her this truth. The truth just kind of strolled right into her mind.

If John could do without her, then she could do without him.

Rising to her feet, she turned and began to make her way back through the forest. Benjamin followed after retrieving the chickens, but he said nothing. He was probably afraid he'd set her off if he said a single word, like pulling the string of one of those birds.

They hadn't walked for more than five minutes before Harriet had a sudden idea. She set down her tote bag and pulled out the new suit coat she had purchased for John. Benjamin watched as she held up the jacket, plucking at the arms. The suit was a little wrinkled, but it looked as good as new.

Then she reached back into the sack, pulled out the hunting knife and jammed the blade into the jacket, near the pocket by the heart. She drew the knife down, cutting a long, ripping incision.

She heard Benjamin gasp behind her.

Harriet balled up the jacket and tossed it into the trees, aiming for a muddy puddle, but missing. Then she yanked out the spanking new pants, balled them up, and hurled them to the side as well. This time they landed in the puddle.

Wiping her hands of John, Harriet turned and noticed Benjamin staring at the new set of clothes. Was he thinking of retrieving them for himself? He better not.

Benjamin looked over at Harriet, and must have seen the fury in her face because he just gave a shrug and walked over to his sister, leaving the balled-up clothes where they lay. Harriet turned, and they began the long march back to her campsite.

Just like that, John Tubman dropped right out her heart.

•••

Harriet sat in front of the campfire and watched the flames snap, flinging up a flurry of angry sparks. Man is born to trouble, as the sparks fly upward, the Good Book says. Woman is born to trouble too, she thought.

Benjamin stayed by her side throughout the entire afternoon, risking the wrath of Eliza Brodess. He helped to prepare one of the chickens for dinner and now that the meal was over, they warmed their hands at the fire.

"You oughta go back north, now that it's dark," he said.

Harriet grunted. Off and on throughout the day, she had contemplated going back to the cabin and tearing out Caroline's hair or heart —or kicking her husband where it hurts the most. But she was too weary to budge. Benjamin was right, though. She needed to use the night to her advantage and get moving before word got out about her.

But before she could move, the sound of voices suddenly came from deep within the woods. The voices were low enough to make Harriet wonder for a moment if she had dropped off into one of her visions and was hearing the voices of angels.

But Benjamin heard it, too.

"You hear that?" he asked.

She nodded.

Fear has a way of knocking the weariness out of a person's bones, and Harriet leaped to her feet. Quickly, she began kicking dirt onto the campfire, smothering the flames.

The voices became louder. Harriet pulled out her only weapon—the hunting knife—and Benjamin grabbed a thick stick from nearby. They crouched side by side in the dark, waiting for trouble to come. The crunching of footsteps on undergrowth grew louder, and it came at them from two different directions.

Harriet saw a moving light in midair, swinging back and forth like a glowing pendulum. Then a crowd of people, not just one or two, was suddenly and surprisingly upon them, coming out of the darkness. Relief washed over Harriet. The faces were black, and they glowed in the lantern's light. There had to be close to a dozen of them, both men and women, and the one holding the lantern shoved the light toward Benjamin and Harriet. The man broke into a grin.

"That you, Harriet?" he asked.

"Who wants to know?" she demanded.

"It's Gideon Williams," the man said, moving the light a little closer to his face so she could get a good look at him.

"Well, glory be, it is," said Harriet.

"Evenin' Gideon," added Benjamin. "What you doin' out here in the middle of the night? Master Gibbons won't be pleased."

"No less pleased than Miss Eliza would be if she knew *you* were here!"

The slave turned and swung his lantern back and forth, casting light on the others gathered with him.

"We heard you come back home to rescue people," Gideon said.

"Who told you that?" Harriet demanded.

"Everyone's sayin' it."

Harriet looked at her brother Benjamin, who began to smile. She had come back to fetch her husband, not with any big plan to rescue a whole gathering of people. But God had other ideas. Then another voice spoke up from the darkness. It sounded like Gideon's wife, Sister Lori.

"If you're goin' back north, we're goin' with you."

Harriet's heart began to flutter again. Was it out of nervousness or excitement? It was bad enough trying to escape with her two brothers dragging her down. What would it be like fleeing with a dozen others? Would some of them lose heart along the way and want to go back, like Henry and Benjamin?

"It'd be extra dangerous, with so many of us runnin' together," Harriet said.

"There were a lot more in the stampede," said Sister Lori.

She was right about that.

"It's dark," said Gideon. "We can't waste no more time. Harriet, lead on."

Harriet stared back at them, uncharacteristically at a loss for what to do or say. As she stood there, it suddenly struck her that maybe God had another reason for sending her back south. It wasn't to bring John to free soil; that insect deserved to stay on Egyptian ground with the other locusts. Maybe God had brought her here to strike the Pharaoh with her staff.

She turned to Benjamin. "You wanna go with us, too?"

"I can't. But you go. Take them."

For once, Harriet resisted the urge to browbeat her brother. "I'll be back, Benjamin. I'll get you eventually."

"You do that, sister."

Harriet turned to face Gideon, Sister Lori, and the others squarely. "I don't want no stragglers, and I don't want no one turnin' yellow and sayin' they wanna go back. I'll kill 'em before I allow that."

"Agreed," said Gideon.

A few others murmured their approval, but Harriet couldn't tell how many voices spoke up.

Harriet fetched her walking stick, which leaned against a nearby tree and then gave a good hard look at each of the slaves, although several were lost in shadow. She could see there were no infants among them, and that was a blessing. She didn't have any paregoric to knock them out. The youngest appeared to be a girl of about nine.

"You know how to stay quiet, girl?" Harriet said to the nine-year-old. The girl was almost as tall as Harriet, and they looked each other straight in the eyes.

The girl nodded, not saying a word. She was shaking all over.

"There ain't nothin' to fear," Harriet said, hoping to calm the girl. "We can't die but once."

The girl's eyes widened at those words, but Harriet couldn't understand why her words seemed to have sparked fear. *We can't die but once.* To Harriet, that was a reassuring thought.

Without another word, Harriet turned north and began to lead them out of Egypt.

MOSES

"I had crossed the line of which I had so long been dreaming. I was free; but there was no one to welcome me to the land of freedom. I was a stranger in a strange land, and my home after all was down in the old cabin quarter, with the old folks, and my brothers and sisters. But to this solemn resolution I came; I was free, and they should be free also."
— HARRIET TUBMAN

27

The Bellefield Estate, Cambridge, Maryland

Benjamin found a spot on the front bench in the makeshift church. He'd had to sprint to get there before the opening prayer, and he was badly out of breath. The church was tucked in among a cluster of work buildings on Dr. Thompson's Bellefield estate on the edge of Cambridge, and he'd covered the ground as quickly as he could.

Church for slaves was held every Sunday morning in a blacksmith building on the property—a fitting location indeed. When the Spirit got moving, the small group of worshippers kicked up as many sparks as a smithy's forge. About twenty-five souls filled the place, and already some of the regular shouters in the group were making heaven ring. When Nate Johnson got to moving and shouting, Lord he could make the dust fly. Horace Steele dropped down on his knees, and he too began to stir the sparks.

"We bow at your footstool, Lord, to thank you for our spared lives!" Horace said in his deep, gravelly voice, like he was talking from the bottom of a well. He waved his right hand in the air and said, "We thank you that we were able to get up this morning clothed in our right mind. Through your goodness and mercy, we been spared to assemble ourselves here once more to call upon a Captain who ain't never lost a battle. Oh, throw 'round us your strong arms of protection. Oh Lord! Oh Lord! Oh God, our Captain and King, search our hearts, and if you find anything there contrary to your divine will, just move it from us, as far as the east is from the west. Now, Lord, you know our hearts. You know our downsitting and you know our uprising, Lord, you know all about us because you made us. Lord! Lord! Let us down into the deep treasures of your Word, Lord, yes!"

Throughout Horace's prayer, worshippers threw out words of encouragement, like tossing wood on a fire until the blaze was roaring and rising. Multiple voices began praying out loud, their words mingling. Next, the songs came in, softly at first, and soon the congregation was shouting and singing so loudly that dirt shook loose from the rafters and sprinkled down like rain from heaven.

> *"Don't be weary, traveler, come along home to Jesus;*
> *Don't be weary, traveler, come along home to Jesus.*
> *My head got wet with the midnight dew, come along home to Jesus;*
> *Angels bear me witness too, come along home to Jesus."*

The refrain kept going and going, building steam, building strength, until it seemed that the Spirit was going to fling a flame onto every single person's head, lighting them up like candles, just as it happened in Scripture. Benjamin didn't often get caught up in the shouting and singing but today he almost thought he was going to be yanked right out of his shoes and whisked up to heaven barefoot. When Benjamin saw Jane slip in through the door, he was pulled out of the Spirit, and he felt himself suddenly come crashing back down to earth.

He and Jane had been courting for the past few months, but he was still shocked to see her here. Was she mad to be taking such a risk?

The Jones Plantation, where she lived, was only about a mile away. But her master, Horatio Jones, didn't tolerate his slaves worshipping and praying because the man didn't believe the Spirit of God could burn in the soul of a slave. If Horatio Jones knew she had slipped away to worship on the Thompson place, he might beat her half to death. She once told Benjamin how Jones would punish his slaves by making them stick their heads through a hole in a fence, while he lashed their backside, cracking the whip like a man possessed.

"Where to go, I did not know, come along home to Jesus;
Ever since He freed my soul, come along home to Jesus!"

Benjamin slipped around to the rear of the blacksmith church, and he slid beside Jane on the backbench. It was nice to be by her side, and he reached out and touched her hand, which was warm and soft. She looked scared, and for good reason.

"What you think you're doin' here?"

"Worshippin' God, same as you." She tried to speak defiantly, but he noticed the catch in her voice. She turned away, couldn't look him in the eye. The singing was so loud that they could barely hear each other, so Benjamin leaned over and whispered into her ear.

"Please, worship back at your place by yourself. Jones can't stop you prayin' all by yourself, and God don't care if you pray to Him alone or in a group."

"But God *does* care," Jane said, the heat of anger in her voice. "He don't like seein' His people scattered. He wants us whole."

Benjamin had a hard time arguing with that, so he came at it from another angle.

"The Lord don't want to see you punished by a devil man, though. Go back home before Jones notices you gone."

"God'll protect me."

Jane almost spoke with as much conviction as Harriet.

"But if Master Jones lays a hand on you…"

"God'll get his vengeance. He always does. When Master Jones leaves this life, God'll settle the score."

That wasn't soon enough for Benjamin. If Horatio Jones did anything to Jane, he would settle the score himself. Since he and Jane had begun courting, she assured him that the master hadn't laid a hand on her, but he always wondered.

Benjamin thought about how Nat Turner had pounced on his master's family in the middle of the night, like an avenging angel slipping into Egyptian houses and leaving with a blood payment. That's the kind of vengeance Benjamin would seek if Jones harmed one solitary hair on Jane's head. But would Benjamin really have the nerve to do such a thing? He wasn't sure.

Just a few months before, Benjamin and his brother Henry had tried yet another escape, but as always they lost confidence and turned around. They thought they were being tracked, so they rushed home before they could be caught away from the plantation. But as it turned out, they hadn't even been missed. Now, he wondered if he should try again, only this time he would take Jane with him. The very idea was terrifying. If Jane were caught escaping, there's no telling what Horatio Jones would do to her.

Jane locked her arm in his and joined the singing.

> *"And the moon will turn to blood,*
> *And the moon will turn to blood,*
> *And the moon will turn to blood in that day—O-yoy my soul!*
> *And the moon will turn to blood in that day!*

> *"And you'll see the stars a-fallin',*
> *And you'll see the stars a-fallin',*
> *And you'll see the stars a-fallin' in that day—O-yoy my soul!*
> *And you'll see the stars a-fallin' in that day!*

> *"And the world will be on fire,*
> *And the world will be on fire,*
> *And the world will be on fire in that day—O-yoy my soul!*
> *And the world will be on fire in that day!"*

28

Wilmington, Delaware
Autumn 1852

T homas Garrett leaned forward in the stuffed chair in his personal library, poring over a book on botany. The book, which he'd just acquired, was spread open on a small table. Thomas had lost virtually all of his possessions, including his books, when he was convicted and fined for helping escaped slaves four years earlier. But since that time, he had slowly built back his modest library, volume by volume.

Thomas was sixty-three years old, a stocky brick of a man, wearing an off-white Quaker waistcoat with a long line of buttons. The buttons barely met in the middle as the material strained over his midsection. It was evening, and he read intently by candlelight. He was so absorbed that when he heard a faint thumping on his back door, the sound reached his ears but didn't register in his mind. When the pounding increased in volume, he finally sat up straight, slipped a bookmark between the pages, and pushed himself out of his chair, groaning like he were lifting a heavy rock.

The pounding persisted.

Thomas shuffled into the kitchen and peeped out of a window; he could make out figures in the dark, but he couldn't see any faces. If it were a lynch mob, they would not have bothered knocking, so he assumed they were friends, and he opened the door.

To his astonishment, Harriet Tubman was standing on the threshold. She was blinking up at him with a big grin. She charged into his house, a stream of nine black folks of all ages rolling in behind her. Escaped slaves, most likely.

"Come in," said Thomas, a rather useless invitation seeing that Harriet and all of her guests were already inside. "I am pleased to see thee, Sister Harriet. It appears to me thou hast been busy again."

"Yes, and I am in fitter shape than last time you saw me. But I'm famished, and I believe we all could use some victuals."

Always straight to the point. That was Harriet.

By this time, Thomas noticed that his wife, Rachel, had appeared in the doorway. Without a word, she set about gathering bread, cheese, and milk. He thanked the Lord every day that he had a wife as committed to the cause as him. She did her work with much less fanfare than he did.

This wasn't the first time Harriet had come to his house with escaped slaves in tow, and it wouldn't be the last. As Rachel began to serve the slaves, who were lined up at their dining table, he couldn't help but notice his wife's eyes flitting to the revolver strapped to Harriet's waist.

"I see that thou hast obtained a weapon since thy last visit," Thomas said. Although a Quaker, Thomas wasn't entirely sure what he thought about the justification of using a limited form of resistance, but Rachel was a staunch believer in no violence under any circumstance.

"You be happy to know I ain't had cause to use it," Harriet said. "But I will use it, if I gotta. Sorry to say it in a good Quaker home like this, but if the Good Lord tells me to put a bullet in the belly of a slave hunter, I obey."

Rachel very nearly dropped a plate at those words. But to her eternal credit, she said nothing and kept on serving. The food disappeared almost the moment it was set on a plate.

Thomas's eyes drifted down to the floor, where he noticed that Harriet's shoes were being held together by a hunk of rope. Thomas had given her those sturdy brogans during her last visit, and he was amazed she had already worn them out.

"Dost thou seekest a new pair of shoes?" Thomas said with a smile.

Harriet didn't even look up from her plate. After swallowing a mouthful of cheese, she said, "I could use some money too."

She never was one to mince words.

"I have always been liberal with thee, and wish to be," he said, laughing lightly. "But I am not rich and cannot afford to give thee much."

This time she hit him with a stare. "But God tells me you have money for me."

"Has God ever deceived you?" he said in jest.

"Never."

"Well then! How much does God want?"

Harriet put aside a piece of bread and chewed over that question a spell. "About twenty-three dollars," she finally said, turning back to her food.

The Lord can be quite specific when it came to Harriet Tubman. But Thomas Garrett exceeded her request, and later that evening he handed her twenty-four dollars and some odd cents.

"Thank you," she said. "I can also use some new shoes."

"For thee, anything."

...

Harriet had come and Harriet had gone, and once again Benjamin and his brothers had missed the train north. She had swooped down through the Bucktown area, and just like that, several slaves disappeared with her.

"How many gone missin' this time?" Henry asked Benjamin, as they loaded firewood into the back of a wagon on the Brodess place.

Miss Eliza had brought them back to work for her directly because her feud with Dr. Thompson was heating up; she didn't like the idea of hiring out her slaves to the enemy.

"I'm not exactly sure, but close to ten escaped I heard," said Benjamin.

This time, their sister hadn't even tried to coax them to join her, and that made Benjamin a little depressed. Had she completely given up on them after so many false starts? Henry was married now, with one child, and Benjamin had Jane in his life, so running wouldn't be easy. But Harriet wouldn't understand these complications.

"The way I hear it," Henry said, "folks say she just walked through the woods and started in singin'. Like, as a signal for people to join up with her."

Benjamin had heard the same thing, but he wondered if it was so much hokum. Harriet was becoming something of a legend around these parts, and legends have a way of attracting stories of questionable accuracy. But still, it sure sounded like something Harriet would do. They say she came through the area, singing: "When that old chariot comes, who's goin' with me? I'm goin' with you…"

Hearing the song, people just put down whatever they were doing and ran off in the direction of the music, and they hadn't been seen since.

"People are callin' her Ole Chariot," said Benjamin, tossing two more logs into the wagon. "Others say she's Moses."

When Benjamin turned to pick up another log, he noticed a horse and rider sauntering down the narrow trail that weaved through the forest. It was easy to tell it was Master Thompson; being such a short man, he was dwarfed by the huge animal. Dr. Thompson's personality hadn't changed much over the years; he remained a stern sort, who worked his slaves hard. But his beliefs had been undergoing a slow transformation. Benjamin credited it to the influence of his daughter-in-law, a Quaker girl. Why, Dr. Thompson even put those new beliefs into action when he chose to knock down the emancipation age for twenty-seven of his slaves. He declared that these slaves, all of them women and children, would be free on the

New Year's Day immediately following their thirtieth birthday. Robert's wife, Mary, was one of Dr. Thompson's slaves, and she now had ten years to wait until her freedom at the age of thirty. Henry thought Dr. Thompson had done it just to keep his slaves from running away, but Benjamin liked to think his motives were purer than that.

"Morning, Benjamin. Morning, Henry."

"Mornin', Master Thompson," said Henry.

"Sure sorry we ain't workin' on your place no more," said Benjamin in complete honesty.

"I am, too. But that is exactly what I want to talk to you boys about."

"Are you wantin' to be hirin' us again?" said Henry. "We'd like that, sir."

"I'm aiming for more than that. If you two are agreeable to my idea, I was going to approach Miss Eliza and offer to *buy* the two of you."

Benjamin very nearly dropped his armful of logs. He felt a bubble of hope rise up in his chest, but tried not to get too excited. Life had a way of shoving him to the ground whenever he got too optimistic.

"I couldn't think of nothin' better," said Henry.

"Happy to hear it," said Dr. Thompson. "And you, Benjamin?"

This time, in his rush to respond, he dropped a log on his toe and very nearly let out a curse.

"Yes, sir, I would welcome that, sir," he said, after finally wrestling the wood back in place.

Thompson tipped his hat and smiled. "Very well, boys. I am bound for Miss Eliza's, and I will put an offer on the table. I think I can make the deal very worthwhile to her."

"Thank you, sir!" Benjamin wondered if he spoke too excitedly. He hated it when slaves gushed and groveled, but he couldn't help it. The idea of getting away from Miss Eliza Brodess was almost too good to be true. Under Thompson, maybe their emancipation ages would be reduced, just like he'd done with the others.

Benjamin tossed his armload of wood into the back of the wagon and wiped his hands while watching Thompson continue on his way through the forest.

"If Master Thompson buys us, we might have no more need to run," Benjamin said. "We could just wait for our emancipation day."

That statement wiped the smile from Henry's face. "Listen to yourself, Benjamin. That's just what Thompson wants us to think. He wants his slaves to give up notions of ever runnin'. He wants us to sit back and wait for freedom to come to us, so we don't snatch it for ourselves."

Benjamin realized his brother was right. Harriet would have been severely disappointed to hear what he just said. But what else was new? She was always disappointed in him.

···

Thompson made the offer, and Miss Eliza shot it down.

Benjamin heard tell that Thompson tried to take advantage of Miss Eliza's dire need for money, and he gave her a low offer to buy the two brothers—insultingly low. Thompson had the larger, better-run operation, and he probably figured he could wield that power to get her to sell at any cost.

But Benjamin knew all about the stubborn spirit of Miss Eliza, and she would rather lose everything she owned than be insulted by someone like Thompson. So Benjamin and Henry remained the property of Eliza Brodess, and they ran again. But this time they didn't run far; they fled into the swampland that riddled the land south of Bucktown.

They settled in. They created a makeshift shelter using a fallen tree as the spine of their new home. By day, they foraged for food, secure in the knowledge that most people steered clear of the interior of the marsh. The trek into the swampland took them a little south, not north, but it was the ideal place to hide until they could figure out what they wanted to do. It was a dense and forbidding land, a great place to get lost.

Benjamin wasn't sure he wanted to make the final push north

without Jane by his side. With Henry having a wife and child, staying put in the swampy land seemed a good compromise. They could steal back and see their women whenever they liked, and yet they lived a life where they could be their own masters.

It was now spring of 1853, which was not a good time to run, with all of the activity on the plantations and timber operations around them; with so many people laboring outdoors, you took a much bigger risk of being spotted. But although spring was not a good time to run, it was a good time to hide, with vegetation thickening and the temperatures tolerable.

The marshland stagnated with a brackish mixture of salt and freshwater. But a narrow freshwater stream also gurgled nearby, where Benjamin loved to watch wildlife: the raccoons, which seemed to be everywhere, the many varieties of snakes, an occasional river otter, and the red bats at night.

He was most taken by a neighborly beaver family that worked steadily on an impressive dam. He would watch for hours as beavers gnawed into the sides of trees, trying to reach the sugary substance beneath the bark with their iron-strong teeth.

One fine April morning, Benjamin and Henry lay on their stomachs at the edge of the river and watched as a beaver chewed away at some green leaves, his chestnut fur glossy and matted in the water. Henry slipped off his shoes and slid into the river.

"What you doin'?" Benjamin asked.

"Just gettin' a closer look."

"You think that's wise? The beavers might think we're stormin' their fortress."

Henry just grinned and began striding through the deepening water.

Reluctantly, Benjamin followed his brother into the frigid stream, although they were careful not to get too close to the animals. One bite from those enormous teeth could open an artery.

Benjamin was just beginning to get comfortable swimming close to the beavers when they suddenly heard what sounded like the snort of a horse coming from the woods. And if there was a horse, there was surely a human. It would be difficult getting a horse this deep into the swampland, but there were places to tie up an animal not too far away and then move closer by foot. Benjamin and Henry slid behind a partially submerged tree, trying not to make any splashing sounds. Benjamin heard the crunch of underbrush, and he could tell it wasn't a deer moving through the woods. It sounded like human footsteps.

Peering over the top of the log, Benjamin spotted a man nosing around the shelter they had built. He was investigating it from all sides, but Benjamin couldn't see the fellow's face. Then the man called out.

"Benjamin! Henry!"

It was Dr. Thompson. How in the world had he tracked them down?

They didn't answer. They didn't dare.

"I come to give you fair warning!"

Benjamin and Henry looked at each other. Should they trust him? Over the past year, he had been changing in many ways, but he was still a slave owner.

"I know you're around here somewhere. Show yourselves! I have important information you need to know. It's a matter of life and death!"

Benjamin and Henry exchanged looks again, and this time Benjamin slowly nodded his head. Then they both put their hands on the muddy bank and hauled themselves out of the water. A breeze cut through Benjamin's wet clothes, nipping at his skin. When Dr. Thompson spotted them padding in their bare feet across the forest floor, soaked from head to foot, he smiled.

"Taking a bath, were you?"

"You can say that," Benjamin said through chattering teeth. He and Henry stood in front of Dr. Thompson, dripping and shivering.

"Your shelter looks like a fine piece of work, boys, but I suggest you pull up stakes and run," he said. "Run north."

Dr. Thompson was full of surprises. A white man, a slave owner, was telling two slaves to run north? Benjamin had never heard of such a thing. Dr. Thompson despised Eliza Brodess, but even hatred wasn't usually enough to get one slave owner to encourage another person's slaves to run.

When Benjamin and Henry didn't respond, Dr. Thompson explained. "Word has gotten out about your whereabouts. So you can't stay here. Go north."

"Does Miss Eliza know where we are?" Benjamin asked.

"Not yet. But she will soon. There is no time to lose."

Benjamin shifted the weight on his feet and scratched the side of his face.

They knew they would have to face a decision point sometime, but Benjamin dealt with tough choices by putting them out of his mind and hoping for the best. They had lived in their swampland hideaway for a couple of months now, and he was content to just let the time drift by.

He hated decisions.

"I made another offer to buy y'all," Dr. Thompson said, leaning up against a tree. "But Miss Eliza said no once again."

"Thank you for trying, sir," said Henry.

"I thought this time she might give in and sell the two of you to me, especially seeing that you all had fled. Selling two slaves who had run off seemed like a deal she wouldn't resist."

Then Dr. Thompson added the words that made Benjamin burn with shame.

"But she told me she wouldn't sell because she knew you two would come slinking back to her eventually."

Benjamin felt his face redden. Had they become laughingstocks for lacking the courage to make the final break?

"If you're unsure how to get north properly, your father sent a message to help you," Dr. Thompson continued. Their Papa, now a free man, still lived near the Thompson property, only now he had Mama with him. He had bought her freedom for $20. Mama was supposed to have been freed a long time before at age forty-five, but Eliza Brodess still managed to squeeze Papa for cash. He was willing to pay it—anything to ensure her freedom.

"Pa knows we're here?" Henry said.

"Like I said, word's getting around. That's why you need to act now. Your pa said he knows a man who can lead you north."

Benjamin liked the idea of being led out of Maryland, rather than doing it on their own steam. If this man directed them north, maybe they would be less likely to turn around, for fear of looking bad in front of a stranger. Harriet can be intimidating, but she was still their sister, and her judgment was never enough to keep them from reversing direction and returning to the Brodess place.

"How can we find this man?" Henry asked.

"He'll come to you. Your father says to be at the Bucktown general store come dark. The man will be there, and he'll lead you north."

"He a white man?"

"No, a free black. He wears a top hat and stands about five feet, six inches, skinny as a rail. His name is Daniel."

Benjamin looked down at his feet and felt himself shrinking in Dr. Thompson's presence. He was humiliated that they couldn't do this on their own—like their sister had.

"Thank you most kindly," Benjamin said, unable to lift his head and look Dr. Thompson in the eyes.

"You have to choose, boys. You can't live here forever."

"Yes, sir."

"Go north while you have the chance." With those parting words, Dr. Thompson wandered back the way he had come, his horse moving off through the underbrush.

"What do you think?" Benjamin asked.

"I don't think we have a choice. Papa's decided for us."

Good point. The choice was already made for them, and this made it so much easier for Benjamin. If they got caught fleeing north, he wouldn't have himself to blame.

So Benjamin decided he would go with the flow of time, and he would see where it carried him.

...

The man never showed up.

175

Benjamin and Henry snuck to the Bucktown store, just like Dr. Thompson said, and they waited all night. But the man their father promised would help never appeared. So, instead of running north on their own, they waited until morning and then slowly and reluctantly slogged their way back to the Brodess place.

Benjamin had told himself that if the man didn't show up, he would take it as a sign from God that he shouldn't flee until he could take Jane with him. But he suspected this was just an excuse to cover up his inability to make a final decision.

When Miss Eliza saw them coming, she stood in the middle of the path, hands on hips, with a superior smirk on her face. And when they finally appeared in front of her, she gave them each a hard smack in the face and said, "I knew y'all would come back. I knew it."

Benjamin had never felt so low in all his life.

29

Philadelphia
Winter 1854

The horses were on the move again.

Harriet saw herself standing in the middle of a wide, flat expanse—not a single tree or hill in view. It was like standing in the middle of an endless, hollow land. No people. No animals. Not even a trace of wind.

Then she saw a small cloud appear on the far horizon, a brown cloud rising from the ground and stretching from side to side like a long, moving wall. When she heard the distant thunder of hooves, she just stood and watched as the dust cloud grew larger. It expanded both upwards and outwards like a brown blizzard. For the longest time, she could not see the creatures kicking up the dust, but soon vague shapes began to appear—a line of horses stretching from one side of the horizon to the other. Unbridled animal power charged toward her with unfathomable strength.

"I can't die but once!" she hollered.

Then the horses were suddenly upon her, and they rushed by on all sides, coming within inches. She kept her arms pressed flat to her sides, knowing that if she extended them out even a small distance, the horses racing by would snap them off like branches. The noise became deafening, and although she continued to shout "I can't die but once," she could no longer hear herself yell.

As the horses stampeded past in a never-ending stream, she suddenly saw that slung over the backs of the horses were dead bodies. It was like she was seeing a cavalry of lifeless men, dead from battle, with their bellies slung over the saddles and their heads pointing at the ground. Their arms flopped about like dangling ropes.

Then one of the bodies suddenly came to life, and a man raised his head as the horse galloped past her. The man, still slung over the back of the horse, raised himself up high enough to look directly into her eyes. Harriet realized, to her horror, that the man was her brother Benjamin.

When she snapped out of the vision, she found herself back in the kitchen of the Philadelphia hotel where she worked as a cook. She was sitting on a small stool, and workers scurried past her on all sides, balancing plates of food.

"'Bout time you come back to us, Miss Harriet," said one of the waiters. "I been trying to stir you for the past five minutes."

Nodding her apologies, she rose to her feet and smoothed out her apron. She tried to concentrate on her work, but all she could think about were her brothers. She was sure they were in trouble.

···

Benjamin was in a mood to murder. Jane was slumped on the floor of her cabin on the Jones Plantation, sobbing, her face buried in her hands.

"I'm gonna snap his neck!" Benjamin declared, making a move toward the door. Jane moved quickly, springing to her feet and taking hold of Benjamin's shirtsleeve.

"Promise me you won't do nothin'!"

He turned toward Jane, and she looked up into his face. He was almost afraid to look at her directly because her left eye bulged with a purplish swelling. Her nose was cut and clotted, while the slash on her right cheek still dribbled blood. That's where her master, Horatio Jones, had smacked her hard with his ring hand.

Jane had been caught sneaking away to Sunday worship at the Thompson place this past week. She had been coming to church whenever she said the Spirit needed unleashing, and she had always gotten away with it—until two days ago. Jones caught her, and he had made her pay.

"That man deserves to die," Benjamin said.

"But *you* don't deserve to die, and they'll kill you if you lay a hand on Jones."

"How could you stand to be with a man like me if I don't stand up for you?"

"These wounds will heal, but I'll never get you back if they hang you."

"But you won't never feel peace till I get vengeance."

"Please don't, Benjamin. If somethin' ever happened to you, I think I'd kill myself and save Jones the trouble. Let God take care of vengeance."

"He's too slow in actin'."

Benjamin broke free of Jane's grip on his shirt. He began to pace back and forth in the small cabin, trying to decide what to do. If Jones had struck a white woman, the husband would have beaten him to a pulp, and the town would have applauded. But if Benjamin so much as touched Jones, he would forfeit his life. He kicked over a table, sending two metal pots clanging to the dirt floor.

"What's the ruckus in there?" came a voice from outside. It was Horatio Jones. Had he come back to punish Jane even more? If so, he was a dead man. Benjamin snatched up a fireplace poker and moved for the door.

Jane cut him off, giving Benjamin a shove and a glare. She put a finger to her lips, signaling him to keep quiet, and then she flew out of the cabin. Benjamin stared at the closed door of the cabin, his chest heaving. Then, edging closer to the door, he listened to every word.

"Sorry, Master Jones, I just tipped over some pans by mistake," he heard Jane say.

Benjamin put his ear even closer to the wood. If he heard a slap, he vowed he would barge out of the cabin and kill Jones on the spot.

"Well, what's takin' y'all so long to get to the house and start cleanin'? The missus and I got guests comin' this evenin'. If you don't get it done properly, I'll give you a fresh black eye to match the other."

Benjamin put a hand to the doorknob, contemplating whether he should get it over with while he had the chance; he should just jam the poker through the man's gut. Closing his eyes, he tried to control his breath. His body seemed possessed, and it began to shake, like he had ten devils inside. He clenched his left hand so hard that his fingernails dug into his palm.

"I'm sorry, master, I'll get right to work," Jane said. He could hear her go running off to the Big House. That left only Horatio Jones and Benjamin, separated from each other by the cabin door—just two inches of wood. That's all that separated Benjamin from murder.

Should he kill him?

Benjamin decided to put God to the test. If Jones walked through the front door and entered the cabin, he would take it as the Lord's approval. It would be God's way of sending the man to be executed. But if Jones walked away, he would let it pass—for now. Benjamin would leave the decision up to the Almighty.

He put his ear close to the door once again. Holding his breath, Benjamin could sense that Jones was right there, just on the other side of the door. Was God putting a thought in the man's head, telling him he should enter the cabin? Was the Lord sending him into this trap?

Benjamin put his left palm against the door, and he envisioned how he might kill Jones to inflict the greatest amount of humiliation. He decided he would go for the man's eyes. He would drive the poker through Jones's eyeball; he wanted the man to suffer before he killed him. Benjamin bit his lower lip so hard that he tasted blood.

He listened as Jones spit and hacked and coughed, drew saliva, and spit again. Then he heard the man begin to move away from the cabin.

Benjamin still had a chance. If Jones was returning to the Big

House, his back would be turned, and he would make an easy target. Benjamin could kill him and then run north, this time for good.

But he had made a vow to God. He said that if Jones walked away, he would take it as a sign to let him go. Benjamin closed his eyes once again and tried to will the howling devils out of his mind. He slowly walked across the cabin, set the fireplace poker in the corner, and sat down, burying his face in his hands.

He couldn't go on like this. Something had to change.

...

Harriet pounded on the door of Miss Lucy's house. A prosperous black woman in Philadelphia, Miss Lucy often helped Harriet obtain funds for slave rescues; she was the widow of a wealthy black businessman and part of a growing group of well-to-do blacks in the city. William Still had introduced Harriet to her at the Anti-Slavery Society office, and Miss Lucy took an immediate interest in this small, powder-keg of a woman.

Impatient, Harriet was preparing to knock even louder, this time using her walking stick. Miss Lucy opened the door just as Harriet was bringing her walking stick down, aiming for the center of the door. Harriet managed to stop the movement in mid-air before she smacked Miss Lucy squarely in the forehead.

Backing up a step, Miss Lucy stared at the walking stick, which had halted a foot from her face. Then she quickly recovered her bearing, smiled brightly, and said, "Morning, Harriet."

"Mornin', Miss Lucy." Harriet didn't give Lucy a chance to offer an invitation inside. She just walked right in and headed for the parlor. Still smiling, Lucy followed her into the room.

"How can I help you, Harriet?"

"I need a letter written."

Harriet vowed that she would learn to write someday, but she still had not mastered the mystery of the alphabet. So, she relied on others to handle her correspondence. Miss Lucy was an educated woman and often wrote letters to the newspaper on behalf of the Moyamensing Temperance Society, one of the lady's many causes. In fact, Harriet heard that she was still writing letters about the temperance movement's infamous celebration three years earlier—a double-barreled celebration that aimed to garner support for the temperance cause while also celebrating the anniversary of the abolition of slavery in the British Empire. But an angry mob of Irishmen attacked the celebration, setting fire to the abolitionists' headquarters on Lombard Street and the Second African Presbyterian Church on St. Mary's Street.

Lucy was a veteran of many battles and was more than happy to help on all fronts. She was well respected in the Bethel AME Church, and she put on an impressive front. Her clothes were simple but elegant, and today she wore a pelerine, a cape-like collar that was all the rage.

Miss Lucy picked out a clean sheet of paper, along with a pen and inkwell. Then the fine lady took her seat at a small writing table. Harriet stood directly behind her, placing her right hand on Miss Lucy's shoulder. Whenever Harriet had someone write a letter for her, she kept a hand on the person's shoulder to get that Holy Spirit connection, transmitting not just her words, but her feelings, onto the paper.

"All right then," said Miss Lucy. "How do you want to begin?"

"Address the letter to Jacob Jackson," Harriet said. "This letter will be comin' from his stepson, William Henry Jackson."

Miss Lucy smiled. "You don't look like William Henry Jackson to me."

"I sure hope not."

"Does this William Jackson even exist?"

"Course he does. It wouldn't do no good to write to Jacob Jackson using the name of a non-existent son."

"So why are you writing in the name of William Henry Jackson?"

"To send a coded message to my brothers, of course."

Miss Lucy stared at her, as if she didn't fully comprehend. She blinked a couple of times and then looked down at the paper.

"All right then. What is this coded message?"

"I need to send word that I'm fixin' to come down to the Cambridge area to get my brothers. They're in trouble, but we can't let on that this letter has anything to do with rescuing them. The postal folks might be nosin' around and lookin' for abolitionist words. So we can't give nothin' away."

"And yet you want me to let them know you are coming to Cambridge to get them? How can I do that?"

"Through a coded message, I said!"

Harriet shook her head, thinking she had made herself perfectly clear. For an educated lady, Miss Lucy sure needed a heap of explaining.

"All right then, what do you want to say?"

"Tell Jacob Jackson to tell my brothers to be always watching unto prayer, and when the good old ship of Zion comes along, to be ready to step aboard."

Miss Lucy fixed a stare on her and smiled once again. "I take it that *you* are the good old ship of Zion."

"God's the ship, but the Lord made me His captain. And I'll be at the helm when the ship of Zion sails on down to Cambridge."

"Will your brothers understand the meaning?"

"They ain't thick. They'll know this is a notice that I'm comin' home to get them and pull them outta the fire. Now go on—put down those words."

With one hand raised and one hand still on Miss Lucy's shoulder, Harriet closed her eyes and prayed her words onto the paper. She listened to the scratch of the pen and asked the Lord Jesus to hide the meaning of the words from those who would do her harm.

"Will the postal folks see through your secret message?" Lucy asked, pausing in her work.

"Not if God has anything to say 'bout it."

Harriet gave Miss Lucy an outpouring of words. The pen, dipped in ink, ran across the page, eventually signing off with the name William Henry Jackson. Miss Lucy waited for the ink to dry before neatly folding the letter in half.

"You have been trying to get your brothers to come north for a long time now," Miss Lucy said. "Do you think they will finally answer the call?"

"If they don't, I'll force them at gunpoint."

Miss Lucy's eyes widened at the notion, and she cast a quick glance to see if Harriet was carrying a revolver. She wasn't.

"But don't put nothin' like that in the letter," Harriet said, flinging her hand toward the envelope.

"Of course not."

Harriet left feeling drained of emotion. She figured it was fitting, as it had all spilled out onto that page.

■■■

A few snowflakes drifted down, leaving a paper-thin coating of white on the frozen ground. Benjamin blew heated breath on his curled, cold fingers as he snuck onto the Horatio Jones Plantation. Not a soul was stirring, praise God. It was a week before Christmas, and temperatures the past week had been going up and down as if the weather couldn't make up its mind which season it was. Tonight definitely felt like winter, and Benjamin was looking for the warmth of his woman's company. He also had an important question to place before Jane.

Benjamin slipped up to the window of Jane's cabin, which had wooden shutters to keep out the cold as best they could. He could smell burning wood coming from the fireplace inside, as he tapped out a code on the shutters.

A few moments later, the front door swung open, and Jane—just a shadow in the dark—came rushing outside. She was wrapped in a quilt, and to Benjamin's horror, her feet were bare. In the darkness, her black eye was barely noticeable.

"What're you doin'?" Benjamin said, pointing at her bare feet, as she stood with her feet ankle-deep in snow.

"Why are y'all here? You tryin' to get yourself killed by Jones? He will, if he catches you here."

"Go put somethin' on your feet. We gotta talk."

"I'm fine."

"You sure you don't want no shoes on?"

"Quit staring at my feet and talk."

Benjamin worried that she was tempting frostbite. On many plantations, slave children aren't issued shoes until they are almost ten, so they get used to going barefoot. But Jane was far from being a child, and her feet had become accustomed to leather. Still, she had a mind of her own. He knew no amount of ordering her around would get her to cover her feet. So he decided to make this fast.

"I came here, Jane, to ask y'all to marry me."

Jane's irritated expression flew away in an instant. "You what?"

"I come here to ask y'all to be my wife."

She blinked a few times, staring at him hard. "Stay there. Let me get me some shoes."

As Jane rushed back inside the cabin, Benjamin sat down on a nearby log, hugging himself for warmth. Within moments, she was back by his side on the log, this time wearing a pair of shoes. Jane snuggled up to him, and Benjamin wrapped his arm around her. She leaned over and kissed him on the neck. He savored the warmth of her breath. They remained that way for a long spell, just sitting and watching the snowflakes thicken on the ground. The snowflakes had fattened to the size of moths. He watched them land on Jane's hair, then melt from her warmth.

"You didn't give me an answer," he finally said.

"Yes, of course I'll marry you."

Benjamin grinned and stared at Jane, not sure what to say next. "So how do we do this?" he finally blurted.

"We get married proper in God's eyes is how we do it."

"God's lookin' down on us right here, so let's get married now."

"It don't work that way," Jane said.

Benjamin was afraid she might say something like that. He was terrified that Jane would insist on a wedding ceremony, which was one of the reasons he had delayed his proposal. On certain plantations, a slave wedding would not be a problem. Some masters allowed their slaves to marry, even though it wasn't legal in the eyes of the state. Some even made a big fuss about slave weddings, but Benjamin was certain Horatio Jones would *not* be one of those masters.

"You ain't plannin' on askin' Jones's permission, are you?" he asked. "Can't we just get married without him knowin'?"

"If we had a secret ceremony, word would leak, and he'd find out. Then he'd beat me half to death if he knew we got married without his permission."

"But he ain't gonna give you his permission. So we *gotta* marry in secret."

"And then what? We'll have to live separate. That ain't no marriage."

"We been living separated for a long time now, so we're used to it."

"But we ain't married. If we get hitched, I wanna live with you."

"But what about Jones? Even if he lets you get married, you think he'll let us live in the same cabin?"

"He might if it's a cabin on Miss Eliza's land. If we live in a Brodess cabin, he'll save a heap of money on feedin' me."

But Benjamin doubted that Miss Eliza would agree to them living together on her land. She had enough money woes without adding another mouth to feed.

"My Mama and Papa lived separate most of their lives," Benjamin said. "They got by."

"I don't want to just get by," she said. "Besides, at least your folks didn't get married in secret. I ain't gonna do no secret marriage."

Benjamin was beginning to regret asking Jane for her hand. He had grappled over this decision for half a year. And now he wished he could snatch back his words. He felt like all of this marriage talk was going to get her beaten—or killed. What was he even thinking in coming here this night?

"Maybe we could just get married with a few witnesses," Benjamin said. "My brothers maybe."

"Word will still get out. Trust me. People will find out. Jones will find out."

Benjamin grunted, and Jane nuzzled her head against his shoulder.

A slight breeze sent the snow spinning. This wasn't how he pictured the night unfolding.

"Ain't I worth the risk?" Jane asked.

"You're worth any risk."

"Then let me ask Jones if we can marry proper like."

Benjamin didn't answer.

"Are you changing your mind 'bout marryin' me?"

Benjamin was tired of making decisions and then changing his mind. He had done it time and time again when it came to escaping. He was weary of letting his fears beat him down.

"Why would I want to change my mind?" he said quickly, before he could stop himself from saying it. "I said we're gettin' married, so we're gettin' married."

"The proper way?"

"The proper way."

By this time, the snow was coming down heavily. Without much of a wind, it fell down straight, filling up the darkness and thickening at their feet.

30

Horatio Jones said no, of course.

Benjamin figured all along that the man would never agree to their marriage. But he also worried that there was more to the story than Jane was revealing.

"Did he hurt you?" Benjamin asked. He studied her face from all angles, looking for any sign that Jones had answered her request by leaving a bruise. But her face told no story of violence, other than the lone scar that had always been there and the fading signs of her black eye.

It was a Saturday night, just two days before Christmas, and Benjamin had slipped over to Jane's cabin once again. The other six folks who lived in the cabin were still toiling at the Big House, so Benjamin and Jane had the small space to themselves. Jane poked at a fire crackling in the fireplace, trying to stir up some heat.

"Jones didn't lay a hand on me," she insisted.

Benjamin didn't respond. He continued to stare at Jane, trying to look for any signs in her expression that she was lying. If Horatio Jones had hurt her, she would keep it a secret from him; he was certain of that. Some masters only left marks where they couldn't be seen, but Jones was not that kind of master.

"Run away with me," he suddenly blurted.

Jane stared at him for a few heartbeats, as if she couldn't believe what had just popped out of his mouth. "Is it for real this time? Y'all understand we can't run and change our minds halfway there."

Her words stung. Had he tried to run away so many times that even his woman no longer believed he would follow through? He fought back the shame. "I won't turn back."

"Horatio Jones ain't like Miss Eliza, who ain't beaten you for all those times you run. If I run and get caught, Jones will *kill* me."

Lord, she was right. Maybe he shouldn't have even asked her to take such a risk.

"My sister is comin' to lead us out," he said.

"Harriet is comin'?"

"She said so in a letter."

"She said it out right?"

"No. But she made it clear."

He explained that Jacob Jackson had received a letter from his adopted son, a free black in Philadelphia named William Jackson. The letter sent greetings to Harriet's parents and brothers, and it said that when the good old ship of Zion comes along, they should be ready to step aboard. Benjamin, Robert, and Henry knew exactly what that meant. Harriet would be at the helm of the "good old ship of Zion," and she was asking them to sail north with her.

"Are Henry and Robert going too?" Jane asked.

"This time, they are as determined as me."

"And Mary?"

Benjamin looked away, studying the palm of his right hand. Robert's wife, Mary, was far along in her latest pregnancy, her belly round and ripe.

"Robert said nothin' to her yet. Not in her condition," Benjamin said. "Mary ain't in no shape to run."

"I know that. But don't she deserve to know if her husband is runnin' off?"

"Now don't you be sayin' nothin' to Mary," ordered Benjamin. "That's between them."

"I ain't gonna say anything."

"Keep it that way."

Benjamin spoke harshly, too harshly.

Jane looked down at her hands in her lap. Then she heaved a sigh and looked up. "You really think I should run with you?"

Benjamin didn't know how to respond. He had a hard enough time making his own decisions, much less for the woman he loved. He wouldn't be able to live with himself if something happened to her.

"It's the only way we'll be together like man and wife," Benjamin said, forcing himself to say the words. He met her eyes and held the gaze without blinking. "And there's one thing I ain't told you yet."

"This don't sound good."

"Miss Eliza is puttin' up notices."

"Notices of sale?"

Benjamin nodded, their eyes still linked. "Miss Eliza is fixin' to sell me, Robert, and Henry the day after Christmas."

That was just three days away—Tuesday.

"It's gonna be a public auction. So you see...This time we *gotta* run."

Everything was converging on Christmas of 1854. The marriage plans with Jane...the secret message from Harriet...and now the notice of sale. Everything was telling Benjamin the same thing—run north.

Jane looked down at her hands. "I'll go," she said softly.

"You'll run with me?"

She nodded. "I'll go. If I die, I die. As Harriet always says, 'I can't die but once.'"

Yes, but that one time could be awful, Benjamin thought.

Benjamin was both happy and terrified that Jane had agreed—all kinds of emotions tumbling together. The moment that Jane agreed to join the escape, he began to doubt himself. He felt the weight of the risk he was asking from Jane, and he contemplated talking her out of it. But he held his tongue. He was too confused to speak.

...

Hat in hand, John Tubman crossed the threshold of Miss Eliza's home. She had summoned him to her house in Bucktown, but for the life of him, he didn't know why. The Ross boys were always being called to her house, but she owned them. John was a free man.

"Stand there," Miss Eliza said, pointing her white-gloved hand at a spot in the center of the house's main room. John knew he should not look a white woman directly in the eye, so he let his gaze drift around the house, which was slowly crumbling from neglect. Miss Eliza had sold her housekeeper, and every horizontal surface had collected a coating of dust like a thin covering of snow. He could smell mold, probably growing in the rafters he guessed, and the windows were blurred by a greasy scum.

But Miss Eliza was dressed smartly in a mint green dress. Her appearance was the one thing she *did* tend to, no matter her circumstances.

Miss Eliza strolled around the room, looking at him from all angles. He had heard that she would sometimes have the Ross boys stand in one place for hours, without saying a word. John's back had been aching these days, and he wondered if he could stand in one spot for that long.

Then Miss Eliza went into another room, and John craned his neck to see what she was doing. She appeared to be rifling through the drawers of a rolltop desk. Finally, she returned, with a slip of paper in her hand.

"Here," she said, shoving the paper beneath his chin. "Read."

John wondered if the lady was mad. Surely, she knew he couldn't read. He knew of only a couple of blacks in the area who could read, and they had learned in secret.

"Read it aloud!" Miss Eliza shouted. She flapped the paper under his chin.

Warily, he took the paper from her gloved hand and stared at the smudges of ink. The words marched in formation from one side of the page to the other, and he searched for any word that struck him as familiar. He knew the spelling of his own name, and he once knew how Harriet spelled her name.

And there it was. It had been a long time since he had seen Harriet's name written out in print, but her first name suddenly jumped from the page and hit him squarely in the eyes. He also noticed a string of numbers along the bottom and a dollar sign. Everyone knew the dollar sign, even the most illiterate.

John could hazard a guess.

"This is a reward notice, Miss Eliza," said John, offering it back to her. She didn't take it. Instead, she made another orbit around him. "I suppose it's a reward for my Harriet," he added.

"*Your* Harriet?" Miss Eliza said. "I thought you gave up Harriet for that other wench. Am I right?"

John bowed his head. "Yes, ma'am."

"What is her name, boy? The name of the other wench."

"Caroline, ma'am."

"But now she has left you too, am I right?"

John stroked his chin. There was no denying it. Caroline, a free woman, had run off on him, and it embarrassed him to no end. They had fought often, and he usually let Caroline land a few good punches before he fought back. But the quality of their quarreling wasn't to her liking, so Caroline had run off on him.

"I have a proposition," Miss Eliza said. "This notice is offering three hundred dollars for the capture of your first wife."

Three hundred! John was floored, but he shouldn't have been surprised. Harriet had been leading regular raids into Maryland, and the slaves she took north were worth a heap more than three hundred bucks. Her capture was worth every penny of the reward money.

"You know your wife's movements, her coming and going. If you help to bring her to justice, I'll make you rich."

Three hundred dollars was a load of cash. But could he betray Harriet? John scratched at his chin and wondered.

"I need an answer!" Miss Eliza snapped.

John raised his head and looked Miss Eliza in the eyes, but he couldn't hold the gaze for very long. Then a smile crept across his face.

"I accept your offer," he said.

John knew it was safest to agree. This would buy him time to properly think it over. He and Harriet didn't always see eye to eye, but could he really betray her like this? For Judas money?

"What are you gawking at?" Miss Eliza said, flinging out her hand as if shooing away a child. "Go! Bring back Harriet, and you will have more money than you've ever seen in your life."

She was right about that. He would need a wheelbarrow to carry it all.

31

A Steamboat
From Baltimore to Cambridge

Harriet tried to pray away the pain, but it felt as if her tooth was on fire. It let out a constant throb, a pulse of pain, and her tongue kept darting to the tooth, trying to soothe it. But every time her tongue touched the base of the tooth, the pain shot through her entire jaw, bringing tears to her eyes.

This was the devil's work, she thought. Satan was trying to stop her by filling her mouth with pain.

Harriet had left Philadelphia with cash in hand and freedom papers prepared by Mister Garrett. She took a train from Philly to Baltimore, where she hopped onto a steamboat bound for Cambridge. She rode on the lower deck with barrels, bales, and animals, as well as passengers who couldn't afford an upper-deck ticket. With it being such a short trip, most of the white passengers chose the lower deck, so Harriet tried to make herself scarce. She found a small spot next to a big fat barrel of grain. She sat down on the deck and squeezed into a corner beside the barrel. After a long spell of just sitting and praying, she was beginning to drift off to sleep when a conversation jabbed her awake.

"You think she's real or just a story?" she heard a man saying to another. The two men, both white, stood only a few feet away.

"She's real all right. She steals slaves right under their masters' noses."

"A voodoo priestess you think?"

"She has to have some kind of magic to slip into town, snatch slaves, and vanish into thin air."

They're talking about me! Harriet was certain of it. For a moment, the fear in her gut made her forget about the pain shooting from her tooth. She became conscious of the revolver she had stashed in the deep pocket of her jacket. If these men should discover that she was armed...She shuddered at the thought.

"You really think she can vanish?"

"It's the only thing that explains it."

"But how can she make all of those slaves vanish with her? Seems hard to fathom."

This gave pause to the other white man. "You have a point. Can witches make other people vanish, or just themselves?"

"Dunno. What's she look like?"

As the man asked this question, he casually glanced over his shoulder, down at Harriet, who was still crouching on the deck. Instinctively, she scooted back a few inches. He had seen her. Her hand drifted down to her jacket pocket, where her revolver lay nestled. If he dared to identify her...

Abruptly, the man looked away, returning his gaze to the other fellow.

"She's tall, built like an Amazon," the man said.

Harriet smiled at that.

"But she comes in many disguises."

"She might be one of those witches that can change form."

"What's her name?"

Harriet tensed.

"Don't know that neither. But they call her the She-Moses."

Harriet wondered if she should just get up and move. But that was a sure fire way to draw attention. So she sat there on the deck, trying to look like she was minding her own business. She continued to feel their eyes occasionally flick in her direction.

Then God told her to do something she never would have considered on her own. *Sing*, He said.

Sing? But ain't that the surest way to draw attention to myself?

Sing, He said. This thought drifted into her mind unbidden. Harriet was sure God had planted it in her mind, so she obeyed. She knew she had a respectable singing voice, and she burst out with sudden song:

> *"The tallest tree in Paradise,*
> *The Christians call the tree of life!*
> *And I hope that trump might blow me home*
> *To the New Jerusalem!*
> *Blow your trumpet, Gabriel, blow louder, louder!*
> *And I hope that trump might blow me home*
> *To the New Jerusalem!"*

Harriet sang so suddenly and so loudly that the two men nearly jumped out of their skin. They both turned and gave her their full attention—one of the men with his mouth open ever so slightly. Then the man grinned and gave his friend a nudge.

Harriet kept on singing, unsure why the Good Lord wanted her to bring so much attention to herself when she should be hiding like a mouse. Harriet stood up and ventured onto the open deck, still belting out her song.

> *"Paul and Silas bound in jail,*
> *Sing God's praise both night and day!*
> *And I hope that trump might blow me home*
> *To the New Jerusalem!*
> *Blow your trumpet, Gabriel, blow louder, louder!*
> *And I hope that trump might blow me home*

To the New Jerusalem!"

Many sets of eyes on the lower deck moved toward Harriet. A small audience gathered, but she kept right on singing. Pretty soon, a few white men started clapping their hands and stomping their feet to the music. And when she finished one song, she barely paused to take a breath before God told her to keep singing. *Keep singing!* So she launched into a new song.

"O rocks, don't fall on me!
O rocks, don't fall on me!
Look over yonder on Jericho's wall,
Rocks and mountains don't fall on me!
And see those sinners tremble and fall,
Rocks and mountains don't fall on me!

"O rocks, don't fall on me!
O rocks, don't fall on me!
The trump shall sound, and the dead shall rise,
Rocks and mountains don't fall on me!
And go to mansions in-a the skies,
Rocks and mountains don't fall on me!"

By the time she finished the second song, she realized the music had done its work. It had taken the men's conversation away from slave escapes and moved it to music.

"Those darkies sure can belt out a song," said one of the white men while Harriet crouched down and slid back into her spot next to the barrels.

As the men continued to talk, Harriet smiled to herself. The smile was temporary, though. A river of pain suddenly flowed from her tooth, cascading down her jawline. The pain brought tears to her eyes, but she made no more sound.

■■■

It was late morning when the steamboat docked at Cambridge. Harriet mixed in with the flow of people disembarking. It was Sunday, Christmas Eve, and many of the folks getting off the boat were greeted at the dock by friends and relatives, welcoming them home for the holiday.

As she moved along the dock, bundled up in her shawl and bonnet, the thump of every footstep rattled her rotting tooth. How in the world was she going to walk forty miles this night if every step jangled her nerves with pain? As she cupped her hand around her jaw, she noticed a young white man tacking a poster to a tree.

"What's that you're announcin'?" she asked him.

"Slave sale, old lady. Take a read."

The boy smirked; he knew perfectly well she couldn't read, and he grinned maliciously.

"Who's up for sale?" she asked.

"Three young bucks. All brothers," he said before walking off, whistling.

Harriet peered closely at the words, asking God to show her their meaning. She had a Holy Spirit sense that the three brothers mentioned on this slip of paper were her brothers, but she couldn't be sure. Her eyes bore down on the words, and she became more and more certain that the brothers being sold were Benjamin, Robert, and Henry. She had arrived in Maryland in the nick of time.

As the people cleared away, Harriet spotted a couple of young black boys who had come to watch the steamboat arrive. Surely no older than ten years of age, they were perched on a fence, kicking their legs and chewing on long stems of grass.

"Boys, you wanna make some money?" she asked.

The two boys leaped from the fence, their eyes lighting up. When Harriet pulled out a couple of coins, they couldn't take their eyes off of the money.

"You see that white boy posting those notices?" she asked, motioning toward the fellow who had just nailed the slave sale announcement to a tree. The two boys responded with eager nods.

"Follow him along the way, and every time he puts up a notice, wait until he's gone and then rip it down."

Their smiles vanished instantly.

"Don't worry, if you wait till he's gone, you'll be safe," she assured them. "You'll also be rich." She took their right hands, one at a time, and placed a coin in each of their palms. The cool touch of the money did the trick, and off they ran, stopping to yank down the first notice. Then they disappeared into the distance, one of them skipping.

Harriet headed for the edge of Cambridge and the Thompson's Bellefield estate, where her brothers had been hired out. But first she made sure she still had the revolver well hidden in the large pocket of her heavy brown jacket. She was going to haul her brothers to freedom, whether they liked it or not.

32

The Bellefield Estate, Cambridge, Maryland
Christmas Eve 1854

Harriet slipped through the trees that wrapped around the barn on the Thompson's Bellefield estate. Her rotten tooth flared up, throbbing and bringing tears to her eyes with every footfall. She trod carefully on a blanket of pine needles. Soft steps would keep the pain away, and they would also muffle her movements.

Crouching behind a tree, she spotted Benjamin moving about outside the Thompson barn, looking all around and rubbing his hands together for warmth. Probably scouting for her. He would be better off staying hidden in the barn.

Still walking softly, she snuck up behind Benjamin.

"I'm here," she said.

She about scared him half to death. Benjamin spun around, looking startled, and then broke into a grin. "Harriet, so glad it's you."

"I got your message to meet at the Thompson barn. You didn't need to be out and about lookin' for me."

"I was just gettin' anxious."

It had been a long time since they had seen each other, and they gave each other an awkward hug.

"Everyone here?" Harriet asked.

"Henry and Robert are waitin' in the barn. I got some food there for you too."

"Thank you. I'm famished."

There were no white folks in sight because the barn was well removed from the Thompson house and screened by trees. So they hurried out of the trees and into the dimly lit barn.

"Harriet!" Henry shouted, leaping to his feet.

"Not so loud," she scolded. Henry gave her a hug, while Robert beamed from the bale of hay on which he was sitting. A couple of cows observed. Harriet sat down on a milking stool, while Henry and Benjamin also took seats on bales of hay. All was silent as her eyes moved from brother to brother. She had a sense of everything coming together; God's plans for her family were falling into place at long last. There was something supernatural shimmering in the air. She could feel it, like the Israelites of old before they left Egypt.

"Tonight's the night," she said. "Y'all ready?"

"Ready," said Henry, and Robert nodded.

"This time...no turning back," said Harriet, her eyes falling on Benjamin. "Do you agree? No turning back?"

"If Jane comes with us, there ain't no way I'm turnin' back," Benjamin assured her.

"Hold on," said Harriet. "Jane? Your fiancé?"

"That's right. I ain't goin' anywhere without her comin' too."

"And she's agreed?"

"She has."

"She knows there's no turnin' back?"

"She knows it more than any of us. If she goes back, Horatio Jones will kill her."

Harriet chewed that over in her mind. She realized that having Jane along would be just the thing to prevent Benjamin from turning around. And if Benjamin didn't get cold feet, she didn't think Henry or Robert would either.

"All right then. Jane is welcome on the Glory Bound train."

Then Harriet directed her fierce gaze on Henry. "No turning back?" She wanted to hear it from each brother, in turn.

Henry responded quickly and firmly. "No turning back. I'm doing this."

Finally, Harriet focused her stare on the oldest brother, Robert. "No turning back?"

He answered with silence. This was not good.

"No turning back?" she repeated.

Robert stared at one of the cows, as if he wasn't even listening to her question. It was cold in the barn, so he kept his hands clenched beneath his armpits.

"Did you hear her?" Benjamin asked. "Are y'all gonna come with us or not?"

"I aim to," Robert answered, but he paused just long enough to cast doubt on his answer.

"You can't just aim to," said Harriet. "You gotta *do*."

"But Mary's time is soon."

Robert's wife, Mary, was getting close to the birthing day. Harriet understood not wanting to leave her at such a pivotal moment but, at the same time, freedom was on the line here.

"Our baby needs a father," said Robert.

"And that's exactly why you should escape," Harriet said, quick to pounce. "If you don't escape, you'll be sold south, and your child will *never* see you. All three of your children won't never see you."

"At least this way you can return and bring them outta slavery at a later time," said Henry. "That's what I'm planning to do with my wife and children." Henry's wife had recently given birth to a second son.

Robert didn't answer, and he wouldn't make eye contact with any of them. He stared into the fire.

"Did you talk to Mary 'bout this yet?" Benjamin asked.

Still no answer.

"Robert! Did you tell Mary about the escape?"

Finally, Robert turned slowly and looked at Benjamin. He shook his head. "I couldn't tell her at a time like this."

"But she's about to have a baby!" Henry burst out. "If she starts gettin' the pains, she's gonna wanna know where y'all are."

"Birthin' is a woman thing."

"But she'll still be wantin' to know where y'all are."

"Trust me, she won't be thinkin' on me. She'll be ridin' the pains. Besides, the midwife's gonna be there for her."

Exasperated, Harriet shook her head. Then she ran her tongue along her teeth, checking to see if her tooth was less tender to the touch. It wasn't. When her tongue struck the problem tooth, she jumped as if jabbed by a fork.

"You all right?" Benjamin asked.

"Right as rain," she said, hoping he didn't notice her wince when she spoke. She brought the focus back on Robert. "You gonna commit or not? What'll it be?"

Robert glanced at both of his brothers, but he wouldn't look Harriet in the eyes. She didn't understand the man's reluctance. He was staring an auction sale squarely in the face. Of course he should escape!

"What'll it be, Robert?" Harriet repeated. She leaned forward and tried to catch his eye. Robert stared at the dirt floor and sighed.

"I'm goin'," he said.

"And you ain't turnin' back?"

"I ain't turnin' back."

"Fine. Then it's settled," said Harriet, standing up and feeling tolerably satisfied with their answers. "So we go tonight. It's too risky for you to be seen with me before dark. So go on and do what you have to do with your families, and I'll meet you just after sunset. Should we meet here again?"

"I already told Jane we're gonna fetch her after dark in the slave garden on the Horatio Jones Plantation," Benjamin said.

"The Jones Plantation!" Robert exclaimed. "That's the worst possible place to meet. The man's a viper."

"The garden is a ways from Jones's Big House, screened by a belt of trees, so we'll be hid. Besides, there's no way we can get word to her to change the meeting place anyhow. We gotta go to her."

"Jesus was betrayed in a garden," Robert pointed out.

"What's that supposed to mean?" asked Benjamin.

"Nothin'. Just sayin' gardens are dangerous places to meet."

"Pfffff," said Harriet, dismissing Robert with a flick of her hand. "We'll meet at the Joneses' garden and head straight for Mama and Papa's place. I've already sent a message ahead for Papa to expect us tomorrow for Christmas."

Their parents still lived near the Thompson property in Poplar Neck, about forty miles north of Cambridge, following the Choptank River. And from the looks of things, it might very well be the setting for a particularly joyous Christmas Day.

"But why'd you tell Papa? He don't lie to anyone," said Henry. "If white folks ask if he's seen us, he'll tell them he has."

"He said if we stay in the fodder house, he don't have to know when we're there or when we leave," Harriet said. "That way, he can honestly deny ever seein' us."

"I still don't like him knowin'," Benjamin said.

"It's our Papa. Don't be frettin'."

"And what about Mama?" asked Henry.

"I told Papa not to breathe a word to her," said Harriet. "He knows better."

They all knew that if Mama were aware of their escape, she would raise a ruckus and beg them not to leave. She'd make such a fuss that everyone within a mile would know what was going on.

"Papa won't let on to Mama," said Harriet.

"So it's settled then," said Robert. He rose to his feet and made for the door, as if gripped by a sudden notion.

"Where you think you're goin'?" demanded Henry.

"Like Harriet said, I gotta check in with Mary before we leave."

"You gonna tell her what we're doin'?"

"I already told you I ain't. But I gotta see her one more time."

And with that, Robert was out the door, heading for his cabin on the other side of the trees. After he had gone, Benjamin, Henry, and Harriet sat there, listening to the sound of a bird flapping in the rafters.

Henry finally broke the silence. "You think Robert's gonna change his mind?"

"He ain't never had a sale hangin' over his head before," said Harriet. "So I think he'll come."

In truth, she had absolutely no idea how the night would unfold. With those final thoughts nagging at her, Harriet slipped out of the barn, leaving her brothers to their own devices. By the time she took a single step away, she was praying that all of them would show.

...

The Ross boys were in trouble.

John Tubman heard they were going up for sale in a couple of days, and he wondered if they were finally going to make a run for it. In John's eyes, the three of them were cowards who would never run. But with a sale hanging over their heads, they might finally work up the courage.

In fact, the thought crossed his mind that Harriet, *his Harriet*, might come down to Cambridge to help them escape. That's why he found himself wandering in the direction of the Thompson's Belle-field estate, where the three brothers were staying. It was late afternoon, and the shadows were lengthening, as he moved along the edge of Cambridge. He hid himself away in the edge of the tree line, staying out of sight.

For John, it was a lonely Christmas Eve without his girl. Although he and Caroline fought like cats and dogs, he always figured she would stay with him. But she was the cat and he was the dog in their courtship, and cats don't care about anyone but themselves. So she had left him.

Feeling sorry for himself, John picked up his pace as he made for the Bellefield estate. He was a free man, but he knew it was not always a good idea for free blacks to wander any more than slaves. Sometimes, he felt like a slave without a master.

With it being Christmas Eve, he figured he would be safe because there wouldn't be any slave patrollers out this evening—at least he sure hoped not. Besides, he knew the patroller routes, and he could find safe paths through the woods to reach the slave cabins where Harriet's brothers were living. Benjamin lived in one cabin with several other slaves, Henry kept a separate cabin with his wife and children, and Robert occupied a third small cabin with his family.

Finally reaching his destination safely, John crouched at the edge of the woods, looking out at the string of cabins. He saw a few children romping around, but no sign of the brothers. He picked up a stone, jostled it in his hands, and then hurled it at nothing in particular. Ever since Caroline had run off on him, he had been dwelling on Harriet.

He missed her.

John would never admit that to anyone. He had trouble enough admitting it to himself, but the truth could be a nag. He kept thinking about what might have been if he had gone north with Harriet. She was becoming famous around these parts because of her exploits, and he wondered if they might have become a legendary team. But she went and ran off on him.

He also thought long and hard about the reward that Miss Eliza had mentioned for his wife's capture. That was a heap of money.

Without any warning at all, John spotted one of the Ross brothers come rushing out of the trees to his left, from the direction of the barn. It looked to be Robert, making a beeline for his cabin at the end of the row.

Crouching, John remained hidden in the woods as he followed Robert's movements. Robert seemed in an awful hurry, but he paused just outside his cabin door, as if debating whether to enter. Only moments after he slipped inside his cabin, John spotted two more figures rushing out of the trees at the exact same spot where Robert had emerged. It was Benjamin and Henry. Had the brothers been meeting in the barn just beyond those trees? With the sale looming, were they planning to run?

John watched as Benjamin and Henry talked to each other for a bit, and they seemed agitated, arms gesturing. Then they disappeared into their respective cabins.

The brothers were up to something, and John was determined to find out.

33

The Horatio Jones Plantation

"Merry Christmas, Jane."

Jane Kane whirled around and there, standing on the threshold of her cabin, was her master, Horatio Jones. The master leaned against the doorjamb, smiling. The only thing worse than a mean and angry Jones was a smiling Jones.

Jones had a wife and seven children, but there were rumors that he had another ten or more yard children roaming the countryside—children from slave women.

"Merry Christmas, Master Jones."

Jane turned back toward the dining table, where she had been folding an extra set of clothing that she was going to take with her this evening. Prudence, a middle-aged slave who shared the cabin with her, sat in the corner sewing a patch on a pair of her husband's britches. The other slaves who shared the cabin were still working at the Big House.

Jane smoothed out the dress that she was folding and slid it across the table, deep into the shadows, and she turned to face him. "You need some chores done tonight, Master Jones?"

"I do, but Prudence can take care of it. Scat on over to the Big House now, Prudence."

Prudence acted like she didn't hear the master's command and kept right on sewing.

"You hear me, Prudence? Scat!"

Prudence looked up from her work and caught Jane's eyes. *Don't go,* Jane thought, but Prudence had no choice.

"Yes, sir," Prudence said, taking her sweet time in setting aside her work. That woman could move awfully slow when she set her mind to it. She groaned as she stood, paused to smooth out her dress, and trudged as slowly as possible out the cabin door.

"Do y'all also need me to do some chores for you in the Big House?" Jane asked, when Prudence was gone.

Jones didn't respond. He sat on a stool in the corner of the cabin and just stared at her.

Finally, he motioned toward the small pile of clothing on the table. "Go on with what y'all were doin'."

Jane had been packing to run, which she couldn't very well continue to do in front of the master. So she turned toward the fireplace, where a small blaze crackled.

She took up the poker and jabbed at the wood in the fireplace. She wondered if she would dare use it if she needed to defend herself. Could she kill a man? She had a hard enough time twisting the necks of chickens.

Master Jones used silence like a weapon. He didn't say a thing. He just kept on staring at her. It was like he was shaping the silence, and then forcing it over her face like a smothering pillow.

"I hear you and the mistress have relatives comin' over tomorrow," Jane said, trying to stir up a normal conversation. But he wouldn't respond. He lit a cigar, and she turned to see a red dot of ash intensify in color as he drew in the smoke. He sometimes used a small, red-hot cigar as a weapon to burn circles in slave skin.

"I think you done poked that fire to death," said Jones, so Jane set down the poker. She immediately looked around for anything else she could use as a weapon if the master attacked her. Prudence's husband,

Calvin, liked to fish, and Jane remembered that he kept a few fish-hooks hidden away in the top drawer of the dresser. So she folded up her clothes and carried them to the dresser and put them away. As she did this, her hand probed the drawer, searching for the fishhooks. Jones went quiet again, just watching.

Jane winced when her hand hit one of the hooks, which pricked the tip of her finger. Ignoring the pain, she wrapped her hand around the hook, removing it from the drawer. Then she turned around to face the master.

Horatio Jones stood up, dropped the cigar stub to the ground, and used his heel to crush it. Jane tensed. Was he preparing to attack? She maneuvered the fishhook in her clenched palm, preparing to use it as a knife. She wished she had let Benjamin kill Master Jones when he had the chance.

Jones took two slow steps in her direction, and she backed up a step. He was still smiling, and she wondered if she had the nerve to slash that smile away with the fishhook.

Then the door swung open, and the spell was broken. Prudence was back, breathing so hard that she could barely get her words out. She must have run all of the way to the Big House and back.

"Sorry, Master Jones, but the mistress is askin' you to help her select the wine that's gonna be served at tomorrow's Christmas meal."

Jones glared at Prudence, clearly irritated by the interruption. Jane was afraid he was going to hit one of them. She had learned the signs of when he was itching to smack somebody around—the fingers of his right hand would ball up and his entire right arm would tense and extend out slightly from his side. But instead of walloping either one of them, he just cursed and barged out of the cabin. When he was gone, Jane collapsed onto the nearest stool, her knees gone to jelly. Prudence came up behind her, wrapping her soft arms around her neck and resting her head on Jane's.

"You can't stay here another day," Prudence said. "You gotta run."

"I know," Jane said. "I know."

...

When the gush of water came, Mary looked almost as shocked as Robert. Robert stared at the floor in disbelief. It was like a bucket of water had just come pouring out of his wife.

The last time Mary gave birth, her water leaked out a trickle at a time, and the labor was long and grueling. But it was sudden this time, and the labor pains attacked her so swiftly and ferociously that Robert was sure something was wrong.

"Let me fetch the midwife!" he said, but Mary latched onto his wrist so tightly that he thought she was going to snap his wrist bones.

"No time!"

"How do you know there's no time?"

"I know what I know!" she bellowed.

Mary backpedaled toward the pallet and lowered herself down, then raised up her legs and let out a scream. This wasn't how it happened before. The last time, the pains came upon her slowly and steadily, and it took half the night before the baby was born. There had been plenty of time for the midwife to take control and for Robert to make sure he was a long way removed from the bloody business.

But this time the pains pounced. Mary was already beginning to sweat and shake as Robert placed a towel beneath her.

"This is too fast, too fast!" Mary shouted, and Robert could see in her face the exact moment when the next labor pain began. He let her take his hand, and she clamped down on his fingers with strength he had no idea she possessed.

Mary let out another scream, and for a moment Robert wondered if she was dying right in front of him. Thankfully, their other two children were being tended to by one of the other mothers, so they didn't have to see all of this.

"Is Mary all right?" came a voice from the door.

Robert craned his neck around and saw that both of his brothers had opened the cabin door and stood on the threshold, obviously afraid to take a step closer.

"Get them out of here!" Mary shouted, stopping her groaning long enough to yell.

"We'll fetch a midwife," Benjamin said, and the brothers were gone in an instant. Robert would feel a lot better when he saw someone wearing a dress enter the cabin. This birthing business was not for men.

"They're goin' after the midwife," Robert assured her, pulling out a handkerchief with his free hand and dabbing Mary's sweat-streaked forehead. Mary was terrified, that's for sure. During the last two births, she didn't show a trace of fear, but this was different. As she started to speak, he could tell the power was coming over her again before she could get the words out. Labor pains could be as merciless as a master, taking ownership of her body.

Her next scream was so loud that it must have been heard a county away. Then, just as soon as one labor pain was gone, another came at her like an attacking force. The birth pains were like lines of soldiers, with one line reloading while the second one fired, so there was no letup in the firepower.

"Help me, Robert! Help me!"

"What do you want me to do?"

But Mary was in no shape to answer. She ripped out a scream even louder than the last one, if that were possible.

The next thing Robert knew, he felt the presence of other people in the cabin. He was relieved to hear the rustle of dresses. Three women had swept into the room, all of them slaves rushing over from the Thompson Big House.

Reinforcements had come. When Mary relaxed her grip on his hand, for only a moment, Robert took the opportunity to let go and retreated to the door. When he looked back, the midwife had taken Mary's hand and was talking her through the next pain.

Robert slipped through the door and out into the cool night, and he ran his fingers through his hair. *What now?*

...

The moment John Tubman heard the first scream, he thought Robert had done something terrible to his wife. But when Benjamin and Henry came rushing over, and the screaming kept on coming, he realized he was hearing the pains of birthing.

John once desired a boy of his own, but now he wasn't sure if he cared. It was hard enough just looking out for himself, let alone a child. When he and Harriet had lived together, he felt burdened by having to take care of her, especially when she was sick. It was one of the reasons he would get so angry and impatient with the woman. He hated the unending chores, and white folks made his job of being a husband so much more difficult. A man's job was to protect and provide, but how could he do that with both hands tied behind his back?

Soon, John saw several women rush up to the cabin, where the screaming went on and on, a torrent of pain. He had heard women holler in labor before, but this sounded worse. He wondered if the mother and child were dying.

John decided to wait and see how it all unfolded. If the brothers slipped away in the night, he would be right behind them, following them every step of the way. He was sure the brothers would lead him directly to Harriet. His wife was out there somewhere—not far away. John could sense it.

34

Poplar Neck, Maryland

Papa Ben Ross was weary. He knew people called him "Old Ben," and he was certainly feeling that way tonight. He lowered himself into his chair and looked around at all he had built. His cabin was small, but it was his own. He had built every stick of furniture in the place with his own hands—the bed, the table, the chest, the dresser, and the chairs. He had also built up a fine reputation among the white folks in this neck of the woods. Why, Master Thompson respected him so much that the man had even given him ten acres of land when he set him free. *Ten acres*!

But now his daughter, Harriet, was asking him to put it all on the line.

A man had come the day before, carrying a message from Harriet that she was fixing to bring Benjamin, Robert, and Henry out of slavery this very night. Papa Ross had a bad feeling about all of it. This was not the Christmas he was expecting.

"What's eatin' you?" asked his wife. Rit had just finished with food preparations for the night.

"I'm an honest man, ain't I?" Ben said, looking over at Rit.

She puffed on her pipe and rocked in her favorite chair. "Course you're an honest man. Too honest, in my book."

Ben waved a hand at their modest cabin. "I created all this 'cause I know how to get along with white folks."

Rit didn't answer. She just kept puffing on that pipe.

"I don't wanna lose all we have," he added.

"Now you're worryin' me, Ben. Why you thinkin' you might lose everything?"

"No reason, no reason," Old Ben muttered, realizing he had probably said too much. Harriet's message had clearly said not to breathe a word to Mama about the escape, and his daughter was right. Rit would make such a stir that their escape would be put in jeopardy. Rit wouldn't do it on purpose. She just couldn't help herself. She would try to stop the children from fleeing, out of concern for them. But in doing so, it would only make things worse.

"You not tellin' me somethin', Ben?"

Old Ben couldn't lie, but he was good at deflecting questions. "I'm just worryin', that's all," he said. "You know that 'bout me. I shouldn't have said anything."

Ben was already trying to figure out a way he could help his children to safety without being forced to lie to Dr. Thompson or other white folks. He had built his life on honesty, and he couldn't compromise it now or he'd be done for. He had to figure out a way to honestly deny he knew anything about his children escaping.

"I got the hog all trussed up for cookin'," Rit said, puffing away and rocking. "I sure hope the children will be here for Christmas."

Every year, the masters allowed their family to have the Christmas meal together, and once again it was Old Ben's reputation for honesty that helped to make that happen.

"I'm sure the three boys will all be here, but I don't think Rachel can make the trip," he said. Rachel was their only daughter left in Maryland.

"Even Robert? Is he comin'?"

"It depends on how Mary's doin'." Old Ben wondered whether Robert would have the nerve to escape when his wife was about to pop. But with the slave auction looming, who knew what Robert was capable of doing? Rit still hadn't heard about the three boys being put up for sale on Tuesday, and he intended to keep it that way.

"It's no secret that our Harriet's been helpin' folks all around here run off. If our other children were fixin' to run away, would you tell the master the truth if he asked you 'bout it?" said Rit.

Her question nearly knocked him off his stool. Did she know something about the escape after all?

"You asked me this question before. We don't need to be discussin' it on Christmas Eve."

"Nonsense! What if the boys decide to skedaddle north after Christmas dinner tomorrow?" Rit said. "Would you tell Master Thompson what happened?"

"I know how to dodge those kind of questions."

"You'll just dodge his questions? You mean you still won't lie, even for your children?"

"The devil is the father of lies," said Ben.

"And you're the father of those three boys. A father's gotta lie when it means protectin' his own."

Old Ben shook his head violently, trying to shake away his wife's words. She was like Eve, tempting him.

"I said I can't lie. Besides, what makes you think the children might be runnin'? They never ran any other Christmas."

Rit sucked on her pipe, then let the smoke come out of the right corner of her mouth, like she was letting off steam.

"Y'all never know when they'll get it in their heads to run," she said. "And if you ever tell on the children to the master, I'll put you on a spit and roast you alive."

"Don't worry none."

"Don't worry? Your truth-telling has got me real worried."

Old Ben leaped to his feet and stabbed a finger at his wife. "Master Thompson give us this land! My honesty made it possible for me to buy your freedom!"

"You don't owe that man nothin' if that's what you're thinkin'."

"I owe him the truth."

"You owe him *nothin'*!"

"I can't lie," Ben said. "If I try to lie, they'll see right through it. But I told you I'm good at dodging questions. So stop worryin'."

"I ain't gonna have you be the cause of our children gettin' caught. I won't have it!"

"It's my reputation that got us what we got! And you want to throw all that away?"

"If it means our children go free, then yes. I'll throw it all away, including this ten acres of land!"

"That's the devil speaking."

Rit moved in on him quickly and beat her fists on his chest. Old Ben just stood there and took the strikes. His wife had once been able to pack a punch when she was younger, but Rit's arms and hands were weak with age. He barely felt the thumps.

When she wore herself out, he tried to wrap her in an embrace, but she shoved him away and strode to the fire. She tossed another log into the flames, creating an eruption of sparks. Old Ben saw a few sparks land on a clump of straw, and he rushed over to make sure it didn't ignite.

Rit watched what he did and then spit out her next words. "If you betray our children for the sake of your reputation, I'll burn this place down with my own hands."

Ben Ross finished stamping on the sparks and turned to face his wife. He believed her. She wouldn't lie about something like that.

■■■

"He still out there?" asked Jane.

"Sure is," said Prudence.

Horatio Jones had returned from the Big House, but this time he had not entered their cabin. He sat outside the slave cabin, sitting on a tree stump in the dark and smoking another cigar. But just his presence, his silence, terrified Jane.

"Whata we do now?" Jane asked. "It's almost sunset, and I told

Benjamin I'd meet him at the garden just after dark. I can't walk outta here with Jones sittin' right there."

Prudence nudged open one of the shutters a little farther to get a good look outside. Shaking her head, she pulled back from the window and put her hands on her hips. She was a stout woman—and strong. Not much seemed to shake her.

"Do you think—?" Jane started to say, but Prudence snapped her fingers.

"Shush!"

Jane shushed.

"I'm puzzlin' this over, but when you talk, my thoughts slip away. So be quiet."

Jane nodded submissively. Holding one hand in the air, like she was in church, Prudence closed her eyes and said nothing. Then, as if suddenly coming alive, she moved swiftly across the cabin to the fire, which was beginning to die down. She poked at the fire, sending sparks flying upward.

Jane wanted to speak her fears aloud, like opening a box of spiders, but she was afraid to break the silence. When Prudence was done jostling the logs in the fireplace, she went back to the window and peeked out again. Then she went over to the corner and lifted up the pair of her husband's britches that she had been sewing. At last, she spoke.

"Stand up," Prudence ordered. Confused, Jane did as commanded.

Jane was completely mystified as Prudence held the pants up against her waist. "I think they'll do."

"Do what?"

"They'll fit," said Prudence.

"You want me to put on britches?"

"Take 'em," said Prudence. She shoved the pants into Jane's hands and then went to the dresser and began rifling through the drawers.

"Ouch!" Prudence said, and she sucked on the dot of blood on the tip of her right forefinger. "Why my husband insists on storing his fishhooks in this dresser I'll never know."

While sucking on her bleeding finger, Prudence used her free hand to fish out one of her husband's work shirts and hurled it at Jane.

"Put it on!" she commanded.

"You want me to wear your husband's clothing?"

"It's the only way you gonna get past that man."

Jane was horrified. Prudence wanted her to dress in men's clothing and stroll right by Horatio Jones?

"Shouldn't we just wait for Jones to leave?"

"Too risky," Prudence said. "Before he leaves, he'll probably come in here, send me away on some errand, and have his way with you."

Jane felt her knees going wobbly once again.

"Y'all need to dress up like my husband."

"Dress as Calvin? But how…?"

"You're almost as tall as him, and Jones won't notice in the dark."

"But don't Jones know that your husband is off at the Big House? Why would Master Jones think I'm him?"

"Jones don't know for sure where Calvin is. For all he knows, my husband coulda come back here."

Jane searched desperately for any excuse not to do this. "But he'll kill me if he catches me in a man's clothing."

"He might do worse if you don't get outta here."

Jane didn't ask what "worse" might be. She already knew. So she quickly began to undress, wondering how in the world she would pass as a man. She prayed for darkness to conceal her form as she started working her way into Calvin's clothes.

35

The Bellefield Estate, Cambridge

Benjamin and Henry found Robert pacing outside his cabin. Inside, Mary's pain continued to come out in a series of screams. The sun was going down, and they needed to get to the Jones Plantation soon. Harriet and Jane will be waiting and wondering.

"How's Mary doin'?" Benjamin asked. As soon as the words were out of his mouth, he immediately realized it was a stupid question.

"Y'all got ears, don't ya?" Robert said.

"Sorry."

Henry was all urgency. "We can't wait no longer. We gotta go, Robert."

"Jane and Harriet will be at the meeting place waiting for us," Benjamin explained. "We gotta get there before Jones finds out that Jane is gone."

Robert put his hands on either side of his skull, as if he were trying to squeeze out a decision.

"So are you comin' with us or not?" Henry asked.

Another scream erupted from inside the cabin. Robert spun around and stared at the door. "If I leave, I'm desertin' my family."

"If you stay and you're sold off, you won't be with your family neither," said Henry.

"But it's your choice," said Benjamin.

"I think Mary would want you to go," Henry said. "If you'd a told her you were runnin' in the first place, she woulda told you to go."

"You can't know that for sure."

"No woman wants to see her man sold off."

"But still…I can't leave till the baby's born."

Henry shook his head. "Okay, stay until the baby comes. Then try to catch up with us."

"I'll do that," said Robert, his voice faltering. "I'll stay till the baby is born."

"All right then," said Henry.

Benjamin said nothing, wondering if this would be the last time he'd ever lay eyes on Robert. He was certain that once the baby was born, Robert would choose to stay in Maryland. Then he would be sold off two days later. It was bound to happen.

Benjamin and Henry took turns embracing Robert before they left.

"We'll see you soon," Benjamin said, although he didn't believe it.

"Tell Mary what we're plannin'," Henry said. "She'll want you to run."

Robert nodded, and then he looked away as Benjamin and Henry turned on their heels and began to trot into the forest. When Benjamin glanced back, he saw Robert squeezing his head again, as if in pain.

...

"Good thing you a tall woman," said Prudence.

Jane felt a fool, standing there in men's clothing, although to her shock, the britches fit well enough. Jane was about the same height as Prudence's husband, Calvin, but she wasn't as hefty. The clothes hung loosely on her frame; the rope belt was the only thing keeping the pants from falling to her ankles. But loose-hanging clothes would raise no suspicions. It's not like slave clothing was tailor made.

"In the dark, Jones won't notice a thing," said Prudence.

Prudence went back to the window and nudged open the shutters, just a sliver.

"He still there?" Jane asked.

"He just lit another cigar, so he ain't goin' nowhere."

"Why's he just sittin' out there, you think?"

"He knows we know he's there. And he knows the worst part is you wonderin' and fearin' and sweatin'."

"Won't he eventually figure out what you done to get me away? Won't you pay the price?"

"Don't you worry none about me, Sister Jane. He's too dumb to figure out how you got by him. Besides, he won't kill me. His wife values me as her best worker in the house. She'd kill *him* if he did me any harm."

Jane prayed she was right.

"You ready?" Prudence asked.

"No."

"Ready or not then. Let's go."

Prudence opened the door and led the way. Jane felt like a Christian saint being led out into the arena, right in front of a starving lion.

■■■

They were late, as usual. Harriet waited for her brothers in the small garden on the Jones Plantation. The garden was used by slaves to grow their own food. With it being the dead of winter, the ground was hard and covered with the last frozen residues of the growing season. She felt the cold nibble at her exposed fingers, which poked through her tattered gloves. She watched as a stoat—a weasel in a white coat—came nosing through the vegetation. When Harriet made a hissing sound, the stoat darted into the dark.

As she watched, that wretched pain flared in her jaw, for she had disturbed her tooth. She thought the pain had been subsiding, but evidently not.

Still no sign of her brothers. If they dared to back out again...

She fingered the cold handle of the revolver, which she had taken out of her pocket and slipped into her belt.

Then she spotted two figures sliding out of the woods. It was hard to make them out in the dark, but she knew the way her brothers walked. But why were there only two? She felt her blood begin to boil.

"You're late," Harriet said, springing up from the ground. She heard Benjamin gasp and saw him backpedal two steps. It was just like when they were young and Harriet would spring out of nowhere and scare Benjamin to tears.

"Where's Robert?" she demanded.

"With Mary," Henry said. "She's gone into labor."

"She givin' birth *tonight?*"

"Mary's in a whole lotta pain."

"*Tonight?*"

"That's what I said. But Robert says he'll meet up with us at Mama and Papa's place soon as the baby comes."

"Pfffff."

Harriet didn't believe Robert would join up with them, not for one minute. She had been certain the Lord wanted her to rescue *all three* of her brothers—to lead them through the fiery furnace, like the three friends of Daniel. So why would God send the birth pains on Mary on this day, of all days? Was the Lord telling her it wasn't in His good will for Robert to go with them?

No. It couldn't be.

She figured the Lord was just testing their resolve. The Lord was telling them that freedom was like birth pains, and making tough choices was like a mother giving birth. It took blood and suffering, and the breaking of waters before freedom came. That's why Mary had gone into labor this night of all nights. It was God's way of forcing Robert to choose. If he really wanted freedom for himself and his family, he had to leave his wife, even in the midst of her suffering. Pain rules this side of Eden, and Harriet's aching tooth was a constant reminder of that truth.

"Let's move," Harriet said. "Robert'll just have to catch up with us."

"I ain't leavin' yet," said Benjamin.

Harriet turned on him, tempted to pull out her revolver and force him to march north.

"I said that Robert will just have to find us at Mama and Papa's place. So let's go."

"We gotta wait for Jane," Benjamin said.

Harriet had completely forgotten about Jane. Her freedom train never waited for anyone before, but she knew the importance of bringing Jane Kane along.

Harriet flung a hand in the air. "What's takin' that woman? We gotta get movin'."

"Somethin' musta happened."

"But my train always leaves on schedule."

"Well, this passenger ain't goin' nowhere till I find out what's happened to Jane."

Harriet gave Benjamin a hard stare and fingered her revolver.

"All right, we'll go find Jane, but we gotta be careful."

So the three of them plunged back into the woods, following a trail that took them a short distance to the slave cabins on the Joneses' property. At the ragged edge of the woods, they peered down a steep slope toward four cabins, staggered along in a string in the clearing. Below, they saw a man sitting on a tree stump. They could smell his cigar smoke, even from up the slope.

"That a white man or black man?" Harriet whispered. It was hard to make out in the dark.

"It's Horatio Jones," said Henry.

"That explains why Jane didn't show up," said Benjamin. "She's trapped in the cabin and can't get past that man."

"Can we create a distraction?" suggested Henry.

Harriet just grunted. She didn't like it when her escape plans were altered, even a little. If the Lord changed the plans, that was one thing, but she wouldn't allow her brothers to change them. They always seemed to find an excuse not to go north.

Harriet had seen enough. "We gotta go. Now."

"I said I ain't leavin' without Jane," Benjamin insisted.

"But *we* are. Let's move, Henry."

Harriet took several steps into the woods, but neither brother budged. Harriet pulled out her revolver and pointed it at Benjamin. "I said move."

Benjamin and Henry both stared back at her, with looks of disbelief. "You threatenin' us?"

"I'm *savin'* you. Y'all are stiff-nicked Israelites, always findin' reasons not to go to the Promised Land."

"And you're crazy. You ain't gonna shoot us," said Benjamin.

Harriet had used the gun before to threaten people who wanted to back out of escapes. And it had always worked, because people knew the threat was real. But these were her brothers, and they knew she wouldn't shoot them. She was here to rescue them, not kill them.

Lowering her gun, Harriet let out a sigh. Lord, her brothers would be the death of her.

Then they heard the sound of a door squeaking on its hinges. Something was unfolding down below at the cabins. Harriet, Benjamin, and Henry dropped down, ducking behind a clump of bushes. Harriet nearly gave out a shout when she knelt on a couple of spiky brown balls, fallen from a nearby sweet gum tree. Jumping back up, she kicked away a clump of the spiky balls, and then moved into a crouch, peeking over the low bushes.

Two people had left the cabin. One man, one woman from the looks of it. But neither looked like Jane.

...

John Tubman followed Henry and Benjamin all the way to the slave garden on the Jones Plantation. He hated the idea of putting even one toe on Jones's land. He had heard stories about Jones, and if half of them were true, the man was a devil. The only thing that spurred him on was the thought that Henry and Benjamin might lead him to Harriet.

And that's exactly what they did.

From his vantage point, hidden in the woods, he saw a shadow in the garden rise up from the ground and greet the brothers. The shadow was a small person— about the height of Harriet. And when the shadow spoke, he was certain. It was his wife.

But now that he had tracked down Harriet, John wasn't sure what to do next. He hadn't thought it through that far. Should he join her and go north? Should he demand she stay in Maryland and share his cabin like a proper wife? Or should he command her to apologize for deserting him when she fled north? On top of all that was the possible reward he could get for letting Miss Eliza know what she was up to.

He waited for a chance to find Harriet alone, but that was going to be tricky. The three siblings kept together like a unit. And when they suddenly began to move out of the garden, they all headed in the direction of the slave cabins on the Jones Plantation. That made no sense at all. North was the opposite direction. They were heading toward the plantation run by the worst man in this neck of the woods.

Were they insane?

With Harriet, you never knew.

36

Jane, dressed in Calvin's clothes, kept her arm linked in Prudence's as they stepped out of the cabin and into the open. Jones stood to his feet, about twenty feet away, still smoking his cigar. It glowed red in the night like a warning.

Jane stared straight ahead, keeping her eyes fixed on the Big House in the distant dark. If she looked at Jones, she might fall apart.

"Where y'all think you're goin'?" Jones asked.

Calvin was a quiet man, which meant that Prudence did most of the talking for the married couple. So she was the one who responded. "Calvin and I are headin' back to the house, sir. Got more cleanin' to do for the big day tomorrow."

"At this time a night?" he said.

Jane could hear the suspicion in his voice. She stared at her feet, afraid to look in his direction.

"It's Christmas Eve, and y'all got an army of folks comin' tomorrow. The mistress wants us to make sure all is right," said Prudence.

Jones made a grunting sound, and Jane could feel his eyes boring down on her, staring directly at her. Did he notice that the clothes hung on her limply? Could he see her womanly features beneath the coat? What if he checked the cabin the moment they were gone and saw that she was no longer inside? She hadn't thought about that possibility.

It was too late to worry about all of that now. *Just keep on walking.* She felt Prudence's grip on her arm tighten, a reassuring squeeze.

It was a long hike to the Big House, a massive three-story place that sprawled to both sides, with rooms spilling into more rooms. When they reached the house, they didn't go in the back door, where servants entered. Prudence steered Jane to the north side of the house, and when they were safely behind a large magnolia tree, they let down their act.

"*Go.* Before Jones sees that you ain't in the cabin," Prudence said. She gently pushed Jane toward the woods to the north. The slave garden was just on the other side of the belt of trees.

"Maybe this ain't gonna work," Jane said. "Maybe we should try another day."

"You got this far. Now go!" Prudence stood directly behind Jane, shoving on her back with both of her hands, like pushing a stubborn ox.

"But—"

"Go."

"But Benjamin—"

"*Go.*"

It was clear that Prudence wasn't going to let her spout any excuses. Jane gave up arguing, and she walked hesitantly into the woods, praying that no one spotted her slipping away. When she was safely concealed behind the wall of trees, she broke into a jog. She found that it was much easier to run in britches than in a long, heavy dress. Men had all of the advantages in life.

But when she reached the garden, she found no one waiting for her, and her stomach did a flip. She was late, but she never would have imagined Benjamin would leave without her. How could he? She rushed up and down the garden boundaries, whispering his name into the dark: "Benjamin. *Benjamin.*"

Jane spun in circles and then staggered to a stop and began to sob. She had risked her life, and now this! Their plan was to head for the home of Benjamin's parents, Ben and Rit, in Poplar Neck, but she would never be able to find their cabin in the dark. She was terrified. She was afraid of the animals she might meet, or the evil spirits that drifted through the forest like a fog. She was afraid of *everything*.

Crouching down, she hugged herself for warmth and wept. Then it started to drizzle, a cold rain. The kind of rain that could kill a person with sickness.

One way or another, she was going to die. She was certain of it.

...

Benjamin, Henry, and Harriet were flat on their bellies on the cold soil, staring down at the cabin below. Two figures that looked like Prudence and her husband Calvin had just strolled past Horatio Jones and headed off in the direction of the Big House. A chilly drizzle began to patter the ground.

No sign of Jane.

"You think Jane's still inside the cabin?" Henry whispered.

"Gotta be," said Benjamin. "She's trapped in there, with Jones standing guard."

"How we gonna get her out?" Benjamin asked Harriet, but when he looked over to where she had been just moments ago, he found empty air. Harriet had vanished.

"Where's Harriet gone to now?" Benjamin remained on his belly as he peered in all directions. She had threatened to leave without them, but would she really do it? Had she given up on them, once and for all?

"Shall I go look for her?" Henry said.

"No," said Benjamin. "We need to stick together till we get Jane out of the cabin."

Back down the slope, Horatio Jones stood a good distance from the cabin, staring at the dilapidated structure and smoking his cigar. When Jones finished the cigar, Benjamin was afraid the man would enter the cabin and corner Jane.

Benjamin would not let that happen. He no longer cared about escape. He cared only for Jane's safety. He had a knife, hidden in his clothes, and he would use it to butcher Jones like a pig before he let the man take Jane. He'd butchered many a pig, so he knew exactly how to do it, beginning with a slice to the jugular.

Benjamin watched as Jones tossed his cigar to the ground and pressed it into the hard December soil with the heel of his boot. Then the man wiped his hands on his pants' legs, straightened up, and stared at the cabin's front door for a few more seconds. Benjamin got into a crouch, preparing to sprint down the slope for the kill.

"What you think you're doin'?" his brother asked.

"I ain't gonna let him get inside that cabin."

"Don't be a fool."

When Benjamin saw Jones take a step toward the cabin, he took off running.

...

This was John Tubman's only chance to catch his wife alone. He had followed Harriet and her two brothers back to the edge of the woods, looking down on the slave cabins at Jones's place. When Harriet slipped away from her brothers, he realized it was now or never.

John followed Harriet as she rushed along the edge of the forest. And when she finally came to a stop, she pulled something from her belt—a gun, he thought. For a heartbeat he thought she had discovered him. She turned and pointed the gun into the woods, and then she fired. John saw the pistol spurt fire, and he hit the ground.

"Don't shoot," he called out to Harriet. "It's me. John."

He remained on the ground, afraid of standing up and giving his wife a tall target. He heard the sound of her steps, moving across the brush, coming directly for him.

Suddenly, a thought occurred to John. Had Harriet heard about his dalliance with Caroline? If she did, and if she had a gun in her hand, she just might shoot him dead.

Rising to his feet, John made a move to run.

...

Before Benjamin could take more than a few steps down the slope leading to the cabin, a gunshot sounded to the right, from about fifty yards away. The blast caught Jones's attention, and the man stopped and stared up the hill, in the direction of the shot. Immediately, Benjamin hit the ground, terrified that Jones had seen him in the dark.

Raising his head just a little, he saw Jones pull out a revolver and begin to dash up the slope. Benjamin was sure Jones was heading right for him.

...

"That you, John?"

Harriet thought she was imagining things when she heard John's voice. She had fired her gun into the forest as a diversion, hoping to draw Horatio Jones away from the cabin. But then someone shouted, "Don't shoot," and out of the corner of her eye she saw a shadow drop to the ground, as if hit by her bullet.

She charged toward the figure, gun drawn.

"Don't shoot, Harriet. I can explain everything."

Thunderstruck, Harriet came to a sudden halt. The voice was definitely John's. But what on earth was he doing here?

John Tubman slowly rose from the ground, holding up his hands like a captured bank thief. That was when Harriet realized she still had her pistol trained on him. She had no intention of shooting him dead, but he didn't have to know that. She liked hearing the fear in his voice.

"Don't shoot me, Harriet," he said, taking another step backward. "I just came back to fetch you and tell you I still love you. Come home with me, Sugar."

Sugar? He dares to call me 'Sugar'?

"Why do y'all need sugar? I thought you had your cinnamon?"

That question certainly seemed to take the starch out of John. He said nothing, obviously startled by her use of the word "cinnamon"—his nickname for Caroline.

"I ain't with that woman no more," he flatly said. "I decided I'd rather be with you, Harriet."

Harriet almost believed him.

"What did she do—leave you?"

When John made a move to turn, she raised her shooting arm a little higher and said, "Don't you dare run now."

"I ain't runnin'. I been lookin' for you. Come home, Harriet. Come home, and we can raise a family."

Harriet felt a sharp pain under her ribs. John had aimed for her weak spot and struck a bull's eye. Harriet had given up on having children, but she still wasn't at peace with it. Any mention of family nearly knocked her off her feet. She thought about how her sister-in-law, Mary, was giving birth to her third child this very night, and how unfair life could be.

"Raise a family? It was you who said I can't never give birth," she accused John.

"That was me talkin' when I didn't have faith. I got faith now… faith that we can have a child."

But there was no "we." John Tubman had dropped clean out of her heart the day she found him living with Caroline, and there was no more room in her life for him. But now he pops up out of nowhere, trying to climb back into her heart. How dare he tempt her with talk about children!

There was no time to think. Harriet knew Horatio Jones would be up here any second now, searching for the source of the gunshot.

"You're like a sore tooth, John Tubman," she said, raising the pistol until the barrel was peering straight into his face. Even in the dark, she could see the panic rise in his eyes. Then she redirected her aim, a little to the left, and fired a second shot, well wide of John. The kickback on the pistol was enough to knock a flare of pain through her ailing tooth.

John took off running in one direction, while Harriet broke away in another. Seemed like they were always running in opposite ways.

■■■

When the second shot went off, Benjamin saw Horatio Jones adjust course. He veered to the right, from where the sound seemed to be coming.

Benjamin stayed low, waiting for Master Jones to disappear into the woods.

The next moment, Henry was there at his side, out of breath and gasping his words. "Go get Jane outta the cabin. Now's the chance."

Henry hadn't even finished his sentence before Benjamin was moving swiftly down the slope in a half crouch. He had only a little time to get into the cabin, bring Jane out, and return up the slope before Jones came back. His heart was thumping in his throat as he stepped onto the cabin porch and eased open the door, just a crack.

"Jane," he whispered through the narrow opening. "It's Benjamin."

He saw a faint glow coming from the dying flames in the fireplace, but no one answered.

"Jane."

Still no response. Benjamin opened the door wider and slipped through the gap.

The cabin was empty. It was a one-room cabin, so it didn't take long to see that the place was completely deserted. But it was dark, so he had to be certain that Jane wasn't hiding in a corner, cloaked in blackness. He spun around in a circle two times, still not believing his eyes. Then he peered into the dark corners but found no one. He was also extremely aware that if Jones returned now, he would be trapped inside the cabin.

"What's takin' you so long?" asked Henry, his voice coming in through the door, which was still slightly ajar.

Spinning around one more time, Benjamin studied every square foot of the cabin. Where was she?

"Hurry," came Henry's urgent plea.

While Benjamin continued to scour the room, Henry barged in. "What's going on?"

"I don't understand it. She's gone."

"We better go then. Jones'll be back any second."

"But where is she?"

Benjamin ignored Henry tugging on his sleeve.

"C'mon, Benjamin. She ain't here. You got eyes, don't you?"

"I don't understand where she's gone."

This time, Henry grabbed him by the upper arm and yanked. But Benjamin still would not be moved.

"Benjamin," Henry hissed. "Jones could walk in here any second. We gotta go."

"Not without Jane."

Henry took a quick look out the cabin window, then rushed back to Benjamin's side.

"We hafta go. Now!"

Finally, Benjamin came to his senses. He felt like he was waking up from a bad dream, only to find himself in a worse reality. This time he let Henry yank him forward, and the brothers stumbled from the cabin and scrambled back up the rise. At the top of the slope, Harriet was waiting for them. Benjamin could smell the gunpowder from her spent pistol.

"You fired the gun?" Henry asked.

"Course I did—to draw Jones away from the cabin. Now let's move before Jones tracks the smell of gunshot. Where's Jane?"

"She wasn't there."

Harriet's voice went cold. "You mean we risked our plan for nothin'?"

"I don't understand it," said Benjamin. "Maybe she's back at the garden, waiting for us."

"We don't have no time to go back to the garden. We gotta go."

"But I ain't leavin' without Jane."

"Then Henry and I will go. You and Jane—and Robert—will have to find us."

"I won't go, neither," said Henry. "Not without Jane."

Harriet still had the revolver in her hand, and for a moment Benjamin thought she was going to slap him in the side of the face with it. It would be a long reach for a five-foot woman but he didn't doubt she could do it. She waved it around to emphasize the urgency of her words, and Benjamin flinched every time the barrel swung in his direction.

"All right," said Harriet. "We go back to the garden, take one last look, and then we leave, Jane or no Jane. Agreed? No more foolin' around."

"Agreed," said Benjamin.

But as they made their way through the dark, Benjamin vowed to himself that he would not leave without Jane, no matter what he just promised. If they could not find Jane, Henry and Harriet would have to go on without him.

Their plan was quickly unraveling, and they could all feel it.

***

Jane heard the gunshots and she instantly panicked. She wondered if that's why she did not find Benjamin waiting for her at the garden. Had he been discovered and chased down—and shot? But who had found him? It couldn't have been Horatio Jones because he was standing guard by the cabin. But she also knew Horatio had several overseers in his pay, and they were as nasty as the master. It must have been one of them doing the shooting.

This left Jane with no idea what to do or where to go. If she returned to the cabin right away, life would go on the same as always, and there was a good chance that Horatio Jones would not even know she had attempted an escape. But she couldn't return to that life. She would rather be dead.

If she stayed here in the garden much longer, that's exactly what she would be. So she had only one choice that made any sense. She would take off and find her way north on her own. She had heard that a string of safehouses had been established all across the land, connected by secret pathways north. But she had no idea where they might be and how to find them. She had no sense of direction and no survival skills.

The man's clothing had helped her get out of the cabin, but the disguise would only raise suspicions along the way. Come daylight, anyone could see she was a woman in a man's clothing, and they would immediately suspect her if they spotted her in britches. Really, what sort of explanation could she give?

Still, Jane had no choice. Man's clothing or not, she had to go. Now.

Jane rose to her feet and stared beyond the garden to a narrow path leading away from the Jones Plantation and into the deep woods. Her Aunt Clara once told her the path through the forest had been created by a massive snake that slithered through the woods, its body twisting and turning to flatten the land and create a trail. At night, Aunt Clara said, this monstrous snake, the width of a tunnel, came out of hiding and opened its jaws as wide as can be, waiting for unsuspecting people to wander straight into its gullet. The story had scared Jane half to death, and it kept her from ever stepping foot into the woods after the sun had set. She was even terrified to walk the path by daylight.

When Jane heard the snap of a twig behind her, she took off running, heading straight for the trail through the forest. But was she heading toward freedom or into the wide open mouth of a serpent?

She would know soon enough.

37

Horatio Jones wanted nothing more than to track down and shoot the neighbors who regularly poached on his property. A couple of scalawags—two brothers—often slipped onto his property to shoot deer. So when he heard the sound of gunshots, he figured the Frank brothers were at it again.

Jones ran off in the direction of the gunshots, but he found no sign of the two brothers or anybody else. But what did he expect in the dark? They could be hiding anywhere. With the cold drizzle coming down, he wasn't about to roam around his woods, hunting for poachers all night. That's not how he planned to spend his Christmas Eve. So he made his way back toward the slave quarters, pausing to light another cigar on his way down.

Jones decided he would send one of his overseers out to see if he could track down the Frank brothers. He had a fellow named Nehemiah that would be perfect for it; Nehemiah would complain, with it being the night before Christmas, but let him moan. In the meantime, what would Christmas Eve be without a good frolic with one of his slave girls? It was an annual Christmas present to himself. His wife knew what he was up to, but she was powerless to do anything but give him frosty glares all Christmas day. Ah, but the glares were worth it.

So Jones returned to the cabin, where he hoped to find Jane waiting for him, huddled in a corner and terrified. He hoped she would fight back. He was drenched to the bone by the time he was back down the slope and approaching the cabin. To dry off, he would order Jane to get the fire going before the fun could begin.

"Hate to keep y'all waitin'," he said, pushing open the cabin door. The fire was almost out, leaving just glowing embers. The cabin was dark, and he figured she was probably hiding in one of the corners. She was going to make this a challenge after all. He liked that.

"Are we playin' hide and seek?" he said, his voice light and cheery.

Jones thought he saw a figure hunched in one corner, but when he pounced, he nearly tripped over the bucket and mop that had tricked his eyes. He liked that she was making him work for his reward, but he soon wearied of the sport and began to get irritated. He looked beneath the table, but no Jane. His irritation sparked into anger, and he hurled the table on its side. Then he picked up a chair and smashed it against a wall. The destruction felt good.

Jones let out a string of curses, and that felt even better. Then he spied the glowing log in the fireplace and had a sudden inspiration.

"If you're gonna hide on me, Jane, I think I need more light in here to find you."

Using tongs, he lifted the glowing log out from the fireplace and held it up to the tattered drapes, which sagged in front of one of the windows. The fire caught, streaming up the fabric, and he stood back and watched his handiwork. His wife was going to be angry that he burned down this cabin, but the spectacle would be worth a few furious words. If the place burned to the ground, he would simply make the slaves build a new one.

By this time, the fire was shedding enough light to make it obvious that Jane was not anywhere in the cabin. The heat drove away the bone-chilling cold, and soon the wall of heat became overwhelming. He stepped out of the cabin, into the dark, strolled up the hill, and took a seat beneath a tree. It protected him from most of the drizzle as he watched the cabin burn.

He watched as people came sprinting out of the Big House, like bees from a hive. The cabin had become a massive torch, beyond saving. But the slaves carried buckets anyway, tossing their pitiful splashes of water onto unquenchable flames.

He pulled out another cigar, lit up, and watched the fun. He figured Jane Kane had slipped out of the cabin while he was off searching for poachers. She was probably in the Big House, working alongside Prudence and Calvin. But he still had plans for her. The fire was only the beginning of his Christmas Eve entertainment.

...

Harriet spotted a figure disappearing into the woods, heading down a trail leading away from the Jones Plantation. It was clearly a man—the clothes gave that away—but she couldn't tell if he was white or black. Still, she felt the Lord nudging her, telling her that this man was on the run, hoping to take a freedom ride on her glory-bound train. That's how her escapes normally unfolded. People would hear she was in the area, so they would latch on to her train. She usually found herself picking up more passengers than planned.

"You see that?" she said.

"See what?" asked Henry.

"Someone just vanished into the forest."

"Was it Jane?" Benjamin said eagerly.

"I think it was a man, and I think he's lookin' for a way north. We gotta get movin' to catch up with him."

"He was a black man?" said Henry.

"Couldn't tell his color."

"So how do you know he's lookin' for a way north? What if he's a white man lookin' for *us*?"

"The Spirit told me he's lookin' to go north."

From the looks on their faces, Harriet could tell that Henry and Benjamin didn't put much stock in Holy Ghost guidance. Their minds were too earthbound, shackled to this world like a second helping of slavery. There were two kinds of slavery in Harriet's mind. The first one was physical, and her brothers knew all about that. But the second one was spiritual, and they were ignorant of it. They were chained to this Earth—limited by what they can see in front of their faces.

"The Spirit told you this man's lookin' for you?" asked Henry, his doubt obvious in his voice.

"You got cotton in your ears? That's what I said, and I'm goin' after him."

"But what about Jane?" said Benjamin.

"This train's waited long enough. It's leavin' the station."

"But why are you willin' to go after that strange man, but not willin' to wait for Jane?"

"'Cause we waited long enough for her. That man, he's on the path we're due to take, so he won't slow us down none. I always pick up passengers on the way north."

"I still ain't leavin'," said Benjamin.

Harriet had already lost Robert on the way and now it looked like Benjamin, and maybe even Henry, might be jumping off of her train. If that happened, she didn't know if she could forgive them—or ever risk her skin to save her brothers again. She wondered if that was a kind of betrayal, but she was too angry at the moment to think it through.

Suddenly, they heard shouting coming from the other side of the belt of trees, off by the Big House. It sounded like alarms were being raised. This was just more evidence that they didn't have time to hang around the garden, arguing and hoping that Jane would eventually wander by.

"You hear that? Sounds like trouble brewin'," she said. "I'm goin'. You two comin'?"

Henry put a hand on Benjamin's arm. "Harriet's right. We can't wait all night."

"I ain't leavin' without Jane," Benjamin snapped back.

"But listen to that ruckus," Henry said. "I think alarms have been sounded. We gotta go."

"I ain't leavin' I said."

"Fine, go look for your woman," said Harriet. "Then maybe you, Jane, and Robert can catch up with us at Mama and Papa's place."

Benjamin nodded, looking as sorry as an old dog.

"Be careful," said Henry, giving his brother a bear hug.

Harriet wondered if she should give Benjamin a hug as well, but she doubted that he would accept it from her. She felt a twinge of sadness, a sense of rejection from both of her brothers. She had risked her life coming down to Maryland to pull them out of the fire, and they didn't appreciate it. Not even Henry. She wasn't sure she had ever felt so alone in her life. No husband. No children. And now she felt her brothers pulling away from her too. She wondered, for one wild moment, if she should have gone back to John when she had the chance.

Shoving aside those feelings, she began to walk for the woods. "Let's go, Henry."

Harriet was afraid Henry would change his mind and stay with Benjamin. If he did, she would be utterly alone. But she soon sensed her younger brother trooping along just a few feet behind her. He didn't come up beside her, though. He remained a few steps behind, not saying a word.

It was like he was intentionally keeping his distance. Harriet got the message.

...

Benjamin backtracked toward the Big House. When he emerged from the woods, he was shocked by what he saw. Down the hill, fire was erupting from Jane's cabin, and a mass of people had gathered—mostly slaves—and could do nothing but stand and stare as flames and sparks rose into the night. It was an eerie sight, like some pagan bonfire.

His first thought: Was Jane inside that cabin?

Benjamin rushed down the slope, mixing in with the other slaves, and tried to see if he could spot Jane amidst the gawkers. He also made sure he stayed a safe distance from the overseer among them. The heat of the blaze was overwhelming, and he felt like his skin had become as soft as wax. Every face he saw was lit up by firelight. Nearly two dozen people milled around the burning cabin. Some of them carried empty buckets that they had used to fruitlessly hurl water onto the fire.

"What you think you're doin' here?" came a voice to his right. Benjamin turned and spotted Prudence barreling toward him, as fierce as flame.

"I've come for Jane," he said. "Is she all right? Tell me she wasn't in the cabin."

Prudence moved in close and spoke in a hush. "Course she ain't in the cabin. She went to meet you at the garden."

"I just came from the garden. I didn't see her there."

Prudence paused, as if wondering whether she heard right. "I sent her off to the garden myself. She was all dressed in my husband's clothing."

Benjamin's chin dropped. "She what?"

"She had to dress in Calvin's clothes to get by Master Jones."

Benjamin stood stock still in wordless wonder.

"Did you hear me? She's in man's clothing."

"You mean she was the one who walked with you out of the cabin?"

"You saw that?"

"Yes! From up the hill, near the edge of the woods. We thought it was Calvin."

Prudence put her hands on her hips and stared at the ground, shaking her head. Then she looked directly at Benjamin. "Did you see anyone who looked like a man at the garden?"

"Lord," Benjamin said.

"What's wrong? Did y'all see her?"

"We saw a man going into the woods just as we reached the garden."

"You fool, that was Jane."

"How was I supposed to know?"

"Then get after her."

Benjamin wheeled around and bolted back up the slope, heading for the belt of trees and the garden beyond. If only he had listened to his sister. He wondered if Harriet and Henry had already caught up with Jane, and whether Henry was on his way back to tell him of their discovery.

He was so fixed on his thoughts and worries that he didn't see a figure moving toward him from his left—not until the man called out.

"Hey you—boy! Where you think y'all are goin'?"

Benjamin stopped in his tracks and saw a figure approach him in the dark. He couldn't make out the man's face, but it sounded like a white man—one of the overseers on the Joneses' place. Nehemiah was his name.

Rooted to the ground, Benjamin had to choose. Face Nehemiah and try to explain what he was doing on the Jones Plantation...or run. Either choice was terrible.

He had no idea what to do, so his body made the decision for him. His legs just started moving.

"Hey! You get back here, boy!"

Benjamin kept running.

38

Harriet spotted the man dead ahead—a moving shadow along the trail. The man slowed to a stop and then suddenly dropped to the forest floor and slumped over. Harriet sped up, with Henry just a few steps behind her. As she closed in on the man, she was stunned to hear him sobbing like a woman.

"Slow down," Henry said, putting a hand on Harriet's left arm as a brake. "What if he's a white man? We could be makin' a big mistake."

But Harriet was confident the Lord had sent her after him for a reason. So she pressed forward, and as they came up behind the slumped-over man, the figure came alive and spun around to face them.

"Harriet! Henry!"

Harriet was stunned: A *woman's* voice came to them from the dark. They moved in closer and could see a lady's face beneath the man's slouch hat. A familiar face.

"Jane?" said Henry.

"But what…why those clothes?" Harriet asked.

Jane slowly rose from the ground, brushing off her pants legs before straightening up to full height. She was tall for a woman, a giant next to Harriet.

"It's the only way I could get past Horatio Jones." Jane peered around. "Where's Benjamin?"

"He went back to fetch you," said Henry. "When we didn't see you at the garden, he thought you were still at the Joneses' place."

"We saw you go off down this path, thinking you were a man," Harriet said, eager that Jane knew the full story. "I told them the Lord wanted us to follow you. But my brothers don't believe in the Spirit's guidance."

"Benjamin and I have no problem believing the Holy Spirit. We just didn't believe *you*," Henry said. "There's a difference."

"Still...if Benjamin had come with us, we'd all be together."

"I gotta go back to him," said Jane, trying to step around Harriet. But Harriet blocked her path, while Henry latched on to Jane's arm.

"Stay here with Harriet," he told her. "It's safer if I go back to fetch Benjamin."

Harriet couldn't believe she was hearing this. "Henry, that's why we're in this pickle—because Benjamin insisted on goin' back. We can't have you or Jane or anyone settin' off on their own. We gotta stick together, like we shoulda in the first place."

"But Benjamin's gotta know," said Henry. "He's huntin' for Jane back at the Joneses' place, and he's gotta know she's with us."

"I'll go with you," Jane said, making another useless attempt to break free from Henry.

Harriet pulled out her pistol.

"Oh, put that away," Henry said. "Is that your solution to everything?"

"People listen to guns," Harriet said.

"But Benjamin needs to be told where Jane is," said Henry.

He did have a point—although her brothers had to be the most ornery and uncooperative passengers she ever brought along.

Before they could resolve this impasse, they heard a commotion coming from down the path. Someone was sprinting down the trail at full tilt. It was a good thing Harriet still had her gun drawn. She raised it and took careful aim at the quickly approaching figure.

"Overseers are comin'!" the voice called out.

Lord, it was Benjamin of all people. As Benjamin closed in on them, his eyes were locked on the figure in man's clothes. When he saw that it was Jane, neither of them said a word. He ran into Jane's embrace while Harriet slipped the revolver back into her belt.

"Enough with the huggin'," Harriet said. "What overseers?"

"I was spotted by one of the overseers from the Jones Plantation," Benjamin said. "We gotta get off this path *now*."

They all paused to listen for the footsteps of a pursuer, but all they could hear were the natural sounds of the forest—bugs whirring and clicking, an occasional owl hoot, and the dripping of water from the branches.

"You sure he's chasin' you?" Henry asked.

"He mighta gone back for dogs. But they'll be comin'."

"We were gonna have to get off the path soon anyway," Harriett said. "Follow me."

For once, both of her brothers listened, and they hurried into the woods. Harriet prayed they wouldn't soon be hearing the sound of bloodhounds. She was sure she could outfox a man, but a bloodhound's nose was difficult, if not impossible, to trick.

...

Horatio Jones was still enjoying the blaze as the final pieces of the cabin collapsed in on itself, transforming wood to ash before his eyes. When one entire wall fell over, it kicked up a spray of sparks, flying into the night like a swarm of fireflies.

A few moments later, one of his overseers, Nehemiah, spoiled his fun, rushing up out of breath and sputtering nonsense.

"What's wrong now?" Jones barked at Nehemiah. The overseer was bent over, trying to catch his breath.

"I spotted a slave fleein' into the woods. I went after him, but lost him."

"You see who he was?"

"Too dark. We'll need dogs."

"But the dogs need a scent, you fool. Why didn't you keep after him to find out who we need to track?"

"I lost him, I said."

"Fool."

There was only one way to determine who had slipped off the property: Gather up his slaves and count heads. All of the servants should be present, because Jones wasn't one of those masters who coddled their slaves and let them spend time with relatives for Christmas. Slaves don't have souls, he believed, so what's the use of giving them Christmas or religion of any sort?

Jones ordered Nehemiah to quickly assemble all of the slaves outside the Big House.

"Is there a reward if we catch the slave?" Nehemiah asked.

"There'll be a reward if you *don't* catch him. I'll shoot you like a dog and give you an eternal reward."

That sent Nehemiah scurrying. Jones lit up another cigar and took one final look at the burned-out cabin, which was now almost completely gone. The flames would flicker for hours. He was irritated that he had to spend his Christmas Eve hunting for a slave, rather than enjoying the final sparks of fire.

When they found this slave, that rascal would pay dearly.

■■■

Harriet's tooth was howling. Every step of her foot sent a shudder through her body and a bolt of lightning through her jaw. She began to groan at every footfall.

"You all right?" Benjamin asked.

"Why wouldn't I be?"

"You're moanin' like you got a nail in your foot."

"I wish I only had a nail in my foot."

"Then what is it?" asked Henry.

"Feels like I got a nail *in my tooth*. A bad tooth is like a bad fence-post, all rotten beneath the soil."

247

"Sorry," said Jane.

"But we really shouldn't be talkin' or makin' any kinda sound out here," Harriet said. And that included moaning. Harriet tried to bottle the natural urge to groan, but that only forced her to concentrate more on the pain. It hurt like fire.

They had forty miles ahead of them to their parents' cabin in Poplar Neck, and it was all through thick woods. The rain had let up, but the sky was cloudy and no stars were visible. Harriet had done this trek enough times that she could now navigate north with confidence, even in the dark without the stars. They still hadn't heard any sound of pursuers. No dog or horse sounds. No sounds from men, either.

"Ahhh!"

The only sound came from Harriet. Her foot caught on a root and she stumbled forward. Pain rocketed through her entire jaw and even behind her eyes. It was like every bone in her face suddenly detonated.

Moaning and holding her jaw, Harriet leaned against a tree to keep from collapsing.

"This can't go on," she said, trying to speak without disturbing the tooth.

"Whatya mean?" whispered Benjamin.

"I gotta deal with this tooth right here and now. If the slave hunters come upon us, and we start runnin', I'll be screaming at every step, leadin' 'em right to us."

"You want one of us to pull it?" Henry asked.

"Oh, God," said Jane, turning away.

"It's gotta be done," said Harriet.

"I'll do it," said Benjamin. "I pulled a tooth or two in my day."

"No," said Harriet. "I'll do it myself. Give me a rock."

Benjamin and Henry stared at her in silence.

Eventually, Henry spoke up. "A rock? You're gonna *knock* it out with a rock?"

"Oh, God," said Jane again, walking off.

"It's gotta be done or I'll be makin' too much noise," said Harriet.

"But a rock? Why don't ya just yank it out?"

"I gotta loosen it up first."

Harriet knew that sometimes you have to go through a heap of pain, all in one fell swoop, to do away with a constant stream of smaller pains—although she wouldn't call the pains she was feeling "small" by any means.

"Just let me try pullin' it," said Henry. He started going for her mouth, trying to poke his dirty fingers inside. That sent Harriet reeling with pain, and she very nearly blacked out while she tried to fight him off.

Harriet held her chin in both of her hands and closed her eyes. Trickles of tears squeezed out from under her eyelids. Her entire jaw blazed.

"Sorry...sorry," said Henry, backing away.

She was terrified that her cry might have carried a mile. But it was further proof that this had to be dealt with now.

"Here's a rock," said Benjamin. "Will this do?"

Harriet took the offered stone in her hand. It was about the size of her fist. She jostled the rock, looking for a good striking surface. The rock had a few sharp edges, which wouldn't do. She wanted it to serve as a hammer, not a knife. But she eventually found a good, flat surface on the underside. She opened her mouth and felt around with her fingers for the suffering tooth. The tooth was on the left side, bottom row, but by now her mouth was so full of pain that it was difficult to trace the source—until she touched it. It was like someone put a torch to her teeth.

She moaned, head lowered, and waited for the pain to subside.

Benjamin and Henry stood on either side of her, and Benjamin rubbed her back soothingly, which she appreciated. She looked out the corner of her eyes and saw that Henry was praying. His lips were moving, mouthing silent words.

Harriet clenched her hand tightly around the rock. She had to do this quickly, without thinking, like jumping into a cold stream. So she brought the rock down on her tooth. It was like a gunpowder charge went off in her mouth. Pain everywhere, flashing through her entire head. She dropped the rock and fell to her knees, cupping her jaw with both hands. Something wet pooled in her mouth, and she spit. It was blood, naturally.

Tenderly, she ran her fingers across her teeth to see if the suffering tooth was loose enough to pull. It was a little loose, but not enough to yank. Breathing hard, she sat back down on the tree trunk, and Henry handed her the rock again.

She whacked the tooth again. She didn't stop to think about what she was doing. She hit the tooth again and again. One of the strikes went wide and slammed against a healthy tooth.

Dropping to her knees on the muddy, cold ground, she reached in and felt the tooth moving, like a tree stump holding on by just a few strong roots. In a fury, she hit the tooth one more time, tossed aside the rock, and reached into her mouth.

Then she yanked. She felt a searing, tearing sensation and a flash of red-hot pain, and she bowed down so low that her head rested against the ground. Her jaw throbbed, like a beating heart in her mouth. Tears streamed down her cheeks, and she began breathing and snorting like a wounded animal. She spit more blood.

Harriet was in so much pain that at first she didn't realize that both of her brothers had their arms wrapped around her. Even Jane, as afraid as she was of what was happening, had come to her side and had a hand on her shoulder.

For the first time in a long time, she didn't feel alone.

She wanted to savor it for as long as she could—to bask in their embrace. It had been a long time since anyone had put their arms around her. But she knew they needed to get moving, so she straightened up, took a deep breath, and unfolded her clenched right hand. Nestled in her palm, like an oyster's pearl, was her tooth. Her hand was sticky with her own blood.

Harriet slipped the tooth into her pocket, to keep as a reminder of what it meant to suffer, and then she rose to her feet.

"If we got pursuers, they mighta heard my screamin'. We better move."

They resumed their flight, and for a little time, Henry and Benjamin kept their arms linked in hers, one on either side. She liked that, but as the forest thickened, they could no longer walk arm in arm, so they split apart and walked two abreast through the forest.

Her jaw throbbed, but the worst of the pain was clean gone.

39

Horatio Jones watched everything from up on the front porch of the Big House. The cold rain had returned by the time Nehemiah had all of the slaves rounded up and standing in a ragged line in front of the house. The pungent smell of burnt wood wafted over them, carried on a slight breeze from the slave cabins. Jones had hoped to line up his slaves indoors so he could get out of the cold and the rain. But he thought it best to stay as far as possible from his wife, who was furious that he had decided to celebrate Christmas by torching a cabin. So he found a dry spot in the rocker on the front porch, and he watched and waited for his overseers to do the head count.

Nehemiah went down the line, counting out the twenty-seven slaves. He pointed at the slaves, one by one, and counted on his fingers. After he finished the first count, he and another overseer, Cooper, consulted together. Then Cooper also went down the line, pointing at each slave and counting out loud.

"Whatja get?" Nehemiah asked.

"Twenty-six," said Cooper.

When Jones heard Cooper's final tally, he jumped to his feet. "How many did you get?" he asked Nehemiah.

"Twenty-six, sir."

So one of the slaves had run after all. Nehemiah said it was a man he saw slipping off into the woods, so Jones told the overseers to count the men. "See who's gone."

Frustrated that his Christmas did not look like it was going to be peaceful in the least, Jones came down from the porch and into the drizzle. As he approached, the overseers had the men step forward. Cooper held up the lantern as he and Nehemiah went down the row, looking into the faces of each and every male slave. Most of the men glared straight ahead, oblivious to the rain dripping down from their hair, streaking across their faces.

When Nehemiah and Cooper had finished the count of males, Nehemiah capped it off with a curse. Then he scratched the back of his head. "Don't rightly know who's gone. They're all here, I think."

"Check again."

This time, Jones hovered behind Nehemiah and Cooper as they progressed down the line, holding up a light to the faces of each male slave. As Jones called out the name of each one, he kept track of the numbers on his fingers. There should be twelve men, and when they reached the end of the line, his count said twelve.

"I thought you said the one who run was a man," said Jones.

"It sure looked like a man to me," said Nehemiah. "Britches and all."

This time, Jones had the women step forward. There should be fifteen of them, children included. Once again, the count was made, and Jones stared into the face of each and every woman and girl.

Fourteen. One gone.

Like a door swinging open in his head, it suddenly dawned on Jones which one was missing. He cursed himself because he should have seen it coming.

"Where's Jane?" he asked.

When he received no answer, he charged toward Prudence, who stood staring at the ground near the end of the line.

"Where's Jane?" he demanded.

"The last I knew she was at the cabin, sir. Calvin and I went to the

Big House to work, and she was in the cabin. I sure hope she weren't in the cabin when it went up in flames."

That couldn't be. Jones was sure he had checked every inch of the cabin. There had been no sign of her. But it was dark. Could he have possibly missed her hiding in a corner? But even if he had failed to spot her, surely she would have run out of the cabin when the fire started—unless she preferred death over what he had planned for her this night. Or maybe the smoke fumes overwhelmed her before she had a chance to flee.

On the other hand, maybe Nehemiah, the fool, was mistaken. Maybe the slave he saw disappear into the woods was a woman, not a man.

Snatching the lantern from Cooper, he decided to go back to the cabin and search the rubble for any signs of bones or burnt flesh.

"You get the dogs," he snapped at Nehemiah, "while I check the burnt-out cabin."

"You think the She-Moses swooped down and took her?" asked Cooper. Jones hated hearing the hint of awe in the overseer's voice.

"You mean Harriet Tubman?" Jones said. "Use her name! And if you call her Moses again, I'll have you thrashed."

"Sorry, sir," said Cooper, diverting his eyes. Jones felt the power of his authority, and he smiled at the man's reflexive subservience.

"But you might be right. It could be Tubman. We need to track them down! Nehemiah, why aren't you getting those damned dogs?"

Nehemiah, who had been standing there listening to the theories, took off running.

Then Jones wheeled back in Cooper's direction. "If Jane's gone, she was probably aided by Harriet's brother, Benjamin. But whether it was Benjamin or Harriet doing the snatchin', they might be headin' for the house of Ben and Rit Ross up near the Thompson land. When Nehemiah comes with the dogs, y'all head north toward their cabin."

"Yes, sir, but..." Cooper began.

"Out with it, damn you! If you got your words stuck in your throat, I'll cut them out of you!"

"I don't rightly know the proper way to their cabin," Cooper said.

"Especially in the dark."

"I can help with that," another voice said in the darkness.

A figure stepped into the meager light being shed from the cabin windows. It was a black man—John Tubman, Harriet's former husband, of all people.

"Where'd you come from?" Jones demanded.

"Just passing by when I saw the fire, sir."

"You can help?"

"I can. I'll lead you right to 'em."

...

Harriet, Henry, and Benjamin made steady progress, aiming to reach their parents' cabin in Poplar Creek before sunrise. Harriet's tongue kept darting to the vacant spot once occupied by her aching tooth, and she praised God Almighty that the pain was gone, though she was still spitting out blood. They followed the Choptank River east from Cambridge and kept the water to their left as the river arced north, pointing them to Poplar Neck.

Harriet carried a walking stick, the same one she had used when she strolled off of Dr. Thompson's property five years earlier. *Thy rod and thy staff comfort me, even in the valley of the shadow of death. I will fear no evil.* Her staff truly was a comfort, carrying her through the valley of dark night, directing her, protecting her.

"I'm tired," Jane said. She and Benjamin brought up the rear. Harriet had noticed some time ago that she was slowing down.

"Can't stop now," said Harriet. "Got a long way to trudge."

"How long?"

"Hours. Be grateful y'all wearin' britches. Wish I had me a pair. It'd make this hike a whole lot easier."

Her long, heavy, brown skirt was annoying, especially when crossing streams waist deep, but at least she had on a sturdy new pair of shoes, thanks to Mister Garrett.

Harriet suddenly put up a right hand, and the small group stopped dead still. She crouched low, and so did the others.

"Whadya see?" whispered Henry.

"You see that cabin over yonder?"

Henry and Benjamin both rose up a little higher and peered straight ahead.

"Where?" whispered Benjamin.

Harriet was astounded that they couldn't make out the black traces of a cabin among the trees.

"Trust me, it's there," she said. "We gotta skirt around it. Follow me."

A cabin in the woods meant there were white men in the area. The cabin showed no sign of light and was barely discernable in the thick forest; it had a lonely, abandoned look, but it was dangerous to assume it was deserted. Harriet decided to make a wide loop around the east side of the cabin. But as they did, Jane stepped on a brittle branch, and it snapped, like the crack of a gun.

Harriet put a finger to her lips to tell her to be quiet, and Jane looked horrified.

"It's all right," whispered Benjamin. Harriet flung her hand back, whacking her brother in the arm to tell him to be quiet.

A few minutes later, it seemed they had been discovered. Harriet heard movement coming from behind them—multiple cracks and crunches. Whoever was coming toward them wasn't even trying to disguise their approach.

Harriet quickened the pace, and Jane began to whimper softly. Harriet gave Jane a warning glare to quiet down, but in the dark the woman probably couldn't see the fierceness in her face.

Soon, they heard another series of cracks, but now it was coming from in front of them, not from behind. Harriet made a sharp turn right, moved east a spell, and then motioned everyone to a halt. They all crouched low behind a thicket of evergreens, the smell of needles enveloping them.

A lantern light appeared in the distance, moving through the woods, circling them and searching. Then came moving shadows, two of them, weaving back and forth, and twigs cracking underfoot. Most remarkable of all, a voice began to sing softly.

"Sister Rosy, you get to heaven before I go.
Sister, you look out for me, I'm on the way.
Travel on, travel on, you heaven-born soldier.
Travel on, travel on, go hear what my Jesus say."

Harriet stood up and pushed aside the evergreen branches, emerging from the trees and beaming bright. There, standing before her, were two black men, fellow passengers hoping to hop onto her freedom train. Henry, Benjamin, and Jane also left their hiding spot, moving out from behind the trees into the small circle of light.

The two men were silhouettes behind the lantern light. One of the men held the lantern at full arm's length so they could get a good look at Harriet and the others. This man was as tall as Benjamin, the other much shorter.

"You must be the She-Moses," said the tall man.

"How'd you know we would be passin' by?" asked Harriet.

"Word gets around."

"We been out here all night, huntin' for y'all," said the other. "It's a miracle we found you."

"You aimin' to go north with us?" asked Harriet.

"If y'all will take us," said the tall man.

"There's always room aboard. Douse your lights, and we'll be on our way."

"Where you escaping from?" asked Benjamin, but Harriet waved him off with a flutter of her hand.

"Ain't got time for introductions, and we need to keep our tongues silent," she snapped. "We gotta get to Mama and Papa's before mornin' light, and then y'all can chat like schoolgirls."

For some reason, the short man found this amusing. He let out a little bark of laughter.

"No laughing neither," snapped Harriet.

"Yes, Moses."

"Sssshhh! Let's get a goin'."

Then the two men stepped into line as the group continued north, now six strong.

...

Robert spent the entire birth pacing in front of their cabin, listening to the sound of suffering. Sometimes, he'd wander a little farther off to get out of earshot of Mary's shouting, but it didn't work. The sound pursued him. The light, steady rain had soaked him to the bones, but he wasn't about to enter the cabin for shelter; nothing on earth would get him inside there while Mary was hollering.

There were brief pauses in the screaming, but during the final push, the shouting was constant. And when the noise abruptly ended, he wondered if his wife or the baby had died. Life or death: One or the other had won out.

Finally, he heard a cry, but not from Mary. Robert moved closer to the cabin door, but he didn't dare enter. Not yet at least. He heard another muffled cry. Definitely a baby. But what about his wife?

As he leaned in closer, the front door suddenly swung open; he tried to pull back, but it whacked him in the side of the head, stinging him in the ear.

"What you doin' blockin' up this doorway?" said the midwife, Lydia.

Robert massaged the side of his head, trying to rub away the pain. "Mary and the baby...are they all right?"

"C'mon in. See for yourself."

Soaked to the skin, Robert cautiously entered and found Mary propped up on the pallet, lit by a candle. She had a new life in her arms.

"It's a girl," said Mary, beaming.

Their first girl.

Robert moved tentatively across the room. He sensed that every step toward his family was a step away from Harriet, Benjamin, Henry, and freedom. How on earth would he be able to catch up with them by this point? His siblings were long gone, probably halfway to Mama and Papa's house. He said he would join them later, but he was no longer sure.

"She's a bit of a mess, ain't she?" said Robert, staring down on the baby girl, who was bloody and slick with moisture.

"You're the one who looks a mess," Mary said. "Dripping all over."

True. He was as soaked as the baby.

"Sorry." Robert crouched on the floor next to the pallet, while the midwife moved about, gathering up a couple of bloody rags and taking them out of the cabin. "How're you feelin'?"

"Tired, but happy. Ain't you happy? You don't look it."

He wasn't. He had finally made the decision to leave with Harriet to go north, and then this happened. He was cold and weary and afraid of the forces that were hurtling down on him. In just two days, he would go up for auction. He felt like he was trying to get out of the way of a roaring locomotive but his foot was stuck under a railroad tie, and the train was bearing down on him, whistle blowing.

"I'm just tired. But not half as tired as you must be after givin' us this beautiful baby."

Mary smiled and said nothing. As she stared at the baby (they hadn't come up with a name yet), her eyelids began to droop. Pretty soon, Mary's mouth slightly parted, and she breathed heavily. When she seemed to be asleep, Robert rose to his feet, thinking this might be his best chance to slip away and rejoin Benjamin, Henry, and Harriet. He could just disappear and send word back to her when he was safe.

But as he took a couple of steps toward the door, he was stopped by Mary's voice. "Where y'all goin', Robert?"

He turned. Smiled.

"Nowhere. Just thought I'd clean up some of the mess in the room."

"Since when you worried about messes?" Her words came out slurred, half-formed.

Robert returned to his spot on the floor, by her pallet.

"I'm right here."

But she was already asleep again. This time, her heavy breathing became light snoring, and the baby in her arms was also asleep. He waited to make sure the snoring didn't let up, and then he slowly rose to his feet and tiptoed toward the door.

"Where you think you're off to?"

Mary must have the sensory skills of a bat, able to detect movement in the pitch dark, even when she was asleep.

Robert slunk back to her bedside.

"I was gonna head to the Big House and see if I can get hired out by someone needin' work."

"But it's Christmas Day tomorrow!"

"People need extra help on Christmas, and we could use the extra money from me bein' hired out. Especially now that we got another mouth to feed."

Mary stared at him in silence. He was afraid she could see straight into his skull and know what he was really thinking—that this might be his last chance to escape. Maryland was close to the freedom states, but if he got sold south, it would be an impossible distance. Come Tuesday, if the auction went as he feared, Mary would be losing a husband, and his children would be losing a father. The only way to save his family was to save himself and get them out later.

But he couldn't say any of this to Mary. She might think him a coward, running off when they needed him most.

The baby woke up and suckled, and then she dropped off to sleep on her mother's breast. Soon after, Mary followed the baby into sleep —yet again. This time, Robert waited a good long time before he made his move. This time, when he got up, Mary didn't wake. Neither did the baby. This time, when he walked to the door, they slept on. Carefully, he turned the handle and heard it softly click. He looked back to see if either his wife or the baby had awakened. Seeing that they both still rested peacefully, he slipped out into the night.

The drizzle had stopped, but a slight breeze cut through his soggy clothes. And then he heard crying, but not from the baby. It was Mary, sobbing.

Robert didn't hesitate. He rushed back into the cabin, and he returned to her side, offering no explanation for why he was outside.

Mary looked at him directly. "You're leavin' us, ain't you?"

Robert started to offer up another excuse, another lie. But he was sick of falsehoods piling up.

"I gotta run. I'm bein' sold on Tuesday."

Sobbing even harder, Mary shook her head. Eventually, she managed to stutter out a few words. "Stay. I don't think Miss Eliza will sell you far, if she sells you at all. She's said she was gonna sell you before, and she never did."

"This time it's real."

"How do you know?"

"Harriet said it was."

"Harriet?"

"She come down to get us. The Lord sent her."

"Since when do you believe her visions from God?"

Robert shrugged. "She's right a lot of the time. Besides, if I get free, I'll come back for you and the children. I promise you that."

Mary began to cry again, chest heaving. Robert just sat there and said nothing, like waiting out a storm. When Mary finally settled down, she ran her hands across the back of their newborn's head.

"Go," she finally said.

Robert wasn't sure he heard right.

"Go, I said."

"You sure?"

"Course I'm not sure. Who's sure about anything?"

She looked up at him, her face half in shadow. The candle was almost burned out, but enough light shone to see part of her face, like a half moon. Robert leaned down and kissed her on the forehead, because he didn't think she would accept a full kiss. Then he gently kissed the top of his little girl's head.

"Pick a good name," he said.

"How 'bout Harriet?"

Robert smiled. "Harriet's a good name."

Mary looked down at the baby, and she wiped away a tear as it made a trail across her cheek. Then she looked back up at Robert and said one final, "Go"—one last permission to run.

So Robert did. Before he knew it, he was outside, running like a man being chased by every demon in the dark.

40

Poplar Neck, Maryland
Christmas Morning 1854

I t was still dark when they reached their parents' cabin. The cold
rain had fallen on and off throughout the night, sometimes heavily, and the six runaways were frozen wet. On the way, they had
learned the names of the two men who joined their band of fugitives
—John Chase and Peter Jackson. They also learned that both men had
escaped from the Cambridge area.

The sky had cleared of cloud cover, and moonlight shone down on
the family's corncrib, a small, squat, gray building. The corncrib was
narrow at the bottom but widened as it rose from the ground. Their
father had painted a white cross on the front because Papa always
thought their corn would get extra protection against thieves if they
kept Jesus in clear view. The corncrib stood within sight of their
parents' cabin, which lay just down a gentle slope.

"We gotta stay hidden all day, then start movin' again come
night," Harriet reminded them. She turned toward Jackson and
Chase and added, "That means we also gotta stay outta sight of our
Mama."

"You jokin'?" asked Jackson. "Why ain't you greetin' your Mama on Christmas?"

"'Cause she ain't to know about us. If she knew we were escapin', she'd try to stop us."

One by one, with Harriet leading, they crawled into the cramped confines of the corncrib. They clambered up a heaping pile of corn, which filled the crib about a quarter full. There, they found some biscuits and butter, wrapped up in a basket—provisions left by Papa. Benjamin went to work distributing the food. Henry didn't even wait to butter the bread before ripping into it.

Soon, morning broke, and the sun began to send yellow shafts of light into the eastern sky. Outside the corncrib, the world was still dripping with rainwater, but the roof was watertight. The slats that made up the walls had thin gaps between them, allowing them to see what was happening at Mama and Papa's cabin. They couldn't see the Christmas pig roasting on the spit, but they could sure smell the heavenly scent. My, Harriet was hungry.

About an hour passed before they spotted movement. It was Mama, stepping out of the cabin. At first, Harriet was sure that Papa must've told her about their presence. But Mama walked right on past the corncrib, without even giving it so much as a sidelong glance.

"You sure you don't wanna greet your Mama?" asked Jackson.

"Hush," hissed Harriet.

Mama hobbled down the narrow road leading off of their property, and peeked around a bend. She was looking for them, expecting the brothers for Christmas dinner, as always. Mama looked so forlorn, staring off into the distance. It had been five years since Harriet had seen Mama, and she wished with all her might that she could slip from the corncrib and fold into her arms. She ached for physical comfort.

Eventually, Mama turned around, with the saddest look on her face, and she trudged back to the cabin. For a second, her head turned in the direction of the corncrib, and Harriet drew back from the slats. But Mama just kept on trudging, past the corncrib, down the slope, and back to the cabin.

Harriet felt the urge to stretch out on the corn and drift away because daylight was their only chance to sleep. But it seemed as if she had closed her eyes for only a moment when Benjamin nudged her in the side.

"Papa's comin'," said Benjamin.

Sitting up, Harriet wondered how long she had fallen asleep. Her mouth felt gummy as she leaned forward and peered through the gaps between the slats.

"What in the world is your Papa doin'?" said Jackson.

What in the world was right. Papa was approaching, but he was walking *backward* toward the corncrib. Occasionally, he would glance over his shoulder to gauge his direction, but he walked all the way to the corncrib backward.

"You have one strange family," said Chase.

"Won't deny it," said Harriet.

"Papa, why you walkin' backward?" Henry whispered through the slats.

Papa still wouldn't turn to face them. "'Cause I don't want to lay eyes on y'all. If I don't see you, I can tell the truth when I tell folks I ain't seen my children."

"But why—?" Chase started to say, but Harriet cut him off.

"Papa's got this thing 'bout tellin' the truth."

"I'm leavin' y'all some pork and more biscuits." Then Papa scooted backward a little closer and laid a basket on the ground, not far from the corncrib entrance. "I'll bring more shortly. Y'all be silent now. Your Mama don't suspect nothing, so keep it that way."

"Is Mama's still expectin' us for Christmas dinner?" asked Henry.

"Course she is. But you keep out of sight. We can't have her gettin' upset."

"We will, Papa," said Harriet.

"Fine, fine."

Then Papa strode off, walking forward this time, back to the cabin. Harriet watched him go as the light streamed through the slats, painting the inside of the corncrib with striped shadows.

They would eat, sleep, and wait for dark. Then it was north. Always north.

...

John Tubman crouched at the edge of the forest, peering out on a lone cabin. Nehemiah and Cooper, the two overseers, flanked him on either side. Meanwhile one of the two dogs took care of nature's call in a nearby bush. The second dog strained at the end of its leash.

"There it is," said John. "The cabin of Ben and Rit Ross."

"Don't see nobody nowhere," said Cooper.

"Maybe they's all hidin' inside," said John.

"Could be."

"Let's take a looksee, but be quiet about it," said Nehemiah.

The three men and two dogs emerged from the forest and into the sun-drenched clearing. The sun had finally come out after a night of persistent drizzle, and the drying powers of the light felt good. Judging from the position of the sun, it looked to be close to midday on Christmas Day.

"You stay back," Nehemiah told John, and he was happy to oblige. There was no telling if bullets were going to start flying.

Both Nehemiah and Cooper had their pistols drawn by the time they reached the cabin. The windows had been shuttered, to keep out the winter cold, so they went to the door, where Cooper tested the handle. The doorknob turned, and he threw open the door. Then he craned his head around the door and peered into the cabin before entering.. Nehemiah followed right behind.

John crouched on his haunches and waited for the sounds of arguing. Nothing. No shouting. No breaking furniture. No gunshots.

It wasn't long before the two overseers were back outside and heading in John's direction. John's mouth had gone cotton dry with anticipation and fear. Did the men know? Had they figured it out? Were they going to put a bullet in his head and be done with him?

"They ain't here," said Nehemiah, walking right past John, without batting an eye.

"Did the place seem occupied?" John asked.

Nehemiah came up short and turned toward John. "Of course it looked occupied. Why wouldn't it be?"

"Just askin'. Ben and Rit Ross sometimes work on other Thompson property, so I wondered if they might be there."

Nehemiah shrugged. "The fireplace still gave out a bit of heat from the ashes. So somebody's been there recently."

John nodded, afraid to say anything that might trigger suspicion. Then they all slunk back into the forest, where they would wait for Rit and Old Ben. John hadn't prayed in a long spell, but he prayed now. He prayed that whoever lived in this cabin would stay away for the rest of the day. He also prayed that if the people in this cabin did return, Nehemiah and Cooper wouldn't whip him for leading them to the wrong place. But most of all, he prayed they would believe him when he said he had made an honest mistake taking them here.

The truth of the matter was that cabin they looked out upon was a good deal east of where Rit and Ben lived. John had no idea who actually lived in this cabin, but he was grateful to God they had found the place empty.

If John wound up being whipped for leading the overseers on a wild goose chase, he would take it like a man. Just as long as Harriet was long gone by the time they discovered they were at the wrong place. Then it would all be worth it.

•••

This time, when Harriet was nudged awake, she knew she had slept a long spell. But when she opened her bleary eyes, she was shocked to see that it was Robert who had done the nudging.

"Robert!" she exclaimed, breaking into a smile and giving her third brother a hug. "Y'all made it."

"You probably never thought I'd come," he said.

That's right, I didn't, Harriet thought. But she had the good sense not to speak it. "You're here," is all she said. "And Mary...?"

"She gave birth last night to a baby girl."

Another twinge of jealousy hit Harriet. Mary already had two young ones, and Harriet was as barren as an empty cupboard. But she managed a smile for Robert's sake.

"We named her Harriet," he said.

This time, Harriet's smile was for real. She beamed. "We'll come back for Mary and the children," she reassured him. "Mark my words. We'll be back."

"Thank you, Harriet."

"Robert made it here 'bout an hour ago," Benjamin said. "But we thought we'd let you sleep."

"Did you warn him to stay outta sight of Mama and Papa?" she asked.

"We did."

Jackson shook his head and smiled to himself. "Strangest family I ever seen."

41

John Tubman thanked the Lord Almighty that the cabin was deserted. Whoever lived there did not return until just before darkness fell. Two figures emerged from the woods, one of them carrying a dead deer over his shoulders. Both of them were white men —a father and son, from the looks of it.

Nehemiah and Cooper simultaneously turned their eyes on John. "Do either of those men look like Ben Ross to you?" Nehemiah snapped.

"I don't understand, sir. Maybe Ben and Rit moved off somewhere else. I coulda sworn this was their house."

"You playin' us for fools?" asked Cooper.

"No, sir. I thought this was Ben and Rit's place. Looks just like it."

"It's a cabin, you fool," said Nehemiah. "Cabins have a way of lookin' all the same."

"Sorry, sir."

"You're gonna be even sorrier."

"But maybe Ben and Rit used to live here. Just ask the men."

"We intend to. And then we'll deal with you."

Nehemiah and Cooper left the cover of the woods. As they stepped into the clearing, the father and son looked up sharply from their work. The father heaved the bloody deer onto the ground, and he reached for his rifle. Nehemiah held up his hands to show he meant no harm.

Meanwhile, John remained at the edge of the woods, watching all of this unfold and wondering if he should just turn and run. Nehemiah and Cooper had their backs to him, and all of their attention was focused on the rifle the stranger aimed in their direction. There wouldn't be a better chance to run than this. He didn't need to wait around to find out what Nehemiah and Cooper might do to him for leading them on a wild goose chase. He took one step backward, trying not to make a sound. A second step, a third step, and a fourth step backward, and then he turned and slipped off into the darkness of the forest.

At first, he moved slowly and silently. But when he heard Nehemiah let loose with a curse, it was like a gunshot went off in John's mind, and he started running full steam ahead. He headed south, tearing through the forest. He dodged stones and jumped over ditches as if his body anticipated every obstacle well before he reached it. As he fled, John perked his ears for any sounds of overseers pursuing him, but he was making such a racket, crashing through underbrush, that he couldn't tell if they were coming after him or not. If they did chase after him, that would only help Harriet and her brothers, because John intended to lead them in the opposite direction of where Harriet was headed. He would give her all the time in the world to get away.

John had never felt so free as he did at that moment; his legs moved faster than they had in years. He almost felt like he was in one of Harriet's dreams, the one in which she dreamed she was flying high, winging her way north. There was no way that Nehemiah and Cooper would be able to catch him today.

But would they catch him tomorrow? And what would they do to him then? He decided he would worry about tomorrow when it came. Today, he was free as a bird.

■■■

Harriet woke to the powerful smell of roast pig as she emerged from a long, hard sleep. She had gone back to sleep, trying to snag as much rest as possible before the next leg of their journey. Her back ached from snoozing on corncobs that dug into her side, but the scent of food more than made up for the pain.

Benjamin and Robert were already awake, but the others were still out like a light.

"Evenin', sister," said Benjamin.

"Evenin.' How long did we sleep, you think?"

"Don't know, but I been awake nearly an hour."

"And Mama?"

"She's come out to the road lookin' for us twice just in the last hour. No tellin' how many times she came out here lookin'."

Darkness was fast approaching. Soon they would be gone, and Harriet would no longer have to fight the temptation to greet Mama. As the shadows lengthened across the field, they heard another slam of the cabin door, and there was Mama trudging, trudging, trudging. Mama puffed on her pipe and stared at her feet, as if she were afraid to look up and be disappointed again. But she eventually raised her head to stare down the road. Then it was a dismal slog back to the cabin, Mama looking so mournful that Harriet almost busted out crying.

"Why don't y'all just say hello?" Jane said. "It's killin' me watchin' her like that."

"It's killin' us too," said Benjamin.

"Then just greet her, tell her you're fine."

"But we ain't fine, and we won't be fine till we're free," said Henry.

"We can't let her know we're here," Harriet said. "It's as simple as all that." She tried to put all of her force behind her words so Jane would stop tempting them. "Mama can't keep a secret if her life depended on it. She'll talk and talk, and she'll let out that she saw us. And then the wrath of the white world will fall on her and Papa."

It was certainly an odd predicament. They had a Papa who would not lie and a Mama who would lie like the blue blazes for her children. But Mama might give away the truth through the constant flow of her reckless words.

Papa brought out more roast pork, walking backward to the corn-crib, of course. Mama had outdone herself with this Christmas feast. Pork, red peas, sweet potatoes, black coffee, and hunks of steaming hot bread. They knew they had to be quiet, but it was tough containing all of the sighs and gasps over the hearty meal.

Finally, darkness came down like a black veil. Papa came out one last time, carrying several sacks of food supplies for the road. But this time, instead of walking backward, he came cautiously toward them with a *blindfold* over his eyes.

"That's close enough," Harriet called through the slats, afraid their blindfolded father was going to walk straight into the side of the corncrib.

Papa set down the sacks and then called out softly. "Y'all can come out now. I'm as blind as a bat. I can't see ya."

"What 'bout Mama?" Harriet whispered from the corncrib.

"Don't y'all worry, she's asleep in her rocker. She's bone weary from worryin' 'bout y'all."

Tentatively, the six corncrib occupants crawled out of the small structure and approached Papa, who cocked his head like a bird, listening to their movements.

"I wanna walk a ways with my children," he said. "I figured I could do that if I was blindfolded."

"Understood," said Benjamin. He took his father by the right arm and carefully turned him around.

"I can hear your voices, and that's all I need to make me happy," he said.

"Is the blindfold tight, Papa?" asked Robert.

"I know how to tie a strong knot. Y'all should know that 'bout me."

That was true. Papa's knots were as true as his words. They were strong and firm and couldn't be pulled apart. With Henry holding one arm and Benjamin taking the other, Old Ben walked among his children as they passed noiselessly past the cabin.

"From what I'm hearin', there seems to be a whole lot more of you than I thought," Papa said.

"Two men joined us on the way," said Benjamin.

"We thank you, sir, for the food," whispered Peter Jackson.

"Hope there was enough for the extra mouths."

"There was plenty, sir," said John Chase.

"Mind if we take one last look at Mama?" asked Benjamin.

"Have at it, boys. No tellin' when you'll see her again."

"You sure she's asleep?" Harriet asked. After spending an entire day cooped up in a corncrib, just to stay out of sight of their parents, she didn't want to be spotted by Mama at their moment of departure.

"You know your Mama," said Papa. "When she's down, she's down cold. She won't wake for hours."

Benjamin quickly slipped up to the window and peeped inside the cabin. "She's sleepin'."

Then, one by one, like mourners paying respects to the deceased, they went up to the window and peeked inside. Even Jane, Jackson, and Chase passed by the window, casting glances at Mama. Chase made the sign of the cross as he did.

When Harriet took her turn—the last one to go—she saw Mama sitting in her rocker by the fireside. It was just as she had seen her almost every evening of her childhood. Every night, the rocker would be creaking, and Mama would be puffing away on her pipe, lost in thought and occasionally smacking her lips and sighing. She would rock and puff and sigh and smack until she drifted off to sleep, her pipe dropping out of her hand. It's a wonder she never set herself aflame falling asleep that way. Harriet always knew the exact moment that Mama dozed off—when the rocker would come to a rest, and she could no longer hear the creak-creak of moving wood. The sound of the rocker was like Mama's heartbeat, and when it finally stopped, she was dead to the world. Sometimes, Mama would sleep the entire night in that rocker, but she would wake up in the morning with new life, like Lazarus shaking off his grave clothes and bounding into a new day.

When Mama was young, she had incredible energy, but Harriet

was struck by how small and frail she now looked. Mama seemed worn down, like the broken-down shoes Harriet repaired with string, as the sides split and holes appeared on the underside.

Mama was coming apart, held together by prayer. But just as Mister Garrett was sure to give Harriet a brand-new pair of walking shoes, Harriet was sure the Good Lord was going to someday give Mama a brand-new body, strong as youth.

Harriet's eyes burned with tears, and she wiped them away with the sleeve of her jacket before any of the drops could streak across her dust-covered cheek. Her throat felt locked up, and she sensed a mounting sadness fall over her shoulders like a mourning shawl. She also felt her brother's hands gentle on her shoulders, and she felt the comfort of family. It was Benjamin's hands.

Everyone was quiet until their father said, "Y'all best be on the road while you have the night to hide you."

"Yes, Papa."

So they left the cabin, and they left Mama, and they moved along a narrow path leading into the woods. Benjamin continued to steer Papa, holding on to his right elbow.

"I been fastin' for you all day," Papa said.

"Thank you, Papa."

He always fasted every Sunday, as long as Harriet could remember, but it was now Monday—Christmas Day—and he had fasted for a second straight day! Harriet was amazed by his ability to resist roast pork on a day like this. He was one determined man.

"Y'all take care of yourselves," Papa said. "I love each and every one of you."

"I love you too, Papa," said Harriet. She tumbled into his arms, weeping uncontrollably. What was the matter with her?

"Careful now. Don't want to knock off my blindfold."

"Yes, Papa," Harriet tried to say, but the words caught in her throat.

With Papa spending most of his life on a different plantation, she never had much chance to fall into his arms as a little girl. His embrace was like a big bear's—warm and strong.

"The Lord lead your feet in a straight path," he said, before turning around and placing his back to his children. Carefully, he reached behind his head and picked apart the knot he had tied, and the blindfold fell from his eyes.

Harriet watched him wander back down the path with a slight limp, and she wondered if he might cheat a little and look over his shoulder and take a peek—just a peek—at his departing children. But he never looked back. He couldn't. Not if he wanted to tell white folks, in all honesty, that he never saw his children.

Once more, Papa called out and said he loved them, and then Harriet and the others moved forward into the forest. As the path made a loop to the left and they tramped far from the sight and smells of home, Harriet nearly crumbled under the weight of her sorrows. It was good thing she still had her walking stick to keep her upright.

42

B en Ross knew they would eventually come. But he was relieved it wasn't a slave catcher. Dr. A.C. Thompson showed up on Tuesday, the day after Christmas, while Ben was stacking wood outside the cabin.

"Mornin' Ben," said Dr. Thompson, leaning forward on his saddle. He didn't dismount from the horse, but stayed up high in the saddle. If he had dismounted, he would have stood a head shorter than Ben Ross, and he wouldn't like that.

"Mornin', Dr. Thompson! What brings you out this day?"

"Your sons do."

Ben set aside his ax and wiped his forehead with a handkerchief, giving himself time to think. "I thought my sons was bein' sold away today."

"So did John Brodess and his mother, Miss Eliza. They thought they were sellin' your sons, but Robert, Henry, and Benjamin weren't anywhere to be found."

"That's very strange. They never had the gumption to run before."

"That's true. But this time they might've. You know anything about this, Ben?"

This was the question that Ben had been preparing for ever since his children arrived on his property and hid in the corncrib. He took off his hat and tried to speak in the most confident tone of voice.

"I haven't laid eyes on my children for goin' on a coupla months," he said.

"You didn't see them pass through here on the way north?"

"No, sir. I never saw them."

"What about Harriet? There's word going around that she came south to get your sons."

"I ain't laid eyes on Harriet neither. Not for a long, long time."

"What about Rit? Has she seen your children?"

"I'll fetch her."

Ben disappeared into the cabin and told his wife that Dr. Thompson had come, looking for Robert, Henry, and Benjamin. She flew out of the cabin.

"Do you know their whereabouts? I been lookin' for them!" she shouted to Dr. Thompson, rushing toward his horse.

"I thought they usually spent Christmas Day with you," he said.

"I thought so too, and I cooked me a whole hog for the feast. But they never showed!"

Rit was a poor actress, and if she had tried to lie, she would have given it all away. But this was no act. She was truly heartbroken, and Ben had no doubt Dr. Thompson could hear it in every word.

"We're sorry we can't help you any more than that, Dr. Thompson," said Ben. "But we ain't seen them."

Dr. Thompson tipped his hat. "Thank you, Rit. Thank you, Ben. If I discover their whereabouts, I'll be sure to let you know."

"Thank you, sir," said Ben, bowing before the man.

So Thompson rode off, completely convinced as far as Ben could tell. After all, Thompson knew that he would never lie to his face. His word was gold.

···

By this time, Harriet could map the route north in her sleep.

She led them northeast from Poplar Neck and passed by Denton just before they crossed into Delaware. Then they skirted a string of towns—Sandtown, Camden, Dover, Smyrna, Blackbird, Odessa, and New Castle—before arriving in Wilmington. There, they were greeted by her old friend, Thomas Garrett.

Garrett replenished their supplies and then sent them on their way; they were now only about ten miles from the Pennsylvania border. The brothers had never been so close to freedom before. But several miles later, Harriet sat down to rest—a big mistake. She was so dog tired that she should have known she would be overcome by sleep the moment she sat down. She tumbled into a terrible dream about a monstrous snake with the head of an old man. He had a long, white beard, and he kept trying to talk to her, but no words would come out. Then the snake sprouted two other heads, younger heads, and a pack of soldiers attacked the serpent, striking down the younger heads.

Harriet woke up being shaken by Benjamin.

"Harriet! Y'all are havin' a terror dream."

"When you started shoutin' somethin' 'bout a snake, we thought it best to rouse you," said Henry.

Harriet stared around at the others, feeling uncharacteristically embarrassed to have been observed sleeping and dreaming and mumbling in her sleep. Fuzzyheaded, she checked out her surroundings. She was sitting with her back against a rock. The others had gathered in a semi-circle around her, like they were gathered around her deathbed.

"We thought it time to be makin' the final push to Pennsylvania," said Peter Jackson. "Only a few miles away. Don't want nothin' happenin' this close to freedom."

"You're right. I shoulda known I'd fall asleep if I sat down," she admitted. "Let's get a move on." Benjamin and Jane helped Harriet to her feet. She shook the twigs from her dress and took off marching with a surge of new energy. The others had to jog to catch up.

Harriet led them toward Kennett Square, just over the Pennsylvania border—a place swarming with Quakers and other abolitionists. Soon, a house came into view. It was a sturdy stone structure, two stories high with five fine windows all across the front. The Agnew house.

Using her walking stick, Harriet rapped on the front door. It was answered almost right away by Allen Agnew, a serious-looking man with a long, narrow face and high forehead. His modest sidewhiskers were speckled with gray. Harriet pulled out a note that Thomas Garrett had written out for Mister Agnew, and then marched right inside the house before the man even had a chance to read the message. Harriet couldn't read, but she knew the note said that Garrett was sending him "six bales of black wool." The message assured Agnew that he had sent these slaves; they were not sent by some crafty slave catcher hoping to lure them into a trap.

Mister Agnew led them up a ladder and into a loft, which took them down another ladder into a square room—a secret room built between a large fireplace on one side and the west wall of the carriage house on the other. The room had no doors in or out, just a ladder leading up to the loft.

"We have provided thee with food and blankets," said Mister Agnew when they were all squared away. "Rest up. Tomorrow, it's on to Philadelphia and William Still's Anti-Slavery office."

After showering him with their thanks, all six of them bid Mister Agnew good night, and he disappeared back up the ladder.

"We done it," said Benjamin. Somewhere along those final five miles, they had crossed an invisible line separating slave from free.

"We finally done it," said Henry.

After all of the false starts and failed attempts, the brothers had reached the North.

Only Robert looked like his feelings were all jumbled. Harriet could tell he was trying to smile, but the smile kept slipping away like it couldn't stay in place. She knew exactly what was eating at him.

"You'll be back with Mary and your children in no time," Harriet said. "You believe that, don't you?"

Robert just shrugged.

"Well, believe it. We'll make sure y'all are together. This ain't my last trip south, you know."

Robert wrapped Harriet in a big hug. He squeezed so tightly that she thought he might snap a rib. Harriet squeezed back, and she marveled at how she had never felt so accepted by her brothers as that moment. Benjamin, Henry, and Robert had always been like the Israelites who never believed they would actually get to the Promised Land. But they had finally made it after so many years wandering around in the desert.

"Thank you, Minty," said Benjamin, using her childhood name in affection.

The name "Minty" set off an avalanche of emotions. She thought about all that had come her way—the whippings of Miss Susan, the sickness that nearly killed her when she used to wade through cold water checking muskrat traps, the piece of lead that nearly split her head.

Harriet wanted to shed tears, but she fought them back. "Every place that the sole of your foot shall tread upon, that the Lord has given unto you," she said. "So be strong and of good courage. He will not fail or forsake us."

She thought that speaking Scripture out loud would keep away the tears, but they broke through her defenses, and she fell apart in the midst of her brothers.

"Do not be dismayed, for...for the Lord God is..." Harriet paused, her words broken by sobs. "The Lord God is with thee...is with thee whithersoever thou goest."

All of her brothers gathered around her, along with Jane and their new friends, John Chase and Peter Jackson. They drew their arms around her, forming a fortress of protection and comfort. Then Henry began to shed some tears, followed by Jane, Benjamin, and Robert. That made it even more difficult for Harriet to get her emotions under control. She cried like she hadn't in years.

When she was spent, a weariness settled on her, and the pains she had been ignoring in her feet and back became more demanding. She was not even forty years old, and yet she felt like a broken-down old bridge that had been carrying a heavy load of people south to north, slave state to free state. She needed rest.

It took a good quarter of an hour before she could get control of herself, and when she did, they all sat down to share in the food left by Mister Agnew.

"We been thinkin'," said Henry, as they passed around the bread and marmalade. "We all been talkin', and we think we should change our names."

Harriet perked up at this notion. "New names?"

"I would be James Stewart, Henry would be William Henry Stewart, and Robert would be John Stewart," said Benjamin.

"Stewart." Harriet chewed on that name, working it over in her mind. Stewart was a powerful name back in Maryland.

"We need free names now," said Robert. "Even Jane is changing her name."

"From Jane to Catherine," she said.

"I'm going with the name Daniel Loyd," piped in John Chase.

"And I'm gonna be Tench Tilghman," added Peter Jackson.

Daniel Loyd and Tench Tilghman were also the names of rich, powerful white men.

"My! All these names," Harriet said. "I ain't sure I can keep y'all straight."

"You ever think 'bout changin' your name, Harriet?" Benjamin asked.

She had already changed it once. From Minty Ross to Harriet Tubman. Many a time, she had thought about shedding the name of "Tubman" after all that John had put her through. But she clung to it the same way she clung to the hope of someday being loved by a faithful husband and a child of her own.

"I'm content with Harriet," she said finally. "If I keep changin' my name every whipstitch, I might forget who I am."

"I don't think that'll ever happen," said Jane.

"But free names is good," she said. "So Stewarts you'll be."

And with that, Harriet held up her cup of milk as a toast.

"To the Stewarts and the sunrising side of Jordan!" she declared, drinking her fill of the cool, sweet milk.

AUNTIE HARRIET

"I've been fixing a long time for my journey but now I'm almost home. God has shown me the Golden Chariot, and a voice spoke to me and said, 'Arouse, Awake! Sleep no longer, Jesus does all things well'...Tell the women to stand together for God will never forsake us. I am at peace with God and all mankind."
— HARRIET TUBMAN

43

1902

L ord, Harriet was weary. She was eighty years old, but she felt a
thousand. She had shriveled in size, and her hair was as thin as
straw and all white. She once had full, apple-round cheeks, but now
they had sunk in, showing her cheekbones prominently. Her forehead
was creased with wrinkles, but they didn't hide the scar where the
hunk of lead had smacked her as a child.

She still had visions, except nowadays she couldn't be sure if what
she was seeing was actually a vision or whether she had died and was
on her way to Heaven. Whenever she climbed out of a vision and
found herself back in her skin and bones, she was always a bit disappointed.

But another day of life had given her another chance to tell her
stories. She loved to spin her tales. She admitted that she sometimes
painted in some extra details that may or may not have truly
happened, but she figured she had earned the right to do that. Besides,
she couldn't really know for sure what was embellishment and what
wasn't. Her memory had started playing tricks on her.

Today was one of those days when she got to tell her stories. She was out in the field behind the house of her niece, Margaret Stewart. Margaret, who was in her forties now, brought along her daughter, Alice. They had gathered out in the back yard, a good distance from the house because Harriet said she wanted to be close enough to the trees to hear the birds and feel the breeze. A field of tall grass separated the yard from the trees. The grass swayed, making a gentle click-clack sound as the wind-swept grass rubbed up against each other, dipping and swirling in the breeze.

"You put butter in my tea, I hope," Harriet said to Margaret.

"I never forget, Auntie."

Auntie. It was always "Auntie." Only one person had ever called her Mama, and that was Gertie, the child of her second husband. Harriet finally got herself a husband who loved her completely, and she had adopted his daughter, Gertie. His name was Nelson Davis, and she married him four years after the War Between the States. But he had been dead now for fourteen years.

Harriet was alone once again, but she was used to it by now.

Harriet was ready for death to claim her, because she had done what she was called to do. She brought her family out of slavery, along with dozens and dozens of others. She had even managed to finally help her parents escape north back in 1857. Her parents had helped some slaves escape, and the authorities were closing in, preparing to arrest them, when Dr. Thompson, of all people, warned them. That was when Harriet swooped down and pulled them out. She had a tough time convincing Papa to leave behind his tools and Mama to give up her feather bed, but they made it. Glory!

But then there was Rachel...Harriet's last remaining sister. The memory burned like hot tar. Harriet had tried several times to get her out, but her sister wouldn't go. Harriet persisted, and she had been planning another attempt to rescue Rachel when she was knocked flat by terrible news.

Her sister had died. Harriet had failed her.

Harriet had gotten out everyone else in the family—even Robert's wife, Mary, and their children. But not Rachel. No one had ever died on any of her rescues; that was something to hold onto, wasn't it?

But Rachel had died before she could help her. It would always haunt her.

"Go on off and play," said Margaret to her daughter, Alice.

Obediently, Alice scampered off. Margaret started saying something to Harriet, something about the work she was fixing to do on the house. But Harriet's eyes were on Alice, who looked to be playing with some invisible person off by the oak tree. Alice was talking to someone. Maybe it was God, for Harriet had had the same kinds of conversations all her life. She and the Lord were still good friends.

Harriet nibbled on the edge of the sweets that Margaret had served her. Margaret always remembered that she loved her sweets. Harriet was sure to avoid the empty space where she had knocked out her tooth with a rock, though she hardly even noticed she was doing it anymore, for it had been so long ago.

Margaret kept on talking about some blame thing, but Harriet was too busy picking up the pieces of sweets that had crumbled in her lap. Harriet was dressed all in black—a full black skirt and an old black hat. It wasn't like she was in constant mourning. She just liked black.

Margaret was saying something about her husband when Harriet noticed, in the corner of her eye, that little Alice had entered the grassy field. Alice strolled through the tall grass, running her right hand across the tops of the blades. Harriet had done the same thing as a little girl, feeling the grass tickle her palm. My, Alice was so like her.

Margaret had switched from talking about the house to talking about the weather, but Harriet had heard enough. She decided to get out of her chair and have herself some fun. As she raised herself slowly out of her chair, her head began to spin, and she thought she was going to topple. Margaret leaped up and put out a hand to steady her.

"Well, Auntie, what on earth are you doing?" asked Margaret, like a mother talking to a child.

"Ssshhhhh," Harriet said, putting a finger to her mouth. "Don't say a thing."

"But Auntie…"

"Ssshhhhh!"

Harriet crept over to the edge of the field and got down on all fours. Oh my, she hadn't done this in years! She crawled into that field of grass, staying low to the ground. It reminded her of the day she crept through the sea of grass when she crossed over into Pennsylvania for the first time.

She could hear Alice singing to herself, and she crept silently, like a cat, closer and closer to the child. Then Harriet got on her belly and began to squirm like a snake. She wondered if she might throw out her back doing this at her age, but she didn't really care. Besides, she was sure the Good Lord would hold her together for this bit of fun.

She slithered in the direction of Alice, who was still singing to herself, obviously unaware of the creature stalking her. The good earth felt cool and comforting beneath Harriet's body, and it smelled rich and bountiful. The scent of soil and grass was her favorite perfume.

Slither, slither, slither...

Alice's voice became louder and louder.

All at once, Harriet struck. She shot out her right hand and latched onto Alice's ankle as she shouted, "Got you!"

Alice let out a squeal, and she fell backward on her behind and burst out laughing. She rolled onto her belly, laughing so hard that Harriet thought she might choke. Harriet rose onto her knees and tickled Alice beneath the ribs.

When Harriet peeked her head above the tall grass and looked back toward the house, she could see that Margaret was staring in their direction and laughing. While Harriet sat there on the ground, catching her breath, Alice tried to climb on her shoulders.

"Alice, no!" Margaret shouted. "Auntie Harriet can't carry you on her shoulders. You're going to hurt her!"

Margaret was right, of course, but Harriet realized that one more hurt wouldn't make much of a difference. What was one more aching bone?

Margaret came out into the field, and she and Alice helped Harriet back to her feet. Then they held hands—a string of three souls making their way back to the yard. Alice walked between them and swung their linked hands back and forth like a jump rope.

Easing back into her chair, Harriet closed her eyes and smiled. Her legs were sore, but a good kind of sore.

"You know, Alice, I got by many a sentry in the war by crawlin' on my belly just like that," she said. Harriet loved talking about her time in the war working as a scout.

"Did they ever catch you?" the little girl asked.

"I never got caught. Not in all my adventures. I was too smart."

"Not once?"

"Not once. The enemy soldiers would see the grass swaying, but they'd think it was just an animal. In the dim flicker of the campfire, I appeared only as a small shadow."

Alice sat there spellbound, her chin propped on her hands, as Harriet launched into another one of her stories. Lord, she had plenty of them to tell.

"I wish for you, and all your offsprings, a through ticket in the Gospel Train to Glory." — HARRIET TUBMAN

DOUG PETERSON'S

UNDERGROUND RAILROAD SERIES

Check out Book 1 and Book 2 of the Underground Railroad series:

The Vanishing Woman tells the incredible true story of Ellen Craft, who escaped slavery by pretending to be a white man, while her husband posed as her slave.
The Disappearing Man is the true story of Henry "Box" Brown, a slave who escaped by mailing himself in a box from Richmond to Philadelphia.

 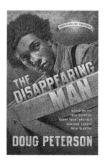

Sample an excerpt from *The Disappearing Man*, which you can find after the Acknowledgments.

AUTHOR'S NOTE

I never planned to write a novel about Harriet Tubman.

I had written two earlier novels about the Underground Railroad, *The Disappearing Man* and *The Vanishing Woman*, but the subjects of those books were lesser-known figures—Henry "Box" Brown and William and Ellen Craft. I had specifically chosen people whom most people had never heard about.

But Harriet Tubman? Almost everyone knows Harriet's name, so why select someone so well known?

When I began to dig into her story, I realized that most people may know her name, but many probably do not know the details of her story. The movie, *Harriet*, released in 2019, went a long way to bringing the details of her life to people's attention, but it didn't touch on her childhood, nor did it delve into the relationship with her husband and her brothers—which I found intriguing.

Also, when I did some background work to find out what had already been written about Harriet, I discovered a lot of non-fiction and plenty of children's books. But I was shocked to find that, as far as I could tell, no one had written a novel for adults or young adults about her life, other than a little-known book published over one hundred years ago. That may soon change since the release of the movie, *Harriet*.

Because I was especially intrigued by the dynamics between Harriet and three of her brothers, that became the primary focus of the story. Harriet is believed to have rescued about seventy people in thirteen raids into the South to help slaves escape. But I decided to focus more narrowly and concentrate on Harriet and her three brothers, who really did have a history of turning back—just as I depict in the novel.

Much of what you read in *The Tubman Train* reportedly did happen because there is no shortage of compelling stories when it comes to Harriet. However, I did change the location of two characters during the brothers' escape scenes. It is believed that Harriet's brother Robert and his wife, Mary, were living a little farther north, in Trappe, Maryland, when the brothers' escape took place. As a plot device, to keep all of the brothers in the same starting place for the escape, I took the liberty of relocating Robert and Mary near Cambridge, Maryland, with the other brothers.

Also, I added a few twists to her brothers' escape, which is the climax of the story. For example...

Benjamin's fiancé, Jane Kane, really did dress up as a man as she made her escape from the Jones Plantation, but I found no explanation for why she put on the disguise. I also knew that her master, Horatio Jones, had a brutal reputation for violence, so I combined those two elements and had Jane put on the disguise as a way to sneak by Jones. Prudence, who helped her don the clothes, is a fictional character.

It was true that Harriet and her husband John had a strained relationship and that when Harriet went down to rescue him, she found him with another woman. And she did buy a set of clothes for him to wear on the escape. It was also true that Harriet's brothers worried that John Tubman might give everything away. But I added the complication of John pondering the possibility of turning in his wife for reward money. In addition, John's decision to lead the two plantation men on a wild goose chase to protect Harriet was a fictional twist.

It's true that Robert's wife, Mary, went into labor on the very night of the escape, and therefore Robert had a difficult time leaving, just as depicted. In addition, Harriet's father had a reputation for never lying, which was why in real life he approached the corncrib walking backward just so he could honestly say he hadn't seen his children.

I sprinkled throughout the book some of the numerous anecdotes about Harriet, such as the time she used a rock to bust loose her sore tooth, and the time she used two live chickens to distract a white man. These stories happened, but probably not during the instances when I show them.

In addition, we know nothing about the courtship of Harriet and John or Benjamin and Jane, so those scenes are fictionalized. And finally, it is true that John Bowley and his family hid in a home along High Street in Cambridge following their escape from the slave auction in front of the courthouse. However, we do not know who sheltered them on High Street. Therefore, the Trout siblings are fictional creations.

Once I had completed a rough draft of *The Tubman Train*, I undertook a self-guided driving tour along the Harriet Tubman Underground Railroad Byway. This trail takes people to forty-five different sites, including the Dorchester County Courthouse, where Harriet's niece, Kessiah, and her husband, John Bowley, escaped with their two young children. The byway also took me to the Jacob and Hannah Leverton House, the Quaker house where Harriet stopped during her initial escape in 1849, as well as to the farm once owned by the Brodess family.

My most memorable stop was at the Bucktown Village Store, where Harriet had been struck and nearly killed by a two-pound weight. The Meredith family has owned the general store since 1855, and I was given a tour by Matt Meredith, a young man in his thirties. When Matt was thirteen years old (the same age of Harriet when she was hit by the weight), he and his father were digging through the dumpster of a house where an estate was being cleaned out. They found a stack of old newspapers, and while Matt was paging through the papers, he came across a runaway ad from 1849, offering a reward for the capture of "Minty," which was Harriet's name growing up. Remarkably, this turned out to be the only known copy of the reward advertisement for Harriet Tubman.

In doing this research, I also found there is no shortage of nonfiction sources about Harriet's story. I invite you to take you own journey into her past, by sampling the ones I used:

- *Harriet Tubman: Bound for the Promised Land*, by Kate Clifford Larson, Ballantine Books, 2003.
- *Harriet Tubman: Imagining a Life*, by Beverly Lowery, Anchor Books, a division of Random House, 2007.
- *Harriet Tubman: The Life and the Life Stories*, by Jean M. Humez, the University of Wisconsin Press, 2003.
- *Harriet Tubman: The Moses of Her People*, by Sarah Bradford, Dover Publications, 2004 (originally published in 1886 by G.R. Lockwood and Son).
- *Harriet Tubman: Myth, Memory, and History*, by Milton C. Sernett, Duke University Press, 2007.
- *Harriet Tubman: The Road to Freedom*, by Catherine Clinton, Little, Brown, and Company, 2004.
- *Scenes in the Life of Harriet Tubman*, by Sarah H. Bradford, Forgotten Books, 2012 (originally published in 1869).

ACKNOWLEDGMENTS

The Tubman Train, like my other two Underground Railroad novels, is first and foremost a story about family. Therefore, my acknowledgments begin with family.

I'm grateful for my wife of forty-four years, Nancy, who is ever faithful and patient in reading multiple drafts of my novels. I'm also thankful for our sons, Michael and Jason, the treasures of our life, along with their amazing wives, Ingrid and Kristen. And, of course, there's our first grandson, Jackson, to whom this novel is dedicated.

I thank my sister, Kathy, and brother, Ric, who read *The Tubman Train* in early draft form. I'm also grateful for my mother, Irene, who is going strong as she closes in on 100 years old. She and my father encouraged me with my writing beginning in grade school, when I decided to become a writer and wrote close to 100 books of my own, with titles such as *The Man From A.U.N.T.I.E.* and *Twenty Thousand Leagues Under the Swimming Pool.*

Beyond my family, many thanks to Heath Morber and his son, Cavan, who read and reviewed drafts of *The Tubman Train*—and to Tom Hanlon, for his editing eye on the early chapters. I also can't forget my Gideon Media Arts family, several of whose names show up among the fictional characters scattered throughout *The Tubman*

Train. They're minor characters in the novel, but major characters in my life.

My thanks go out to Vincent Davis II and Conor Franklin for their promotional expertise, to Barry Napier for his deft editing touch, and to Hannah Linder for her design of the interior pages. Kirk DouPonce provided yet another masterful cover in keeping with my other four novels.

Last but not least, thank you to my church family at Cornerstone Fellowship and to my prayer partner, Scott Irwin, because as Harriet knows, prayer is what holds us together like a well-bound book.

Doug Peterson

THE DISAPPEARING MAN
EXCERPT

Richmond, Virginia
March 23, 1849
4:00 a.m.

Henry Brown ran his eye down one edge of the small trick box. He turned the box over in his hands, admiring it with a woodworker's attention to detail.

The drawer slid in and out smoothly, as it did when he had first used the box to perform magic on the Hermitage Plantation so long ago. John Allen busted the box a couple of weeks earlier, but Henry had painstakingly pieced it back together. Seemed like he was always piecing one thing or another back together.

The trick box with the false bottom was for making things disappear. A coin. A hatpin. An apple. This one had been with Henry since he was twelve, when a traveling magician showed him how to construct it out of pieces of good, solid ash. His master at the time had supplied him with the wood to make the magic box. Those were kinder days.

Setting the box aside, Henry used a knife to pry up two loose floorboards in the corner of his home. It was a stark, one-room home in the Shockoe Bottom neighborhood of Richmond, not far from the docks of the James River, where a large number of slaves and free blacks boarded. Henry's home was the lower level of a two-story tenement, adjacent to a row of decrepit shacks, all leaning in different directions as if in danger of imminent collapse. Henry's roof leaked, and the air whistled through the walls any time the wind kicked up. But this back-alley room gave him more privacy than he had ever known in his thirty-four years. Still, he wouldn't miss the place.

Henry set the trick box carefully under the floorboards and pounded them back down as best he could. He was ready to go.

As Henry looked out his window, lightning lit up the maze of tenements in Shockoe Bottom, followed by rolling thunder. He could smell the rain, feel it deep in his bones, cold air sneaking in over warm, stirring up the night like a witch's brew.

He pulled his straw hat down tight and eased out his back door, into the alley. Henry knew the wind would soon swing around to the north just before the clouds let loose, as it always did. His left hand, wrapped in a bloody bandage, ached with every movement. He prayed that infection wouldn't set in. He had seen people die from cuts not nearly as bad.

Henry made his way north through the dark alleys behind the buildings along Fourteenth Street. The darkness was heavy like a tomb, giving Henry a dread sense of confinement. It was a closing in, a boxing in, an uneasy feeling that he might bump up against an impenetrable wall at any second.

He picked his way along the buildings until his night eyes came to him. The streets appeared desolate, but he knew this was deceiving. Richmond maintained a small army of patrollers who watched for slaves roaming at night. So Henry stayed to the shadows and the pitch-dark alleys. Briefly, he was illuminated by the lightning of the fast-approaching storm. Still no rain.

A sudden bang, and Henry flattened his back against the wooden wall of a small, lopsided building. He made out the ghostly image of a door slamming shut in the breeze, then slowly squeaking open on its hinges, only to be slammed again. He moved on.

Henry was in a hurry, but he made himself go good and slow, so he could avoid any obstacles or confrontations. Yet when Henry reached the end of an alley that spilled out onto Broad Street, someone grabbed his shirt and yanked him backwards.

"It's a colored!" the man shouted.

Henry didn't dare turn and show his face. Panic seized him just as fiercely as the hand on his shirt, and he tore loose, his shirt ripping as he took off. He was now flying, sprinting across Broad Street. A flash of lightning gave him away, followed by deafening thunder.

"Shoot him!" hollered a second man. Then a gunshot.

Henry was moving so fast that he wondered if he might outrun the bullet at his back.

"That way!"

"I see him!"

Henry pulled off his hat to keep it from flying away and made his way toward Monumental Episcopal Church. It wasn't his church. The First African Baptist Church was just east on Broad Street. Monumental was a white church, but Henry knew the lay of the place. He ran for cover in the church's portico and slid quietly behind the dismal monument for which the church had been named. With his hat in one hand, he ran his other across the cold face of the stone marker. He couldn't read or write, but he knew there were seventy-two names carved into the marble, the names of whites and blacks, all killed when the old Richmond Theater burned to the ground. All were buried beneath the church, and Henry could feel their eyes looking up at him.

His heart was thumping so bad he was sure he'd wake the dead. He knew he'd have to get himself quieted down or he'd be found out for sure.

"You certain he went this way?" said one of the voices.

"I'm sure of it."

Henry recognized the first voice: Callahan, one of the overseers from the tobacco factory. Of all the people to stumble into...

They were near. Henry could hear their footsteps as they made their way into the covered entryway of the church. If they caught him, he would surely be subjected to "the thirty-nine"—the same number of lashes that Jesus received.

"Spooks me out here at night," Callahan said.

"Don't tell me you're thinkin' of the spirits of the dead."

Callahan didn't answer.

Henry pressed himself against the cold monument, wishing he could melt into the marble like a ghost. The two men had split up, and Henry could hear them working their way around the monument, coming at him from both sides. If he didn't do something soon, he'd be trapped for sure.

And so he bolted.

Callahan leaped backwards and let out a yelp, as though the sudden rush of movement was more ghost than flesh.

"Grab him!"

But Henry was flying again. He was past Callahan before the overseer had a chance to react.

"Did ya get a look at him?" the other man shouted.

"Shut up and run!" Callahan said.

A couple of blocks from Monumental Episcopal Church was Capitol Square, where Henry hoped his footsteps would be muffled by the lush grass. The lightning had let up, and his pursuers soon lost the trail without the flashes to guide them. Henry leaped into an old chestnut tree and crouched on a low branch thick enough not to sway under his weight. He saw two shadows stop not far from the capitol building, which loomed dark and hulking.

"Any idea where he went?" Callahan asked.

"It's like he just disappeared."

A lightning flash revealed Henry perched in the tree only a stone's throw away. But the two men had their backs to him, so they had no idea their quarry was nearly on top of them.

"Let's split up. He couldn't a gone far."

Callahan and his companion broke off in different directions, and Henry waited a safe spell before dropping down from the tree. Then he took off running, having lost all sense of caution. His feet hardly touched the ground, and he didn't slow down or look back until he was knocking on the back door of a narrow, one-story brick house a little east from the capitol on Fifteenth Street. Samuel Smith opened the door, and Henry slipped inside. Samuel was white, a gambler who made a meager living with a shoe shop. James Smith, Henry's closest friend and one of many free blacks living in Richmond, was there too, and he caught Henry as he stumbled into the room.

"What happened?" James asked. "Looks like you seen a ghost. And got chased by one."

"I was spotted," Henry rasped. "Two men. Callahan and another. Lost 'em, though. No way they followed me."

"Did they get a good look at you?" Samuel asked.

"I don't think they saw my face. But they knew I was a slave."

James looked from Henry to Samuel. "Should we go through with this?"

Henry held up his bandaged hand. "I ain't gonna stage this a second time."

"So it's either now or we come up with another plan?" James said.

"It's now!" Henry was unmovable. "I promised Nancy. I'm goin' through with this."

"All right, all right. If we learn that alarms have been raised, we still have time to back out." Samuel looked at his pocket watch. "The driver will be here to pick up the package in less than an hour."

Samuel reviewed the escape route in detail one last time—when and where the box would be carried by train, steamboat, and wagon.

Finally, James took a deep breath and said, "You ready for this?"

Henry didn't even pause. "I am."

He put his hat back on and glanced over at a wooden box sitting in the middle of Samuel's home like a coffin in a funeral parlor. It was smaller than he remembered. The box carried a Philadelphia address, and on another side were the bold words *THIS SIDE UP WITH CARE*.

"Here." James handed Henry a beef bladder filled with water.

"And the biscuits?"

"They're in the box," said Samuel. He handed Henry a gimlet drill. "Just in case you need more air."

"You *sure* you want to go through with this?" James asked.

Henry's eyes drifted back to the box. "Yes."

Standing next to the box, Samuel grinned and held out his hand, like a coachman motioning to the open door of a carriage. "Then your coffin awaits."

With the gimlet and water in hand, Henry stepped carefully into the box and lowered himself. He rested his shoulder and head against one end and braced his feet against the other. The box was only three feet high and less than two and a half feet wide. Henry weighed two hundred pounds and stood five feet, eight inches tall. He put the drill and water down next to the biscuits where he could get to them and settled in.

"You comfortable?" Samuel asked.

"That's a fool question."

"We're sealing you in," said James.

Henry nodded. James and Samuel picked up the wooden cover and placed it over his head, plunging Henry into a tomb-like darkness. *This is it*, he thought. *Boxed in again.*

Henry was being mailed to Philadelphia. No more masters. No more boxes. No more being somebody else's property. Philadelphia was on the other end of the line. Philadelphia was freedom.

Made in the USA
Monee, IL
09 February 2021